continued . . .

Ride the Wind Home

Christina Kingston

JOVE BOOKS, NEW YORK

This is a work of fiction. Names, characters, places, and incidents either are the product of the author's imagination or are used fictitiously, and any resemblance to actual persons, living or dead, business establishments, events, or locales is entirely coincidental.

RIDE THE WIND HOME

A Jove Book / published by arrangement with
the author

PRINTING HISTORY
Jove edition / April 2003

Copyright © 2003 by Christina Strong
Cover art by Judy York
Cover design by George Long

ISBN: 0-515-13510-0

A JOVE BOOK®
Jove Books are published by The Berkley Publishing Group,
a division of Penguin Putnam Inc.,
375 Hudson Street, New York, New York 10014.
JOVE and the "J" design
are trademarks belonging to Penguin Putnam Inc.

PRINTED IN THE UNITED STATES OF AMERICA

10 9 8 7 6 5 4 3 2 1

Prologue

Merlington Park
1814

She couldn't run much longer! Already she had a stitch in her side and her breath was coming in short gasps. Worse yet, she was running out of trees! Up ahead she could see that they were thinning out. The bright blue of the sky showed through them in patches that indicated she'd soon be out of the park's heavily wooded forest.

Then they would catch her.

The tiny form in her arms pressed closer and whimpered as if he understood that he'd soon be back in the clutches of their pursuers again. "No!" Diana assured him without much conviction. "I'll keep you safe. Somehow."

She renewed her efforts, but it wasn't enough. As she burst from the woods onto the shore of Merlington Park's vast ornamental lake, she fell to her knees, completely spent. Tears of frustration and rage came, and she clutched closer and sobbed over the burden she carried.

"Here . . ." A quiet voice spoke from the foot of a large oak. "What's this all about?"

Diana spun around on her knees to see a young man rise with some difficulty from where he'd been comfortably seated, reading a book. He came over to assist Diana to her feet.

He was far too heavy for his height, which, now that she was standing, she saw was only an inch or so more than her own. Their eyes were almost level, and she peered into his, searching for a clue to his character. Would he be as casually cruel as the men who searched the woods behind her?

Her own blue eyes narrowed as she looked into his. Brown, the soft color of warm caramel, his eyes were kind. Diana heaved a sigh of relief. "It's this," she told him, holding out the puppy she carried.

He reached out slowly so as not to frighten the little dog and stroked its head. "This?"

"Well, yes. And them." She gestured behind her toward the noises being made by the group of young men searching the forest for her.

He smiled at her, a warm and comforting smile. "I'm afraid I need a little more information before I can be of service to you."

Diana wondered what one corpulent gentleman thought he could do to stop the wild bunch of fit young bucks who had been chasing her all day. "It's Lord Calverson and his crowd. They have been plaguing me ever since I arrived. Joking and teasing and making innuendoes that I can't understand, but know are improper."

He frowned at that. "Why should supposed gentlemen do such a thing?"

"Because I am only sixteen and just married, I think."

He frowned even harder, disapproval in every line of his face. "Where is your husband?"

"He's here, but he's at the gaming tables with Merlington and his friends all the time. That leaves me fair game evidently." She pouted. "I've never been in such a position, and I don't know how to handle it."

"Not surprising." He smiled at her kindly. "You are only sixteen, my dear."

She raised her chin at him with the hauteur of a queen, and he smiled again. "Believe me, I know ladies far older than you are who wouldn't be able to manage Calverson's bunch of hooligans." He took her arm gently and turned her toward the lake. "Suppose you let me handle them for you."

Her chin went down and tears came to her eyes. "Oh, could you?" Then she blushed to have seemed to doubt his ability to save her and the puppy from the young men bent on recapturing the dog. "I mean, *would* you?"

"Of course I shall," he said with the utmost confidence. "Come." He led her to the brink of the lake and she saw a lovely boat there, rather like the pictures she had seen of gondolas in Venice. Its dark lacquered hull gleamed, and it was almost filled with cushions. Her rescuer settled her and the puppy in the bow. "Are you comfortable?"

"Yes, quite. Thank you."

"Ah, but your eyes are full of questions. Do you feel as if I have put you in a trap?"

Diana blushed, for that came very close indeed to the thoughts she was having. How uncomfortably perceptive this man was.

"But you really can't run any more, can you?"

"No," she admitted reluctantly.

"So you may as well trust me and rest and catch your breath."

His eyes were so kind. And he seemed totally confident of his ability to keep her safe from the young men who were trying to tease her to death and take the little dog from her to torment again. After a moment's hesitation,

Diana finally let her defenses down and gave him a radiant smile. "I *shall* trust you." Then she added an emphatic "I do."

He bowed with a grace she hadn't expected in so rotund a man. "You will not be disappointed. I give you my word on it."

The men looking for her were closer now. Diana couldn't help it; she shot a fearful glance toward the woods. He was one man and they were so many.

She didn't understand some of the comments they both could hear being made by her pursuers. The expression on her rescuer's face told her she was right to think them dreadful, however.

An expression of absolute fury changed his face as he looked toward the forest and the ribald voices. His anger caused Diana to offer a weak defense of her husband's friends. "They didn't mean to harm the little dog. They were just tossing it back and forth between them to keep it from me — just as boys at school toss each other's caps when playing 'keep away.' But it was so frightened — and they weren't thinking of being very kind. Or careful."

The look her rescuer bent on her held none of the fury she'd seen a moment before, but it was so stern that she found herself babbling. "I caught him when one of the men got too close to me, and ran away from them with it. They think it is great sport to chase after me, I'm afraid."

"I'm certain they do," he said dryly. He shoved the boat out from the shore. It stopped when it reached the end of the rope that tethered it to the punting pole jammed into the bank.

"Just rest and calm your puppy and leave everything else to me," he told her with a reassuring smile. Then he went back to the cushion he'd taken from the boat earlier, picked up his discarded book, and settled down to read.

Diana tried hard to calm herself as she sat there, wondering how she could feel so safe a mere ten feet from the shore on which her pursuers still hunted her. She did, though. This rotund young man had managed to make her feel cherished and safe for the first time since her beloved grandfather had died.

With a gulp, she pushed away that terrible grief and the betrayal she felt had followed it when she'd returned home to the vicarage. There, seeking only comfort from her father, she'd met with gentle rejection.

Diana had never understood why her father couldn't abide her presence. She imagined she never would. She'd been only a bewildered child when, on the heels of her mother's death, she'd been sent to live at Belleview, her grandfather's palatial home. When he had died and she'd come back to her father at the vicarage in Smythingdale Village, she'd promptly been betrothed to Baron Huntley. Though she knew he never meant to, in his effort to get rid of her speedily, her father had condemned her to a life she could hardly bear.

Tears threatened. Resolutely she put that part of her life out of her mind. She was married now. To a man she hated. A man who had introduced her to a brutality she had never known existed. Her fate was sealed, and she was left to make the best of it.

Just right now, however, she was being kept safe by this man with the warm brown eyes. It was such a blessing to feel as that made her feel, that she was determined to luxuriate in it. Even as she attempted to do so, her stomach seemed to sink to the bottom of the lake when she permitted herself to wonder why her father couldn't have married her to a man like *this* one.

After several deep breaths, she relaxed and began to fondle the puppy's velvet ears. It snuggled closer and she kissed it on the nose. The dog gave a happy yelp and joined in the game, enthusiastically washing her chin for her.

"Hey!" There was a shout from the forest. "Over this way! I just heard the dog!"

There were answering cries of triumph, and almost immediately Diana's six tormentors spilled out of the trees.

One grasped the rope tying the boat to the pole jammed into the shore and began to pull. "We've got her now!"

"See if you can talk her into sharing." Calverson stood grinning at her.

"Sharing what?"

"Oh, don't be a slow top, Quinby. What's a beauty like that got that you'd most like a piece of?"

An imperious voice announced, "I rather think that's enough of that, boys."

"Boys! Who the hell's calling us 'boys'?" Calverson spun around to face the corpulent figure at the foot of the tree, his face belligerent.

"Ah." The voice was softer now. "Did I misname you? Very well, I apologize."

Diana felt sharp disappointment. Was her hero really going to apologize to these oafs?

"That's more like it," one of the others said as his friend plucked at his sleeve and tried to get him to back away.

The man at the foot of the tree said mildly, "Permit me to rephrase. I should have said, 'That will be enough, *children.*'"

"By hades! I'll . . ." A tall blond started toward the offensive speaker.

"Yes?" The sitting man sounded bored. "You might, of course. Then I'd accept your challenge and choose pistols."

"Come away, if you value your life, Lawson," the man who had pulled at his friend's sleeve urged him.

"That's very good advice," the bored voice assured the man called Lawson. "I never miss."

While Diana sat tense and transfixed among her cushions, all six men stared hard at the man at the foot of the tree. Finally one of them breathed almost reverently. "Omigod, it's Smythington." He turned and cuffed his friend. "Are you trying to bring The Lucky Seven down on us, you fool?"

"I rather thought he was merely trying to get himself killed, myself," the calm voice answered for the dumbstruck young man. "Permit me to assure you that I shall be most happy to give each one of you that opportunity if I ever hear of you harassing this young lady again." He smiled at them, and one of them flinched. "It shall give me great pleasure in every instance, I might add."

Wide-eyed, Diana thought that she had never seen so deadly a smile in all her life. It caused her to shiver in spite of herself.

"If, perchance," the man went on, "I should happen to fail in this endeavor, *then* we will see if the rest of The Lucky Seven wish to get involved."

The six miscreants stood silent before him.

"I believe apologies to the lady are in order."

"Yes, Your Grace," they chorused. All of them speaking at the same time, they made their apologies as hasty as their retreat.

When they had gone, Diana sat bolt upright. "You're the Duke of Smythington!"

"Guilty as charged."

"My father is the Vicar of Smythingdale. Your vicar."

A wide smile lit his face. "Then you're the little girl I saw once in church with your mother."

"Yes. She was Lady Christiane."

"And very beautiful. I thought until now that she was the most beautiful woman I had ever seen."

"Until now?" Then she blushed furiously. He was telling her she was beautiful. Even more so than her lovely mother had been. It wasn't true. She knew it wasn't true. Especially with her hair all pulled down from branches that had snagged it in her flight through the forest and her yellow gown clearly showing the green smudges left when she'd fallen out of the woods then spun around on her knees to look at him. It couldn't be true, but, oh, how wonderful it was of him to have said so!

He was not handsome, because his face was too fleshy, and his corpulent frame was hardly that of someone who could spring up onto his horse and charge off to rescue a damsel in distress, but to her he was all that she could wish and more. He had saved her and the puppy she hugged from the rough teasing of the men who'd just left, and he'd told her she was beautiful. What else could she ask?

"Perhaps I should take you back to the manor now."

"Yes, I suppose that should be next." She touched a hand to her hair and smiled falteringly. "I certainly need the services of my maid."

He tossed his book into the boat and pulled it to shore. When he stepped into it, it rocked perilously. He blushed, aware that his weight had caused her to grasp the gunwales, and she let go of them as if they were on fire. Standing very still and straight, he began to pole them across the shallow lake to the mansion reflected in its waters.

Diana knew he was disconcerted, but she could think of nothing to say. She was young and unhappy and gauche, and she lacked the conversational skills to put her hero at ease.

It would hardly do, after all, for a married woman to tell

a strange man that she didn't care what he looked like. That to her, fat or not, he was her knight in shining armor.

"It looks as if there is a welcoming party on the shore in front of the manor. Perhaps your husband has heard that you were in difficulties."

Diana turned her face away from him. If her husband was waiting, it wasn't to see if *she* had been distressed, she knew. What would Huntley say? That she had caused his friends embarrassment? That by avoiding their pawing hands she had embarrassed *him* by her missish ways? He was certain to say that it was time she grew up. Didn't he say that with a frequency that gave her a headache?

Under his sarcastic tutelage, she was growing up far faster than she had ever thought it possible to do—if learning of the perfidy and cruelty of men was what her husband considered growing up. And she was certainly doing it far faster than she wanted to. In fact, she was already way ahead of the young wives she had met in London society in that respect.

Sad resentment rose in her. Why couldn't her father have married her to a quiet man like the one punting her across the lake? Why not to a man like this—with gentle strength? Instead, her saintly father had chained her for life to a brutal bully.

Instantly, she felt guilty for criticizing her father. It wasn't his fault that he saw neither guile nor beastliness in his fellow man. His parishioners kept him sheltered from such things. They always had. They probably always would.

"Are you all right?"

The quiet question caught Diana by surprise and brought tears to her eyes. It had been a very long time since she had heard that question. Not since she'd left her grandfather's funeral had anyone cared enough to inquire into her feelings or her state of mind. She managed to choke out, "I'm fine, thank you," over the lump in her throat, and heard the soft sound of disbelief he made just before the prow of their boat touched the turf of the mansion's immaculate lawn.

"Wife." The man denied her her name, claiming her as no more than a possession, his voice harsh. "Calverson tells me you have been running through the woods trying to keep his dog from him."

Diana was outraged. "His dog! It most certainly is *not* his dog. And he and his companions were quite unkind to the poor little thing. I was rescuing it."

The men surrounding Baron Huntley sniggered.

Huntley's face turned red with suppressed anger. He turned to his valet, who was constantly at his shoulder. "Ketch. Drown that cur!"

"No!" Diana flinched back against the cushions, hugging the puppy close.

Her husband seemed to grow larger with menace. "Are you defying me, wife?"

Her eyes wide with fear, she stared back at him. She still refused to relinquish the dog.

"No, Huntley," Smythington answered before she could frame a denial. "Your wife is attempting to put matters straight. She was surprised that your friends didn't know the dog was mine. Fortunately, she brought him to me before he could come to more harm than a good scare."

He looked at the men around Huntley, and slowly every smile died from their faces. "Everyone knows how fond I am of my animals," he said conversationally. "I consider them members of my family, you know. If anything unpleasant should happen to one of them, I should feel myself honor-bound to retaliate." Beneath his bored drawl, his voice became steel. "Your lady wife was just trying to keep such an *unpleasantness* from occurring in your life or the lives of your friends."

Diana was struck dumb. She had never expected to see Huntley back down from any challenge. But he did now. It was as if the softly spoken words of the Duke of Smythington were cannon aimed at him. He and his companions paled uniformly. She desperately wanted to laugh, but dared not. She knew she'd pay a heavy price for her laughter later if she did. So, instead, she stood gracefully and offered the puppy to the dear man who had claimed ownership of the scruffy little thing, her eyes full of gratitude. Her voice shook as she told him, "Here is your dog, Your Grace."

He took the puppy from her with hands as gentle as her own. When their fingers touched under the warm little body, a current like lightning surged between them. For a breathless instant, they could only stare into each other's eyes. Then the Duke managed to say, "Thank you for your brave rescue of my pet."

Her eyes spoke of her gratitude as she told him, "I am certain you will take better care of him now."

His lips said, "I promise you that he will have the very best of care," but his eyes assured her of so much more. He would guard her little dog. That was the least his eyes promised. Also, they promised, as far as might be possible to do for another man's wife, he would guard her as well.

His lips drawn back in a snarl, Huntley took her arm in a rough grasp and yanked her from the boat. "Thank you for returning *my* property to *me,* Your Grace," he challenged.

As Diana watched, contempt for her husband blazed from the Duke's eyes, but his voice was calm as he answered, "It was a pleasure to have been of service to her."

His steady gaze held Huntley's until her husband and his sobered entourage turned away from the shore.

When Diana turned her face back over her shoulder to her rescuer, a look passed between them that formed an eternal bond.

Then Huntley dragged her roughly away.

Later in their room, Huntley said harsh things to her, but they were tempered—as if he feared the Duke might overhear. To see that her husband feared someone made her life a little easier.

Diana knew she had no skills, verbally or physically, with which to defend herself from Huntley in any way, but she was emboldened by the friendship she knew she'd been offered. And for the first time since her husband had revealed his true nature to her, Diana had hope. Huntley might not be able to destroy her spirit after all.

Chapter One

The Vicarage, Smythingdale
1819

Marriage! Oh, no. Not again!

Diana had to make up her mind what to do. She couldn't just sit here like a sacrificial lamb and let them do it to her again!

A walk. She'd go for a walk to clear her head. If she were going to plan her escape, she'd have to distance herself from them. Their obvious concern for her welfare was a drain on her determination.

Everything would be so much simpler if they didn't so very much want to do what was best for her.

What was best for her. They'd thought that marrying her to Baron Huntley had been the best thing for her and that union had been a disaster. Of course, they'd had no way of knowing that the bluff, amiable man who'd courted her had been a brute in secret. And she'd been careful never to tell them.

She couldn't honestly say, now that almost a year had passed since she'd been widowed, if it had been pride that had kept her from telling her father and her aunt about Huntley. Had it, perhaps, been a reluctance to admit humiliation? *Or had it been dread that they might try to interfere—and endanger themselves?*

She wasn't even sure in her own mind. She'd been a mere girl then. She'd been an innocent sixteen. Until her wedding night, life had been one long, lovely adventure, marred only by the death of her beloved mother and her father's rejection.

Because of that awful night and the many that followed, she was no longer innocent, thanks to her brutish husband. And every day she worked hard so that soon she would no longer be defenseless.

Her "training," as she called her efforts, was upsetting her father and her aunt, but she was determined to keep her vow to prepare herself to keep safe. Her vow didn't mean she intended to upset any further these two gentle people who loved her, however, and she refused to do so.

She looked across the path to where her father and aunt sat, the sunlight here in the garden turning their hair into haloes around each of their sweet faces. She could never explain to them how she felt. Never make them understand that she would go to any length to avoid reentering the kind of hell from which her late husband's fortuitous death had released her. Her father and aunt were already perplexed enough by the change her marriage had wrought in her personality—from a bubbling, bright, gay sixteen-year-old to a rather grim young widow.

"Dears," she began, searching for an explanation that would serve to give her time to flee their well-meaning plans for her second marriage and also comfort them when she did, "please try to understand that I need more time to come to grips with being a widow before I consider being a wife again. I need time to visit friends, relax with them, and forget my marriage." She corrected hastily, "I mean my loss."

"We know you must be grieving, Diana." Her father looked as if he were going to reach out to pat her arm, then took his sister's hand instead. He didn't have any idea what to do with this beautiful young woman who happened to be his daughter. He never had. She was so unlike her gentle mother. "Your aunt and I both know how wrenching it is to lose the person you love. We respect your grief, dear girl, but life goes on."

Grieve for Huntley? *Love* him? Diana choked down the denial that rose to her lips. She fought to let them keep their illusions when it came to her late husband. Heaven knew *she* had none!

No, nor had she any about the rest of the men she'd met while she'd been his wife. Whenever she thought of them the word *predators* leapt to her mind. She'd sworn she'd never be shackled to one of them again, and she fully intended to keep that vow.

She'd gone to Huntley with a great fortune, and while it was still sizable, it was less than half of what her grandfather had left her. If her unlamented spouse had lived a few more months, it would have been gone altogether.

Worse than the loss of her fortune was the bitter blow life had served her when her protector, the Duke of Smythington, had, after returning safely from the war with Napoleon, been reported missing. Diana had thought she'd die of the grief the news had caused her.

Huntley had promptly attempted to take up his cruelties where the threat of the Duke's retaliation had caused him to leave off. Diana, though, had grown wiser and stronger by then, and her terrible grief at hearing that something had happened to Smythington had caused her to lash out at Huntley so fiercely that he'd avoided her from then until his death. He hadn't, however, stopped gambling away her dowry.

She had no intention of being made utterly destitute by another of his kind. Bitterness she must keep from these two innocents sitting across the path from her welled up, and she had to be careful to hide it from them as she spoke.

"I have no wish to be married again," she told them firmly.

She saw the look of consternation that crossed her father's face. It clearly showed the puzzlement of a man whose marriage had been the greatest blessing of his life. Both he and his sister beside him had known only joy with their spouses. They had no idea that a marriage could be a nightmare.

Diana lost any hope that they might understand as she looked at her father. Obviously this man who wisely counseled so many others had no idea what to say to her. He was a gentle soul, and, like all the pastors she knew, was carefully sheltered from reality by the kindness of his parishioners. Her father had no idea what the real world was like. She hoped he'd never find out. What she did wish, with all her heart, was that he would make an effort— any effort—to find out how she felt.

Diana knew she was, by her very nature, a difficult problem for him. Her presence made his parishioners uncomfortable. It always had.

The granddaughter of an earl, she had seemed out of place from the start. In her father's parish, Diana was, somehow, much larger than life.

Her mother, that same earl's daughter, had fit in perfectly. She had been truly sweet, biddable, and quietly self-effacing. The deep, caring nature she'd been blessed with had won the heart of every parishioner. Wherever her mother had been, there'd been peace.

Diana was another matter entirely, however, and that was the problem. She was bold and blunt and flippant and gay. There was never the remotest chance she could be thought self-effacing. Worse, she was more likely to tell a self-pitying parishioner to "straighten up and take a firm hold on life" than to console them. She had done so. Often. It had always amazed her that no one seemed to take her advice seriously.

Except for the first few months of her marriage, Diana had never had any trouble getting a grasp on life, even as a toddler. As soon as she was out of leading strings, she'd flown about the parish as fast as she could run, getting into one mischievous prank after another with the boys of the village. She had towed them all along in her wake by the sheer magnetism of her personality. From the start, Diana had been anything but peaceful.

When Diana would enter a room, she'd become the center of everyone's attention. She still did, in spite of Huntley's best efforts to change her.

She was quieter now. Far quieter. But it was a quiet that, instead of soothing, made her father—and his parishioners—uneasy.

Diana understood it. Neither her father nor his sister did, though.

She fastened her gaze on her aunt. *Oh, dear Aunt Mary,* she thought. *You were Mother's dearest friend, and I love you. Even so, I know I can never make you understand any better than I can Father. You both keep waiting for me to turn into my mother, and I can't. Much as you and Father want me to, it just isn't possible.*

Because it wasn't possible, they had again arrived at a crisis point. Now Diana was facing the same rationale that had sent her off to live with her grandfather after her mother's death. It had married her to Huntley, and was

working against her again here and now. For the third
time!

Living with her grandfather had been a wonderful, ex-
hilarating life, and Diana had loved every moment of it.
Her second exile, though, had been anything but wonderful. It had been dark and oppressive. She refused to consider for an instant what life might be like in this third
attempt to restore peace to the parish by marrying her
off—*again*.

No, she must escape before it could be done. To make
her plans for just that eventuality, she rose and invited,
"I'm going to walk along the river for a while, won't you
join me?"

Both her father and her aunt declined, still struggling
with her declaration of freedom. Diana had known they
would, and she rose from the garden bench opposite them
and set off quickly, relieved to be alone and at liberty to
make her plans.

Chapter Two

"There's nothing like a stint as a slave to teach you to appreciate your heritage, wouldn't you say?" The slender man in seaman's culottes smiled down at the half-starved dog at his feet. A sharp bark signified the abused animal's eagerness to please this man who'd rescued him from his persecutors.

For a moment the man stood in quiet thought, remembering a previous occasion on which he'd done the same. It had become an almost sacred memory because he'd enshrined it in the innermost place in his heart. He let himself remember that other dog he had helped rescue, and the beautiful girl he'd rescued with it, and his pulse beat faster.

She had been the one to wrest that tiny puppy from its tormentors, and, in the end, he'd had to stand by, powerless, while she had been returned to the captivity of a brutal husband for her trouble.

Long-felt, anger-tinged sorrow rose in him as he thought of her and the hopeless love that had been born in him that day. His love for a sixteen-year-old girl who was another man's wife.

Resolutely he forced the memories from his mind. Now there was this new dog, and the time for memories was past. He looked down at the huge beast so in contrast with that long-ago puppy and smiled. "Let's see about getting you fed, then, shall we, boy?"

Dropping a hand to the dog's shaggy neck, he gave its ruff a brief shake and set off for the great limestone palace that sprawled, glowing in the late afternoon sun, across the ridge ahead of them. His long strides and homesick haste notwithstanding, the distance across the vast park took them long enough to negotiate that the shadows were lengthening by the time they reached the mansion.

The traveler and his newly acquired four-legged companion stopped short of the wide, stone-paved carriage area, and the man stood a moment deep in thought. He frowned at the tall double front doors, glanced down at his worn seaman's attire, and laughed. Dropping to one knee beside the disreputable-looking canine at his feet, he said, "I don't think my butler would let us in, lad. Not even if he recognized me. Jessops is exceedingly high in the instep, you know."

The dog laved his new friend's chin with a long tongue.

The seaman laughed again, and the big dog squirmed from tip to tail with pleasure. "I think we'd best go 'round to the back, old man. I feel almost certain that I wouldn't be recognized, and if I were, poor Jessops would undoubt-edly faint at the sight of me."

The dog whined as if he wished he could help the man solve his problem.

"Thank you, but the dilemma is mine." He stayed as he was, idly scratching the dog behind the ears as he stared at the imposing facade looming over them. After a long moment—during which the dog rolled over on his back in hopes of getting his belly scratched—he left off staring at the myriad windows reflecting the dying rays of the sun and rose.

The dog scrambled to his feet and stood fixedly attentive.

"Well, no sense delaying, boy. Come along. Let's hope Carrington is still in the estate office."

In a distant wing of the mansion, Alistair Carrington, personal secretary of the Duke of Smythington, sat at his desk, his white-knuckled hands folded over the last ledger in which he'd been making entries. His face was set, his teeth clenched against the words that his position forbade him to speak. With grim determination and a hand that threatened to shake with the anger that was coursing through him, he lit the candles in the candelabra on his desk.

Across from him, a handsome young man dressed in that height of fashion that proclaimed him a dandy lounged at his ease in a brocade-covered wing chair. Regarding Carrington's set face, he frowned. His voice when he spoke was the bored drawl of a man about town, but his eyes were as sharp as stilettoes. "I must insist, Carrington, that you begin to take the necessary steps to make me the next Duke of Smythington."

"That action might be premature, Sir Joseph. There is a rumor that His Grace, your cousin, is still alive."

The other waved a negligent hand. "A rumor only, Carrington. Let us be sensible. What chance has an Englishman in the hands of the Arabs? Especially as soft an Englishman as my cousin."

Carrington's lips tightened at the other's scornful tone, but he didn't speak.

"After all, it has been the better part of a year since

good old David disappeared, Carrington. High time something was done."

The secretary still didn't answer.

"Still hoping against hope, eh?" He smoothed one of his cuffs. "You always were fond of him, weren't you?"

"Yes, I am."

"Oh, come now! Using the present tense while speaking of a dead man, Carrington? You begin to try my patience."

"Do I, Sir Joseph?" The inquiry was mild but the gaze he bent on the man slouched in the wing chair was stony with disapproval.

"You do, Carrington. You do indeed." Sir Joseph Ewing rose to his full height and leaned his hands on the desk. Looming over the elderly secretary he said distinctly, "I am going to London to claim my rights. When I am the new Duke of Smythington, you will be the first person whom I dismiss from my illustrious service. You may count on it."

Carrington rose to meet him glare for glare. "If ever you should be the Duke of Smythington, Sir Joseph, you would have no need to dismiss me from this post, because I should have resigned the moment I heard the news."

Sir Joseph reared back away from the desk. "What? You'd refuse to serve me?"

Carrington's chin lifted and he stared down his long nose at his questioner. "When one is accustomed to serving a gentleman, adjustments to lesser men are difficult."

"Damn your insolence!" The dandy lunged across the desk to aim a blow at the old gentleman's chin. Carrington drew back just enough to cause him to miss and lose his balance. Moving with the purpose and speed of a much younger man, he rounded the desk, caught Sir Joseph by his arm, and propelled him from the study.

"Show Sir Joseph the door!" he ordered the footman on

duty in the hall. Then he had to fight against his own wrathful indignation in an effort to close the study door without slamming it.

Returning to the desk, he dropped his head into his hands for a long moment, then lifted it to gaze across the study to the fireplace. Over it hung the portrait of his master, Michael David Lawrence, Ninth Duke of Smythington.

Serenely the kind eyes in the round, amiable face looked back at him. Michael David, the apple of his mother's eye, the sweet boy who was dearly loved by both his parents until their deaths when the boy was ten.

Carrington sighed, remembering. He had taken over then, and served as parent, tutor, and mentor until the young lord had left for school. He smiled to recall how the boy had showed skill in everything he'd turned his hand to. David had ridden like the wind, a veritable part of his horse. His swordplay had been excelled only by his shooting skills.

Carrington had been so proud of him. No father could have been prouder. The fact that David could not abide the thought of hitting with the intention of hurting another person and therefore was sadly lacking in the gentleman's sport of fisticuffs had done nothing to diminish that pride.

Then David had gone away to school. To Carrington's consternation, the once lithe David had come back a chubby young man of seventeen. Having been made miserable there by the young savages jealous of his rank and fabulous wealth and quick to take advantage of him because of his smaller size, David had begun eating a second helping at meals in order to have an excuse to linger at the table until his classmates were occupied elsewhere. It had proved an unfortunate habit.

From his days at school until his disappearance, David

had sought solace in food. Though this deeply disappointed Carrington, nothing could dim his love of the boy.

Tears came to his eyes. "Ah, David, my dear lad, where are you?"

The candle flames flickered.

Carrington's head snapped around to find the source of the draft that had caused the flames to waver and saw the French doors at the end of the room close gently behind a slender figure. A soft, deep voice called out. "I'm here."

With a gasp of delighted disbelief, Carrington rushed to meet the younger man. "David! Dear boy! Your Grace."

"Just 'David,' Carrington," the seaman ordered softly. "Just 'David.' "

The two embraced, holding hard for an instant before breaking away.

"Oh, my dear boy." Carrington held him at arms' length, his eyes anxiously surveying him. "You can't know how dreadful it has been, watching, wondering . . . hoping against hope that you were all right. Clinging to the rumor that you had made it to a British frigate. Praying that you would come safe home!" He whipped out a large white handkerchief and blew his nose. As he restored it to his pocket he said, "Oh, thank God you've come home."

"Indeed. I do fervently thank God that I have," the Duke of Smythington agreed, clapping his secretary on the shoulder and smiling. "Now get the brandy, Carry, and we will talk."

"Yes, yes, we shall." The secretary hastened to the drinks table on the far wall. "Ah, Your Grace, it seems as if you have been gone forever."

David seated himself in the chair his cousin had so recently vacated and waited for Carrington with a twisted smile on his face. It did indeed seem forever that he'd been gone. He'd spent less than a year away, but he'd spent it a *world* away from his beloved England. A world away from the values and mores he'd always taken for granted. To him, even the word *forever* failed to describe his own feelings about his time in exile.

He sighed, closed his eyes briefly, and reopened them to simply observe his well-loved friend. The deep affection he felt for this man who'd been a father to him was clear in his regard as he watched Carrington pour the cognac.

Everything was special now. Every gesture was treasured, every sensation heightened. David gave himself over to it, luxuriating in the simple fact that he was home.

They took up their glasses and saluted each other.

"To your safe return!" Carrington proposed.

David answered his toast with one of his own. His voice rang with it. "To freedom!"

They sat in silence for a while, seeming to savor their brandy, but in reality basking in the overwhelming joy they each felt at meeting again. Finally Carrington cleared his throat to ask, "Where have you been, Your Grace?"

David merely smiled that twisted smile. "Away, Carry. Just away."

"You can't leave it at that, David." Carrington's eagerness was vying with his concern. "There have been the wildest tales, lad. I've been frantic for your safety. Yes, and despairing of it, too. You can't say, 'Just away,' and hope that I will leave you in any peace."

David laughed then. Grinning, he said, "I suppose that's true. Of you, at least, Carry. As for the rest of our world, the story of my prolonged absence would sound like one of those improbable adventures penned by dreamers who seek to gain the public's attention."

Carrington managed a chuckle. "As I recall, gaining public attention has never been an ambition of yours, David."

"Nor is it now, so you must swear secrecy."

"Done."

David smiled at him. "Since you have left off calling me 'Your Grace,' I'll tell you the tale, Carry."

Carrington settled deeper in his chair, his gaze fastened on the man across from him.

"It began when my good friend Michael Mathers, Viscount Kantwell, and I were journeying to visit a friend. He asked if I'd mind a slight detour, as he wanted to go look at a yacht in a little seaport called Clifton-on-Tides." David's gaze turned inward and his eyes went bleak. "Unfortunately, we never got there."

Carrington leaned forward.

"We ran into an unsavory gang of men herding a group of Englishmen in chains. One of the chained men called out to us for help, but Mathers had already leapt out of the coach to go to their aid. I grabbed the pistols from the coach and lumbered down after him." He grinned a bitter, rueful grin and said self-mockingly, "I was still portly then, and of no help at all. After I'd fired the two shots the pistols held, I was easily struck down. Mathers was still fighting when I lost consciousness, but the odds were too heavily against him."

David drained his glass, letting the brandy burn its way down to his stomach. It was no marvel to him that it did so without warming him in the face of recollections so bleak.

Carrington rose from his chair behind the desk and replenished David's glass, his eyes full of concern.

"When I awoke," David went on, "I found myself chained to a wall in a cave. Mathers, very much the worse for the beating he'd taken, was beside me."

"Oh, lad." Carrington's voice balanced between sympathy and outrage.

David looked down for a moment at the brandy he

swirled in his glass. Then he lifted his chin and told his friend, "We were there several weeks, when one of the other prisoners broke out in a fever." He shot a glance at Carrington. "You know how I've always dabbled in healing."

"Yes," the secretary replied. Smiling, he recalled all the sick and injured animals the man across from him had tended in his youth. One corner of the magnificent Smythington stables had always been full of them. The huge conservatory had become an aviary, as well, with the birds the young Duke had rescued and healed flying happily about in it.

Never hurting, always helping God's creatures had been his splendid, soft-hearted David's way. The young Duke had not even permitted hunting on his vast lands. "Yes, I remember," he said, with a fond smile.

"I tried to help the victims of the fever when it became obvious to me that our captors had no intention of doing so."

"Could you have gotten away?"

"No." He scowled down into his glass. "Mathers was the guarantee for my remaining in the cave. They would have killed him had I escaped. Besides, I was needed."

Silence stretched between them. Finally, Carrington asked, "Were you able to save them all?"

"Not all. The weakest of the women and three of the children died in spite of my pitiful efforts."

"Ah." There was deep sympathy in the secretary's voice; he knew the suffering that would have caused David.

"Mathers was the last to come down with the fever. I was frantic to learn whether he survived it, but our captors had decided to ship a load of us out and they forced me to go along to nurse them. It wasn't until my return to England that I knew he had survived."

"Where were you sent?" Carrington's curiosity was weighted with horror.

"To the slave market in Barbary." It was as if he were reliving the experience. His face was stern with the effort it took him to repress his memories of that dreadful time. Of the men stripped to the waist to display their muscles, their mouths forced open to show the health of their teeth. Of women dragged forth naked to be assessed by lustful eyes, and of the children . . . He slammed his mind closed to the fate of the children, unable to face it even now. Instead he recalled the whistle of the slavers' whips that commanded obedience from them all.

Eyes bleak, he hurried on as if speech would conquer remembrance. "I was sold to a sultan of . . . peculiar tastes." A shudder went through him. "When I refused somewhat violently to go along with his idea of fun, I was . . ." He raised an eyebrow and grinned a twisted travesty of a grin. "I was, er, shown the error of my ways and sent to the mines."

"Oh, my God!"

"There I learned more about the dark side of human nature than I could ever have believed existed had I never left our England."

"Boy, please. You don't have to go on." Carrington's eyes were full of pity.

David cocked his head a moment, then said, "I rather think I'd like to, Carry, if you can bear it. It seems to be helping." He stared into his brandy, thoughtful for a moment. "Like lancing a boil, I suppose." But he couldn't sit still any longer. He rose and began to pace the room.

Carrington got up and replenished their glasses. When he'd sat down again David went on. "In the mines, we were worked hard and given precious little to eat." He stopped, faced Carrington, and gestured to his slender form. "Witness the benefit."

"Dear boy . . ."

"No!" He refused his friend's quick sympathy with the single curt word. "I'm here. I survived." His face was grim. "It's enough. There are many who will never return to their homes." He turned and Carrington saw the agony on his face as he demanded, "What are a few whip marks compared to that?"

Carrington was too wise to answer.

David lapsed into silence then, recalling the men he'd slaved beside in the hell of the mines. Head bowed, he remembered them, God help them. Those who were still alive. Or had been when he escaped. He drew in a deep, steadying breath and threw back his head.

"Are you hungry?" Carrington regretted the words the minute they left his mouth.

David turned toward him and laughed. "Food *was* my comfort once, wasn't it?" His laughter died. "No. I'm rarely hungry now. I've seen . . ." He let that thought go. Why further depress his old friend? He'd done too much of that already.

Forcing a smile, he changed the subject. He told his secretary, "It's my intention, Carry, to get lost for a while. To take a long walk through England. I feel the need to walk in freedom and to reacquaint myself with Englishmen. I'm not ready to harness myself into the trappings and duties of the Duke of Smythington just yet. So let us make plans, shall we?"

In his turn, Carrington forced a smile and told him, "It will be difficult to keep your cousin at bay, Your Grace."

"I'll sign the necessary proofs before I go."

"And you will take care?" Carrington couldn't bear the

thought of losing his almost-son again. "Promise me you will take care."

David looked deeply into the eyes of the man across from him. "I will. Never fear, old friend. I will."

"I *won't!* I don't care what anyone says. I won't!" Diana tossed her heavy mane of honey-blonde hair back and glared at her aunt. Why couldn't she make her aunt understand?

She sighed. Life had been very different for her aunt. *She* would have to be the one to understand, Diana admitted reluctantly.

Her aunt Mary had come home to her brother at the vicarage right after she'd been widowed and had settled in, completely at home again. A Baronet's widow, her aunt was properly called Lady Kelington, but Diana found that cumbersome, so rarely used it, preferring to call her "Lady Mary," however much it annoyed her aunt.

Lady Kelington bowed her head a moment and sighed. "I knew it was a mistake to let you grow up at your grandfather's."

"Grandfather has nothing to do with this and you know it, Aunt Mary. My attitude is caused by having been forced to marry Huntley and by that marriage alone." Diana shrugged, a quick nervous movement. "And, of course, Father's having decided to marry me to him in spite of my wishes in the matter." Her nostrils flared. "As if that choice weren't bad enough, now that I'm a widow and fresh out of mourning, he can't wait to marry me off *again!*"

She took a turn about her aunt's small sitting room, her silken skirts flowing out behind her with the anger of her strides. "If only I hadn't made that deathbed promise to Mother to obey him!" She glared at her aunt, daring her to disagree. "And I did obey him. For I was certainly merely obeying Father when I married Huntley. God knows it was nothing I wanted."

Aunt Mary gasped. "Diana! Don't be irreverent!"

Diana's expression was somewhere between a scornful smile and a scowl. "I suppose that *would* be blasphemous here in a vicarage, wouldn't it?"

"Young lady"—her aunt was stung to a firm reply by her niece's seeming lack of respect for her dear brother's profession—"your father was the fourth son of his family, so of course he was destined for the clergy. Regardless of the difference this made in their stations, your mother and he loved each other very much, and she would be extremely displeased with you to hear you speak this way."

"Aunt Mary." Diana's voice was equally firm. "In spite of the fact that I seem to recall that *she* disobeyed Grandfather to marry my father, I kept my promise to Mother. I obeyed Father and I married Baron Huntley, just as he wished. Now I want to do as I wish. And I wish to remain unattached. I don't want to remarry."

"Oh, my dear! Surely you don't mean that you . . ."

"Yes. Yes, I do. I mean that I want to set up my own establishment. Please understand, Aunt Mary. I want to be my own person."

"Oh, Diana, don't let dear Manfred hear you speak like that! You sound so willful. After all, he sent you to live with your grandfather so that you would have all the social advantages your mother had as a girl. He didn't send you so that you would return to him so strong-minded that he despairs of you. You wouldn't want him to hear you say that you want to be"—she shivered delicately—"*an independent woman.*"

"Slight chance of that, Aunt Mary." Diana sank into a chair, her barely hidden anger finally dissipated. "My father hasn't heard anything I've *ever* had to say."

Unfortunately, Mary was not able to disagree with her, so she offered instead, "He's a scholar, you know. A man of the cloth. A man of peace."

Diana stared at her aunt until Lady Kelington had to look away. Then she said quietly, "And that is the whole problem, isn't it?" She sighed heavily. "My father is a man of peace. I disturb that peace, so I have to go."

Her aunt had no answer.

Diana stared blindly out the window for a long moment. When she spoke again, it was almost pensively. "But why must I remarry? And why a man of my father's choosing?" She stretched out her hands in a gesture that might have been one of entreaty. "I was so unhappy as a wife, Aunt Mary. I never want to put myself under the control of another man as long as I live!"

"Husbands are necessary to protect us, Diana." Lady Kelington spoke with the certainty of the cherished wife she had been.

Diana couldn't bring herself to tell her aunt the truth about her marriage to Huntley. Instead she told her, "I don't need protection! I've been training to take care of myself. Should the need arise, I can fight as well as a man." Diana rose and swept her hand down in a movement that indicated her statuesque frame. "And you must admit that I am certainly no dainty miss!"

Her aunt pretended to cough into her handkerchief so as to avoid giving an answer that pained her far more than it would have her niece.

Diana continued, "Furthermore, I command a sizable fortune; I really *could* be mistress of my own establishment." She set about trying to tempt her aunt into joining in her rebellion. "You could act as my chaperone, so that everything would be proper and Father's mind would be at ease. We could have a lovely gem of a house in London—

not too large—something suitable for a young widow and her widowed aunt. We could make it a truly elegant place and entertain all your friends."

She felt as if she were begging her aunt, and didn't care if she was. "I know you've missed Town since your husband passed away. And your Jonathan would have ever so much more to do in the city than there is for a young boy to do here." Words tumbled out as Diana fought for her freedom. "And of course, I can afford a little country place, too. One near here perhaps, so that you could see all your friends in the parish when we came to escape the London heat in the summer. Only think of the pleasant times we could have!"

If she weren't begging, it was as close to begging that Diana had ever come in her life. She held her breath, waiting anxiously for her aunt's reply.

Her aunt's eyes had sparkled when Diana had talked of London, and a smile had curved her lips at the mention of a country house nearby. Those signs gave Diana hope. She kept her fingers, hidden in the folds of her skirt, crossed so hard that they ached.

Lady Kelington sighed, and for a moment, Diana thought that her aunt was on the verge of giving in. But then Mary recalled her duty. Habit and loyalty to her brother as head of their little family were too strong, and she told her tall young niece, "Diana, your father requires you to marry. It is very simple. That is how it must be."

Diana's heart sank as her dreams crumbled. Fighting tears, she managed, "Because he wishes to be rid of me and my outspokenness."

Her aunt gave up. Tears blinded her, too. "Oh, my dear. I'm so very sorry."

Overwhelmed with disappointment, Diana stood looking down at her companion. Finally she said, "Well, I suppose I must thank you for that much at least." She couldn't help it that her voice had an edge.

Lady Kelington flinched.

Then Diana was contrite to have hurt her. She sighed a deep, ragged sigh and said gently, "And I know you can no more change Father's mind than I can, Aunt Mary, more's the pity. I know you would try to make him see my side of things if you thought you could do so." She said the words, not in the least certain that she meant any of them. She only knew that her aunt had managed to stay a stranger to grief except in the death of her husband and her dear friend, Diana's mother, and she was loath to make her sad now, for her own poor sake.

Resigned, she looked away for a moment. Her eyes weren't really seeing the lovely rose garden at which she stared. Instead, she saw a pair of infinitely kind, warm brown eyes. *His* eyes. Her heart leapt, whispered *If only . . . ,* then fell. That, too, was impossible.

Diana's voice was filled with sadness when she turned back to her aunt and told her firmly, "But I won't remarry, Aunt Mary. I shall never, ever marry again. Not as long as I live. I won't! I swear it."

Chapter Three

At Smythington Park two thoroughly pampered days later, David, clad again in the carefully laundered and lovingly mended garb of a lowly seaman, stood looking back at the great house for a long time. Pride of possession surged through him.

Strange. He'd never felt that before. Always until now, he'd taken it all for granted—the sprawling mansion, the great park surrounding it, even the wealth and the privileged position it represented. No more. Not ever again. He knew now just how blessed he was to have been born here in England.

And yet, even with his newfound appreciation, he was leaving it all behind to go on a quest—the quest that he hoped would bring balm to his wounded spirit and peace to his shattered soul.

He had to. The nightmares that haunted him about his time in captivity had to be silenced. The tortures he'd undergone must, somehow, be cleansed from his consciousness—or at least come to grips with.

He couldn't keep on flinching every time he heard the crack of a whip. He'd used up all the courage he had to keep his captors and torturers from seeing his fear of the lash, and now he had none left to keep his body from quailing at the sound of a leather thong whistling through the air.

He gave a derisive snort and the dog looked up at him. "Fine Peer of the Realm I make just now, friend. My shaking like a leaf when a man whips up his team anywhere near me hardly presents a picture of ducal dignity, does it?"

The huge dog regarded him solemnly, unsure of whether or not to wag his tail. Instead, he approached his new master cautiously, watching him carefully. Finally he whined and licked the man's hand.

David let out a soft laugh that quivered in the air between them. "Thanks, boy. I need all the encouragement I can get if I'm to shake this thing, and I have to get rid of it before I'll let myself return home again." He smoothed the great head. "I think we're ready to go."

The Seaman-Duke had seen to it that Carrington had all the papers he needed to keep his unlovely cousin Joseph from usurping his dukedom, and, more importantly for David's true return someday, that Carrington had the measurements for the clothes he'd need when he got back from his trek. Unless he needed them for a tent, he certainly couldn't use his old ones, thank God.

He'd been careful to ask Carrington to inform all his friends—those close friends who, with him, had been dubbed "The Lucky Seven"—that he might be stopping by. Carrington would also warn them about his appearance, of course.

With everything done that he intended to do for now, Michael David Lawrence, Ninth Duke of Smythington, turned his back on the splendor of his home and began his quest. Whistling to heel the scruffy dog he'd ordered fed, bathed, and brushed, he addressed him. "Well, old boy, now our journey begins."

The dog responded with a sharp bark and a gay wag of his tail. The change in David's tone of voice had filled him with relief.

"Good. I'm glad to see you're looking forward to this, too." David grinned at his foolishness in talking to the dog as if he could understand; then, realizing that he would no doubt do so many times before they returned safely, he told his four-legged companion, "I think we must find a name for you."

The dog looked up, tail wagging.

"'Phoenix'?" David suggested, then shook his head. "No. You might be a bit of a resurrection, but I think we'll put all that behind us."

The dog shoved his muzzle into David's hand.

"Yes," David told him, "I'm glad to be with you, too."

He considered the dog as they walked along. The animal was vastly improved by his bath and a few meals, but he still looked travel worn. "How about 'Ulysses,'" David suggested. "He was a traveler."

The dog looked up, bright-eyed with curiosity.

David shook his head again. "No. I don't think so. We aren't going to be gone *that* long."

They swung along in companionable silence for a while, the dog ambling beside the man he had chosen for his master, the man with his arms swinging and a smile on his lips.

Already England was working her magic on him. Much of the tightness around his mouth had disappeared since his first conversation with Carrington. With his dear friend and excellent secretary in charge, he could shed, temporarily, the heavy burden of his station in life, and he found he was relieved to do so. The wary sadness had left his eyes, and a lightness of spirit began to enter his heart.

He bent and scooped up a stone without breaking stride, the weight of his knapsack almost overbalancing him. Resettling it, he skipped the flat stone along the road ahead of them as he wondered aloud what to call his new friend. "Rover," he murmured. "No. Far too common. You deserve better than that if you're going to accompany me on my journey. I'm not always the easiest person to get along with, you know. Not anymore. You'll have to be a special dog to do it." His smile vanished. "Especially through the nightmares."

The dog pressed against his thigh.

David looked startled. Evidently the dog had responded to the change in his tone of voice. He patted the animal's great head gently.

The dog barked sharply.

" 'Beau,' then." He looked critically at the harsh, ragged coat of his friend. "Hmmm. *Beau* is French for masculine beauty. We've a little difficulty there."

Suddenly an idea came to David. He'd been thinking of the wonders of his country and the men who'd produced and protected English freedom, searching for just the right name. He'd already rejected "Nelson" and "Wellington" as too heroic for an untried animal, but now a story came to mind of a fictional man's travels. That man offered the perfect name. "I say, boy! Jonathan Swift wrote a book about the travels of an Englishman—which is certainly apropos here—and the hero of that allegory was named Gulliver."

The dog leapt high to catch at the stick David had picked up as he spoke. The Duke decided to take the leap as a sign of approval. " 'Gulliver' it is then."

He flung the stick far into the field they were walking beside. The newly named Gulliver jumped the wide ditch beside the road and shot across the stubbled field in pursuit.

It was well that he had. An instant later, with a clatter of wheels and the staccato drum of hoofbeats, a yellow-wheeled gig slewed around the curve behind them and came on at a gallop. The horse's eyes were rolling, its coat lathered. Dust boiled out from under its frantic hooves.

On it came, straight for David.

The driver's hat was pulled low over his scowling face to keep it from blowing off. Nevertheless, David recognized his cousin, Sir Joseph Ewing. His face was set and sullen, and he barely gave the man in his path a glance as he whipped his horse to further frenzy.

An instant later, it became abundantly clear to David that his cousin had no intention of even attempting to miss a lowly pedestrian. At the last moment, David flung himself out of the way into the ditch. He landed at the bottom in a heap.

Biting back curses, David picked himself up. When he found he couldn't stand, he gave vent to all the expletives that he'd first refused to hurl at his fast-disappearing cousin.

Gulliver came running. Plunging into the ditch, he shoved against his new master. David went down again, as his injured ankle gave way under him.

Leaning against the side of the ditch, he looked after the careening gig, hating the fact that it had brought his avaricious cousin to mind so forcefully—and painfully. Finally, it was gone in a roiling cloud of dust around the curve far down the country lane. David looked after it and sighed.

Suddenly, his spirit didn't feel quite so light anymore.

Diana's young cousin Jonathan begged for mercy. "Please, let's stop, Diana. I'm hot and I'm tired."

His opponent's eyes flashed. "Don't be such a sissy. *You'll* grow up to be a man, and you can't be a sissy then." She aimed another blow at the cushion to which her adversary clung manfully.

"Oof!" Jonathan fell back from the force of her blow, recovered, and threw down the cushion. "That's it! I quit! You hit too hard."

Diana's frown of concentration fled. Smiling, she swooped forward and caught him to her. Just as quickly, she let him go.

While he tried to catch his balance she shook out her silken skirts, which she'd earlier caught up to free her to spar with him, and crowed, "Oh, that's splendid. That's the first time I've been able to stagger you. Do you know what this means?"

"Yes." Her cousin scowled at her. "It means that you have gotten to be a perfect hoyden. Ladies don't go around pummeling a fellow like that!" He rubbed his chest as he stared at her resentfully.

"Oh, Jonathan, I'm sorry. Truly I am."

"No, you're not." He glared fiercely. "If you were sorry you wouldn't do it."

She took his hand and led him over to the stone garden bench in the rose arbor. "I . . . ," she started and stopped immediately. How much could she say to a child? What did her so much younger companion know of the cruelty of men? How could she destroy his innocence by explaining that she wanted to be able to defend herself if she ever came upon another monster like her late husband?

After all, she had always taken great care to hide her bruises from everyone, especially her family. A combination of stubborn pride and consideration for their feelings had demanded it. It hadn't been hard. Huntley usually took care that the bruises were in places that were easy to conceal. Besides, around Jonathan, Huntley had been bluff and jovial, almost avuncular. Indeed he had seemed a pleasant man to all who had known him. Except Diana. Baron Huntley had saved his brutality for the bedchamber.

Jonathan stared at her from under a thatch of heavy golden hair very like her own. His blue eyes were full of suspicion and accusation. "Why *do* you do it?" It was more a demand than a question.

Diana considered her answer carefully, determined to preserve his innocence. "I want to be able to defend myself, dear." She remembered her husband's strength and wondered if she *could* have defended herself against it. She didn't know. She only knew that the humiliation she had suffered at his hands had left her with the aching need to make herself able to try, if nothing more.

"What from?" Jonathan wanted to know.

She considered the youth seriously for a moment. "Sometimes," she answered thoughtfully, "one finds oneself in a position of mild danger. A place where someone stronger decides to use that strength against one." There, that had been a safe answer. She found she was rather proud of it.

"Why?"

She plucked a rose from the vine that climbed the arbor beside them, and stripped away the thorns. "Why are people hateful bullies? I honestly can't tell you that, Jonathan." She put the rose up to her nose to smell its lovely scent.

"Frankly, I think there is something terribly wrong with them. Some important piece missing from their personality, perhaps."

"Well"—Jonathan's voice held a note of finality—"then I should be the one punching *you*. There's no chance *you* will ever even *meet* a bully, and someday I shall have to go off to school, where there are lots of them! In fact," he went on, warming to his subject, "there are even boys in our very own village who like to torment cats and dogs. Those are the boys that your father says will grow up to be awful men if their hearts don't change. And sometimes they pick on me when I go to the village, too."

He regarded her rebelliously. "There are no bullies in *your* life, Diana, even if you do no longer have Huntley to take care of you. So you don't need to keep punching on me!" With that he jumped up from the bench and ran off.

After a startled split second, Diana hurled the rose at his retreating back.

Chapter Four

Searching along the edge of his ditch, David found the stout stick that Gulliver had gone to retrieve but had dropped when he arrived back at the depression that held his fallen friend. Using it as a cane, David hobbled down the ditch until he came to a part of it that sloped more gently than the steep sides that had sheltered him from his cousin's unconscious attack.

Gulliver ran up and down the bank, barking wildly.

"It's all right, boy. I'll be out of here in a minute," David reassured the excited dog.

The instant he was out of the ditch and on a level with the great shaggy dog, Gulliver jumped up to put his front paws on David's chest. Balancing with difficulty, David brought the knee of his injured leg up and shoved the dog back, saying firmly, "Down!"

As the dog slewed sideways, as off balance as his new master, David limped away from the edge of the ditch. The dog's next affectionate assault, he knew, might put him flat on his back. He'd prefer that it not be in the mire at the bottom of the ditch.

Gulliver whined and spun in a tight circle, wanting more than anything to leap up to where he could "kiss" his benefactor, but a sharp "No" from David kept him on all fours.

The dog's tail, however, was clamped tight between his legs. His eyes were full of a sadness that tore at David's heart.

Slipping his knapsack off, David eased himself down to sit on a fallen tree and called the confused dog to him. Taking the animal's face in his hands, he told him, "You're a good dog, Gulliver. A good dog. You're just too big to jump up on people." He cocked his head and added firmly, "Come to think of it, any dog at all is too big to jump up on people. It's just plain bad manners." He moved his hands down to the dog's neck and gave a shake to the thick ruff there.

Gulliver relaxed, at last, and grinned at him, tongue lolling. His eyes were bright with eager affection again.

"Good boy," David told him, letting warmth fill his voice. "Good boy."

Finally the big dog's tail began to wag. An instant later, he gave a joyous yowl and flung himself away to run in happy circles, barking.

David smiled and just watched him. As the Duke of Smythington, he must own thousands of animals of one kind or another but as a simple wayfarer, he had only this one. This dog, Gulliver. He set himself to enjoy this single animal to the fullest.

Gulliver's coat was a warm tan with a blanket of wavy black fur that covered his back and went all the way out to the tip of his long, strong tail. The back of his neck and huge head were marked with a band of black that tipped his ears and went on across his broad head to end in a V between his eyes. That gave him a ferocious look, in spite of the fact that his large, black-outlined brown eyes were the kindest David had seen in a very long time. With a little more flesh on him, Gulliver was going to be a handsome dog.

Beyond the rest, there was the love and utter devotion that shone from the dog's eyes. David's heart stirred and lifted at the sight.

He wondered if he had ever studied any of the dogs at Smythington Park half so carefully, and knew that he hadn't. They'd been treated with affection and given every care, but they'd been part of the colorful tapestry of his life, not his boon companions.

Well, this was to be a journey of discovery, after all. Didn't he hope that in this slowed pace of life to which he'd escaped he'd be able to contemplate everything around him until he found peace? He chuckled. Why not start with this wonderful dog?

Calling the animal back to him, David stroked him once down the back and told him, "Time to be on our way, boy."

One hobbling step and David knew they wouldn't be going far. He clenched his teeth against the pain in his ankle, and resisted the urge to curse. Was it all to end here, his glorious quest? Was this to be the end of the journey he'd embarked upon to help him forget the horrors of his captivity?

With all his heart and mind, he wanted to explore the land of his birth with his new eyes of appreciation. He definitely didn't want to have to stop some passerby and beg them to take him home.

No! This wasn't going to be the end of his dream. Not if he had anything to say about it!

"We need to find cold water for this sprained ankle,

Gulliver." He glanced at the afternoon sky, wondering if they would need shelter when darkness fell. If they didn't find any, they could always sleep together under his campaign cloak. David smiled and was glad he'd found that war-worn garment still waiting for him at home. "Looks clear for tonight."

Among many other practical things, his brief time as a common sailor had taught him to be acutely aware of the weather. Climbing wet ratlines to stand aloft on slippery footropes fifty feet above tossing decks could do that for a man. Indeed, furling sails while bent double over their yards in sudden storms had taught him more about the weather than a lifetime under the safety of a vast slate roof had done.

He glanced down at his free hand. The tips of his fingers were still tender from having been torn to bleeding from the roughness of the canvas he and the men sent aloft with him had fought to reef against the force of gale winds.

Returning his gaze to his companion, he told him, "We've a few hours of daylight still—let's find a stream. After I've cooled this ankle, we'll seek shelter for the night."

"Woof!"

David threw back his head and laughed in spite of the pain in his ankle. "Yes, Gulliver," he agreed, "woof, indeed."

Diana went to find her cousin. She'd never thought of her rigorous training program from his point of view before, and now that she had she was a little ashamed of herself. After all, fair was fair, and in her own need, she'd neglected to give Jonathan equal time to develop skills of his own. She hadn't given him his own chance to pummel her.

She also felt a little guilty, too, at having injured his masculine pride, if truth were told.

Besides, she'd have no sparring partner if she didn't make peace with him. And she was determined to make that peace, because she was grimly committed to mastering as many defensive skills as she could acquire.

The first person she found was her aunt.

"Have you seen Jonathan, Aunt Mary?"

Lady Kelington pursed her lips. "Indeed I have, and I really must speak to you about that, Diana. The poor boy was complaining of a stomachache from a blow *you* administered, he said."

"Oh."

"That's hardly an explanation, Diana, and I really must demand one. Why did you strike someone so much smaller than yourself? Indeed," Lady Kelington added, "why did you, a lady, strike my son at all? It is most unseemly!"

"It wasn't quite that way, Aunt Mary. I didn't strike *him*, precisely. I struck the cushion he was holding for me to do so. It is a game we play. A game that will help us develop our skills of . . . ummm . . . self-defense." In spite of her convictions, she could feel guilt flooding her face.

Lady Kelington flung her embroidery into the basket at her side. "Diana, I am thoroughly ashamed of you. No doubt your grandfather has given you very strange ideas of what constitutes proper behavior for a young lady." She shook her head so hard her pretty lace cap slewed sideways. Impatiently poking it back into position, she added, "Riding to hounds with him was acceptable, I suppose. At least, several of my friends seem to think it all right for their daughters to do so. And racing a curricle against his on his own parklands might have been marginally acceptable, since at least you didn't make a *public* spectacle of yourself."

Diana saw how hard her aunt was struggling to be fair and loved her for it. She had no illusions that this was anything but a scold, however.

"I should have told my brother Manfred not to succumb to your grandfather's request that you be allowed to live with him at Belleview after your mother died. Some of the things that man encouraged in you were absolutely unacceptable."

Diana tried to interrupt before things got worse. She'd never liked having her sins cataloged, and her loyalty to her grandfather was fierce. Especially since she'd always known that her father, so deep in his own grief he hadn't noticed his child's, had wanted her gone. Her grandfather's kind intervention had kept her from being sent away to some girls' school where she'd have known no one at all.

Lady Kelington had no intention of letting her interrupt, however. "Fencing, for instance, was quite beyond the pale. I shall never understand why your grandfather thought a lady needed to learn to use a rapier!"

This was her chance to change the way the conversation was going, and Diana took it. "To spite my grandfather's heir, Cousin Maxwell?" she proposed with bright, false innocence.

Lady Kelington couldn't help herself. She laughed. The scolding disappeared in their mutual dislike of the distant cousin who'd inherited her grandfather's title — and Diana's beloved ancestral home. Then she sobered and seemed to look back in time. "Your grandfather was so depressed when your uncle Christian was killed. Then the loss of Christian's twin, Christiane — your own dear mother — following so close on his first loss, nearly unhinged him." Lady Kelington fumbled for her handkerchief and touched it to her eyes.

Tears had come because Diana's mother had been

Mary's dearest friend. That was how her mother had met her father in the first place.

Diana knew that the older woman still missed her mother dreadfully, even after all these years. She tried to inject a soothing comment. She was again denied the opportunity.

"Oh, my dear," her aunt Mary hastened to reassure her, "it was so awful to see him so inconsolable after your mother's death. It seemed the kindly, proper thing to do to send you to live with him. To give him a purpose in life, don't you know. He was so disappointed and depressed that your mother had had no son, only you, and of course, you couldn't inherit the title."

Diana blinked, a little taken aback. She'd never thought of herself as a "disappointment," much less as some kind of a failure! And she still couldn't help wondering when it had gotten "proper" for a parent to give away his child!

"Oh, I don't mean you are of no consequence! Your grandfather loved you dearly, as you very well know. The very thought of you being sent away to some girls' school enraged him." She sniffled once and put her handkerchief away. "You gave him a new reason to live, you know."

It was Diana's turn to reach for her handkerchief.

Her aunt went on, "He adored you and took pride in everything you accomplished. And he left you everything that wasn't entailed to the heir to the title, didn't he? But he couldn't leave you Belleview, and I know you miss living there very much."

"True, but it would never have been the same without Grandfather. I suppose I could have gone back there when Huntley was killed, but I could never abide living there with Cousin Maxwell. Nor, indeed, would his wife have appreciated it."

"No," her aunt said wistfully. "Of course you couldn't. She wouldn't." She straightened her thin shoulders. "Naturally, you came home here to your father, and I'm thankful that I'm here to look after you both."

"We're fortunate to have you to do it."

"It's kind of you to say so, dear. The Applebys are very efficient, though, you know," Mary said, complimenting the couple who worked so hard for the Vicar. She would give even the devil his due, and the Applebys were nothing like the devil. They were pearls beyond price.

"Yes, but Mr. Appleby has his hands full teaching Jonathan and the rest of the parish children at the school, and Mrs. Appleby, heaven knows, is more than fully occupied with this great barn of a house." She swept her hand around in a wide gesture. She frowned slightly. "The Dukes of Smythington were more than generous when they built this parish house. There's room for a small army."

"That's an exaggeration, Diana. If your mother and father had had the number of children they wanted, it would have been just a comfortable fit and not the least crowded. Besides, how can you call this a big house when you've been living in your grandfather's mansion?"

"Grandfather had an army of servants, so the size of his house didn't matter. And Father and Mother *didn't* have all the children they wanted. As you said, there was just me." She sighed, then smiled. "And now, even with me back here again, we all rattle around like peas in a washtub."

"Well, we won't this weekend. Your suitor is to come for a visit."

"What?" Diana was stunned. So soon? Somehow she'd thought she'd have had more time. She'd just come out of her widow's weeds. They hadn't even been packed away yet! "My *what?* Nobody told *me!*"

"I suppose the very thought of doing so made them nervous."

Diana scowled at her aunt and rose. She was fully aware that her aunt was as timorous as the "them" she accused of being too nervous to warn Diana that she was about to be besieged by some buck or dandy of the *ton*. Was it her size or her attitude that made them reluctant to tell her things they thought might upset her? Or were they hoping to sneak up on her!

Diana stood quiet a moment, her lips compressed in a firm line. Then she announced, "I'll go ask Father what's going on."

"Don't nag Manfred, dear." Her hands fluttered nervously. "He's busy in the study, and he doesn't need his peace disturbed."

Diana had to be careful not to slam the door as she left her aunt's little parlor, but she couldn't help muttering, "It's not *his* peace that I'm concerned about!"

Chapter Five

Mrs. Appleby was bustling up the main stairway. "Vicar says company's coming tomorrow. We have to air the front bedchamber, Betsy. And hurry!"

The only maid the vicarage could boast flew along behind the housekeeper. "Why? What's afoot? We don't never have guests. 'Specially since Miss Diana came home." She clapped a hand over her mouth, her eyes wide. "I didn't mean nothin' by that. Truly I didn't."

"Well, don't cringe, girl. That's your own opinion, and I surely won't scold you for it. Miss Diana coming home *did* set the cat among the pigeons. Everybody's on pins and needles since she came." She shook her head. "That girl never was a peaceful soul, even when she was a baby. Now she's a widow, she's worse."

"Hush, Missus Appleby, some'un might hear you."

"Well, I'd hate that, as I'd not like to hurt her feelings, for some good things did come with her. 'Twas *her* money that got us you to help with the household chores. She would have gotten us others, too, if Vicar could stand the confusion of more bodies about the place. And you're most heartily welcome, I can tell you. I'm not getting any younger, you know."

The little maid, breathless from rushing up the wide old oaken stairway after her superior, gasped, "Well, you'll never prove it by me."

Mrs. Appleby hid her gratified smile and ordered, "Strip the bed, air the comforter, and replace the sheets." She threw open the casement windows as she spoke. "Set up a good fire, and be sure there's more coal for it, besides. Noblemen like their comforts, and it's not summer yet. And hurry. This Lord Runsford is already on his way."

"Oh, my. Coming so soon? I bet that'll set Miss Diana off right and proper."

"Yes, it probably will. Such short notice is inconsiderate, if you ask me." Mrs. Appleby sniffed. "But nobody did."

"Yes, Missus." Betsy scurried out to hang the comforter to air on the clothesline in the kitchen yard, being careful not to let it drag. She hadn't meant that it was just the noble visitor's lack of consideration that would set Miss Diana off, but she knew that Mrs. Appleby knew that better than she did, so she went about her business, holding her tongue.

When she returned with the fresh sheets, she and Mrs. Appleby made short work of remaking the bed. The comforter would have to be brought back in in the late afternoon, before the mists rose from the river and got it damp. A small fire in the fireplace for tonight, and by tomorrow the room would be fit to welcome a guest.

"Don't forget to bring the comforter in later, Betsy."

"Yes, Mrs. Appleby." She hurried out to the rest of her duties.

Mrs. Appleby surveyed the room, and wondered, not for the first time, what a man of Lord Runsford's importance was doing staying at the vicarage instead of at the Smythingdale Arms just down the street in the village. The Arms was well known to be one of the finest hostelries in the realm. It provided every amenity. The whole neighborhood had long been proud of it. But Lord Runsford had only put his servants there. Why in the world would he want to do that, and then put himself up in a shabby vicarage?

Mrs. Appleby shook her head, muttered, "There's no fathoming these aristocrats," and went down to report to the Vicar.

She found him in his study, his graying auburn hair alight in a stray sunbeam from the tall window beside him. The little halo of light gave him a saintly air.

He was holding a book and looking even more perplexed than usual. She waited a moment for him to sense her presence. When he failed to, she cleared her throat.

"Ah. Mrs. Appleby. There you are." He looked at her distractedly, and returned his gaze to the book he held.

She waited a moment, then broke into his reverie. "Betsy and I have readied the best bedchamber, and I was wanting to know what else you cared to have done."

"Ah, yes." With troubled eyes, he looked up from the book he held. "I should be thinking about that, shouldn't I?" He gave his head a shake. "It's this damned book, Appleby. And I mean that as a true description of it, not as a curse word describing it." He shook his head again and sighed. "I bought it so that no one else could have it, and it has become the bane of my existence. I don't want it, but I can't sell it or give it away for the same reason I bought it."

"'Tis that book of spells and such, isn't it?"

"Yes. And not that I believe in such things, of course, but I don't want it falling into the hands of some innocent and contaminating them." He sighed again. "And I don't seem to have the courage to burn it."

"Whyever not, sir? True, it's beautifully crafted and no doubt worth a lot, but I know those considerations don't have any weight with you."

"No. I'm afraid it's cowardice, pure and simple." He frowned mightily. "I know I should cast it into the fire, but what if this curse on the first page of it has any truth to it?"

"What does it say?"

"That burning it would release the demons contained in the spells. Even though I don't truly believe it, I can't seem to bring myself to take the chance."

Mrs. Appleby quoted, " 'Greater is He that is in me than he that is in the world.' "

"Oh, yes. I stand in no doubt of that! But what if they *were* real and they scattered abroad? After all, even Christ believed in demons. Don't forget those He cast out into the swine. Suppose I were to liberate some by burning this dreadful book? How could I be certain that everyone with whom they came in contact is as firm in their beliefs as we are?" He ran a hand through his hair. "Alas, it's a chance I dare not take." He quoted in his turn, " 'There are stranger things, Horatio, than are dreamt of in our philosophies.' " He frowned again. "I *think* I got that right. Not biblical, of course."

"Well, as to that one, I can't say. I make it my business to read only the Good Book," his housekeeper told him.

The Vicar didn't notice. Putting the book under discussion down on his cluttered desk, he went to find his volume of *Hamlet*.

Seeing her employer had retreated into his own world, just as he always did when researching a new idea struck him, Mrs. Appleby left the study and went about her business. Arriving back at the top of the stairs to make a last-minute check on the best bedchamber, she saw Diana standing in its doorway with a speculative look on her face. She wished she could beat a hasty retreat, but Diana turned and saw her. The sunlight that had been flooding the stair landing faded as the younger woman approached her.

"Appleby! Do you know where my father is?" the younger woman demanded.

"I believe he's in his study, Lady Diana."

"Thank you." Diana passed her at the top of the stairs and plunged down them at a pace that left no doubt in the housekeeper's mind that the Vicar was in for it. She glanced out the window. That the weather seemed to be taking a turn for the worse was somehow appropriate.

At the foot of the stairs, Diana turned left and made a beeline for the study. Throwing open the door, she found her father standing in front of one of the bookcases with a leather-bound volume of Shakespeare in his hand.

"Ah, Diana." He smiled at his only child and said with satisfaction, "I was right. The quote I offered Mrs. Appleby a few moments ago *was* from *Hamlet*."

"Father," Diana began without preamble, "I want to talk to you!"

"Yes, my dear?"

"Mrs. Appleby says that we are expecting a guest."

"Yes. Baron Runsford is coming. Tomorrow evening, I believe."

"Runsford!" Diana remembered the man. She remembered him well. Handsome in a swarthy fashion, he'd been an acquaintance of her late husband. Huntley hadn't particularly liked Runsford as he was rumored to dabble in the occult. Huntley had preferred to keep *his* vices traditional.

Diana hadn't liked Runsford because of the way he'd

always let his gaze slither over her for far longer than anyone else did. That was not saying a great deal, since all her
husband's friends stared at her for longer than decent people considered permissible.

Diana refrained from voicing the questions and, more to
the point, the accusations that rose to her lips. She knew
without being told that her father was going to try to be-
troth her to Runsford. What other reason could there be for
his accepting the man as a guest here in his very own
home?

"Looks like it might rain." Her father, as desirous of
changing the subject as of escaping his daughter's steady
gaze, went to stare out the window at the darkening day. "I
hope the Baron doesn't have an unpleasant trip." Muster-
ing his courage, he turned to face his only child again.
"Did you know him in London, Diana?"

"Yes. The Baron was well known there." Her tone was
not conducive to further questions about her acquaintance
with the gentleman under discussion. Not from a father
who was intimidated by her, at any rate.

"I hope you will be cordial to our guest, Diana. He has
come a long way to see you again, after all."

Diana stiffened for a moment, then forced herself to
relax. She knew better than to argue at this point. Vague as
he was most of the time, her father always knew his own
mind when he felt he was acting in another person's best
interest. And when he thought himself in that position, he
always got his way.

*Well, it doesn't matter how much I love you, my dear fa-
ther, you aren't going to get your way this time. Not if I
have anything to say about it!*

"Runsford seems most eager to renew his acquaintance
with you, my dear. I thought it only hospitable to invite
him to stay here at the vicarage." He cleared his throat ner-

vously. "He really seemed to desire it, and it will give the two of you more time to become, er, reacquainted."

Diana said a fervent prayer that it would also give her innocent father time enough to see the Baron for the lecherous man he was, as well. She hadn't much hope of a positive answer, however. God, being a gentleman, never transgressed the will of His creations, more was the pity. That being so, He could hardly be expected to force the truth on someone who was as determined not to see it as her father was.

Diana only hoped that Runsford wouldn't think the invitation to the vicarage included an invitation to her bed! Her innocent father had no idea of the sort of man he was dealing with. Indeed, if she had not been forced to acquire knowledge of the ways of Runsford's sort in self-defense, she'd never have known either.

She took a deep breath to steady herself and answered her father. "So it might, Father," Diana was careful to say mildly. *It might if I were foolish enough to remain here where he is, at least. I have every intention of being gone at the earliest opportunity, however.*

She picked up a book of poetry and pretended to peruse it. When she spoke, she made her voice casual. "How is it that we had no more notice of his visit than we have been given? Was Lord Runsford in the neighborhood on some other errand?"

"No, I don't think so." The tips of her father's ears were reddening, a sure sign that he had not told her the complete truth. Since deliberate prevarication was beyond him, he was forced to add, "Actually, I've known of his intention to visit for quite a few days, I, er, ..." The rest of the sentence came out in a rush; ". . . just haven't told you."

Diana felt as if she were going to explode, but to let her father see she was furious would hardly be productive. It was apparent from the fact that he'd kept the Baron's visit secret from her that her own father was plotting against her, and no matter how lovingly he did it, she could clearly see that the end wasn't going to be to her liking.

Diana closed her eyes momentarily against the pain of that knowledge, and wished, not for the first time, that her father had taken sufficient interest in his only child to know—no, more than that, to *care*—what her feelings were. No matter how hard she'd wished it, though, he never had.

Now, she only wished she could have had more warning, have had more time to plan her flight. She hadn't even had time to send a message to her Godmother to prepare her for her Godchild's precipitous arrival!

No matter. She would just have to get as much together as she could in the few hours left to her. She had every intention of being well on her way to London before the family arose for breakfast tomorrow morning. That way, she'd avoid Runsford altogether.

She felt a little shiver run up her spine. She wouldn't feel safe from her father's well-intentioned machinations until she was settled in her Godmother's luxurious house in Town. Her dear Lady Bradford would take up the cudgels in her defense, she knew. Her Godmother knew well the character of the nefarious Baron Runsford, too.

She dared not let any of her thoughts show to her parent, however, for fear he would put a stop to her flight. So she kept her voice casual as she said, "Please excuse me, Father. I wish to go select a gown to wear for dinner tomorrow night."

The Vicar beamed. He hadn't expected Diana to cooperate so cheerfully and was more relieved than he could say. "Of course, my dear. You *will* want to look your best tomorrow night, won't you? I shall see you at dinner."

Humming softly, he turned away and went back to his bookshelf.

Diana left with the familiar strains of "A Mighty Fortress Is Our God" following her. Right now, she couldn't help wishing that her father's fortress would collapse on him!

Taking the stairs two at a time, Diana was soon tearing through her wardrobe to find dresses that would be easy to stuff into the small portmanteau she planned to get from the trunk room as soon as the house settled down. Leaving tonight would be the best thing to do. That way her father and aunt would have time to think up an excuse for her absence that would not offend the offensive Oswald Runsford.

Suddenly she stopped. A glimpse of a very familiar color had caught her attention. Carefully she pulled out a dress she'd kept hidden in the back of her armoire for years. It was a pretty yellow summer dress with the smear of grass stains on its skirt.

Diana went still as a statue as memories of the day she had ruined that dress assailed her. The remembrance of a pair of warm brown eyes filled her mind. They'd been kind eyes in a world that had grown hostile. The sound of a never-to-be-forgotten voice followed. A gentle voice that went perfectly with those eyes. The Duke of Smythington.

Quick tears threatened and warmth suffused her as she recalled how that wonderful, gentle man had saved her.

Diana went to stare into the mirror, lost in memories. Strange, how Huntley and all of his friends had known that *she'd* just been made one of the living things that the Duke considered under his protection. In utter amazement, she'd seen them quail and concede that they understood. Even Huntley.

From that moment on, her life had changed because the

gentle Duke had placed her under his protection. Her husband's friends, always leering before, had begun to treat her with a hint of respect, and Huntley himself had stopped his overt bullying.

That respite had given her time to grow up. To grow strong. She was very strong, now, thanks to the Duke of Smythington. She was a woman in charge of her destiny. He had made that possible, and she was eternally grateful.

She remembered bad times, too. Like the awful moment when Smythington's courier, resplendent in the Duke's livery, had brought her his master's letter. He'd delivered it straight into her hands, staunchly refusing to entrust it to anyone else.

The letter had told her that the Duke's leave from Wellington's army was up, and that he was returning to the war. He assured her that he had made very careful provision for the care of her puppy. She had burst into tears to read it.

She'd known, somehow, that he was reassuring her that he had made provision for her, too, though she had no idea how he could. And when she'd read his words, it had been as if his letter and the tears it caused had broken some dam in her heart and spilled out all the dreadful things she'd been hoarding there. His caring had swept them away. Realizing that had allowed her to emerge from the captivity in which her husband sought to hold her.

Clutching the Duke's letter, she had wept all night. She'd wondered then, from the awful pain in her heart, if somehow she had fallen in love with him. She had no idea what it was like to be in love. Never having experienced love of any sort since the death of her bluff but caring grandfather, she couldn't be certain what it was that she felt so acutely. She only knew that his safety was the most important thing in life to her.

Whether or not she had fallen in love with the Duke, though, she'd never yet met a man she considered his equal. She'd found she could hardly bear the anxiety she'd had at knowing he was in constant danger on the Peninsula.

She'd been frantic until she'd heard he'd escaped the French who'd held him prisoner briefly, and had exulted at every word of praise he'd received in the dispatches. Even her husband's sharp disapproval was unable to deter her from the interest she took in the war news.

She raised her gaze to meet that of the woman in the mirror. Smythington—she frowned at how stilted that sounded—had helped the woman she saw there come into being. Without his perception, without his kindness, indeed, without the protection he'd somehow extended over her, she would have been broken by the drunken attacks of her bully of a husband. Instead, the Duke's caring had sent her out into society to make friends. Indeed, she suspected that he had sent several of her dearest expressly to become friends of hers.

Then he'd come home safe from the war, and her heart had rejoiced. She'd experienced a new fear, then, too. She'd been afraid that if she met him, her feelings for him—whatever they were—might show in her eyes. Then the fat *would* have been in the fire! Huntley was drinking almost constantly by then, and was of a very uncertain temper. The stronger and more independent she became, the more he drank. And, thankfully, the more he left her alone.

When she'd read that after the Earl of Taskford's wedding the Duke and a friend had disappeared, she'd nearly died with worry over him. Then his friend, Viscount Kantwell, had resurfaced and she had begun to hope desperately for word of the Duke. Finally, later, the dreadful news had come that Smythington had been sold into slavery.

Diana rubbed her forearms with hands that trembled. Even now, her flesh crawled at the very thought of her kind hero in the hands of slave masters.

Diana wasn't a Catholic, but when news had reached her that the Duke of Smythington had escaped captivity and returned safely to England, she'd gone to the nearest Catholic church. There she'd paid for every candle in the cathedral to be lit in thanks for his safe return.

Though all England thought it was odd that no one except his staff had seen him since his return, he was safe, they said. Diana felt as if she had been holding her breath all this time and only now could draw a full one. How she wished she could see him—to assure herself he was truly safe. Would he even remember her? Would . . .

"Stop it," she ordered her reflection.

With some surprise, she found that she was hugging the old yellow dress to her. She smiled. "Foolish Diana," she chided, "keeping a faded old dress. When will you ever truly grow up and stop holding on to faded dreams?" she asked herself briskly. Then she added softly, "Impossible dreams."

She rose, forcing herself to laugh at her foolishness, and went about the business of collecting those things she intended to take with her to London. Foolish or not, the faded old dress was among those things.

A soft knock at her door caused her to snatch up and sling her comforter over the pile of clothing on her bed. "Yes?" she called.

"It's me, Jonathan. Can I come in?"

"May I come in," Diana corrected automatically.

Jonathan pushed his face around the door and grinned at her. "You already *are* in, Cousin Diana."

Diana smiled in spite of herself. "Yes, I am, and I'm busy, so what is it you want?"

"I wanted to know if we were to do our fencing lesson tomorrow morning?"

Oh, Lord. I won't be here in the morning! She couldn't let her young cousin know that, however. "Yes," she said with some hesitation, hating to lie. "That'll be fine if that's what you'd like."

"I would. Unless it rains." He frowned at the darkening sky outside her window. "I don't want you slipping in the mud and skewering me."

"Imp!" Diana threw one of the pillows from her bed at him. "There are buttons on the foils and you know it. There is no chance of either one of us being 'skewered,' as you so elegantly put it."

"Nevertheless, I'd feel much better if we were always on good, dry ground if it's all the same to you."

Diana smiled at him. She would be gone, but she surely *would have* obliged him if she were going to be here, so she said, "That will be fine, Jonathan, dear."

"Dear." His eyes filled with suspicion and he backed toward the door. "You called me 'dear.'" He scowled at her. "Are you *sure* there are buttons on those foils?"

The weather had deteriorated to a steady rain by suppertime, and Diana watched it worriedly as Betsy helped her dress to go down to dinner. She didn't want anything to delay her departure. She wasn't certain she wouldn't betray her plans if she lingered too long here in the vicarage. Her emotions were in such a turmoil, knowing that her father was about to rid himself of her again without— again—any consideration for what she might want. She felt so unwanted her stomach was in a knot.

If she did decide to make good her escape in the driving

rain, she would probably be drenched to her skin by the time she got on the stagecoach, and would stay soaking wet the whole trip. Arriving in London with a nasty cold was definitely not part of her plan. She'd just have to wait and make her escape after Baron Runsford's unfortunate visit.

"Thank you, Betsy. That will do nicely." She gave the little maid a quick hug, startling the girl half out of her wits. "Don't touch the things on my bed, Betsy," she ordered as she left the room to go downstairs. "I've special plans for them."

Diana had special plans to enjoy her family at supper, too. It would be the last meal she ate with them for some while, and she was going to make it a memory to cherish. She was humming as she went downstairs. The tune was "A Mighty Fortress Is Our God," and this time she was grateful to know that the Fortress was sheltering her.

After supper, young Jonathan, in spite of his best attempt to get excused from doing so, was on his way to the barn to feed the horses. Walking as slowly as he knew how, he kicked a stone along in front of him and grumbled his way to the barn. When the stone landed in a puddle, he left it and trudged on.

Elijah, their gardener, coachman, and man-of-all-work, had brought the horses in from the pasture, as usual, and they stood with their heads hanging over the lower part of their stall doors. As soon as they heard his footsteps, they nickered urgently to him as if they hadn't been grazing on good green grass all day.

"All right, all right. Just be calm. You know I've come to feed you." He paused to stroke the soft muzzle of his cousin's big gelding and wished for the hundredth time that he possessed enough equestrian skill to be allowed to ride him. Hussar was far too spirited for him, however, and he could only trail along enviously behind Diana, trying to keep up with her on one of his uncle's carriage horses.

Diana had seen to it that her father had a very fine pair of carriage horses, but they were gentle ones that would take the Vicar about his parish safely. That suited everybody but Jonathan, who wished with all his heart for a fiery steed to carry him flying after his intrepid cousin. Safely, of course.

He scratched Dasher, the nearest carriage horse, behind the ears and received an impatient shove for his trouble. "All right!"

Crossing the barn aisle to the large grain bin against the opposite wall, he seized the lid and heaved it up, bracing it with his left hand as he scooped grain into the bucket kept there for the purpose with his right. He was bent far over, scooping grain from the bottom of the bin and making a mental note to tell Elijah he needed to get more, when a sudden sound started him. Rearing up, he let go the heavy lid of the bin.

With a resounding whack, it cracked him on the head. It felt as if he'd been dealt a blow from one of the quarterstaffs with which he and his cousin bashed at each other. Stars filled his field of vision and he sank to the floor, his back sliding down the side of the sturdy wooden grain bin.

Immediately, a large, hairy body nudged him, whining concern.

Letting out a yipe that startled the dog into an answering yip, Jonathan threw up a hand to fend the brute off.

Gulliver tried to apologize for having startled him by washing Jonathan's face.

"It's all right, lad. He's friendly," a gentle male voice assured him. Then it asked, "Are you hurt?"

Jonathan looked up from his hairy attacker to see a

sailor leaning on a roughly hewn crutch. He shook his head to clear it of such an incongruous vision. They were pretty far from the sea. The shake hurt, and he grasped his head in both hands and groaned.

"Here, let me see."

"Wh-who are you? And what are you doing in our barn?" Frowning, he peered up at the stranger through pain-slitted eyes.

"We've time enough for that when we've seen to your head. That was a nasty crack you got."

"It was the lid. It's heavy."

"Here, let's put you up here where I can see you." Gritting his teeth against the discomfort in his injured ankle, David lifted the child to sit on the bin. To distract the boy from his pain, he said, "I imagine this lid has to be as heavy as it is to keep the horses out of the grain."

"*That's* what Diana says."

"Oh? Who's Diana?" David didn't really care who Diana was, he just wanted to keep the boy talking. He'd had experience with head wounds, and though the boy wasn't bleeding, he wanted to be certain there were no symptoms of internal damage.

"Diana's my widowed cousin."

"Ah." He lifted the boy's left eyelid gently. He asked, to keep the child talking, "And is she nice?" He lifted the other eyelid. Good, the pupils were the same size.

"No! She's dreadful."

"Dreadful?" David leaned his hip against the grain bin. This standing on one foot was tiring. "Dreadful is a pretty strong word for a woman, isn't it?"

"Not for Diana. She's stronger than any ole word. She's a big bully, and she's as strong as an ox." He pushed up his sleeve to show the sailor the bruise he'd gotten when he'd

failed to parry one of Diana's thrusts during their last quar-
terstaff practice. "See!"

"Great heavens." Even the observation that the boy's
speech wasn't slurred failed to stem David's flood of
anger. The bruise was a big one, and the thought that an
Englishwoman had deliberately inflicted such a blow on a
child outraged him. This was just the sort of brutality he
was running away from remembering.

The boy warmed to his topic. "Yes. And Diana is always pummeling me. She even wants to engage me in
swordplay."

David wasn't sure he believed that.

The child read the skepticism on his face and burst out,
"It's true! Tomorrow we are to have fencing practice.
Whether I want to or not!" he cried, conveniently forget-
ting that he had set the date.

"Fencing!" David's brows snapped down in a frown.
"A woman?"

"Well, she's a great one for wanting to be able to do
damage to others, you see." He squirmed a little and
looked away. Finally he said softly, "I don't mind too
much."

Not mind being beaten up by some belligerent terma-
gant? David was even more reluctant to believe that than
he'd been to believe the boy was fencing with a female.

Now that he saw that the boy had not been truly hurt
when the lid of the bin fell on him, his own concerns came
to the fore. He found himself on the horns of a dilemma.

What to do? He was hardly in any condition to be discovered and thrown out of the barn. He couldn't really
walk yet. It would be a day or so before his ankle healed
enough for him to continue his walking tour, and this barn
was the only shelter for miles. Except, of course, for his
own estate, and he was determined not to go back to

Smythington Park to be suffocated out of his resolve by the loving concern of Carrington and his staff.

"I've an idea."

"What?" Blue eyes wide now, the boy looked up at him.

That certainly made a change from a reverential "Yes, Your Grace?" and it caused David to smile. When he did, the boy relaxed at last and smiled back. "What's your idea?"

"I know a bit about fencing. If you could persuade your cousin to come here and fence in front of the barn, I could watch and perhaps give you a few pointers to use against her later."

"That would be splendid!" The boy was fascinated. "But I didn't know sailors fenced. I thought sailors used a cutlass."

"Ah, yes. That, too. But you said you were fencing. Rapiers, I presume?"

"Un-huh." He cocked his head. "You're very well informed for a common seaman."

"And just how would you know that?"

"I read." He looked smug. "You know everything when you read."

"I must agree that there is a great deal to be gained by reading. Just remember there are exceptions even to what we learn from the pages of books." David was sitting on top of the grain bin beside the boy now.

"Yes. I suppose that is true."

"You may depend upon it."

"Uncle Manfred says that knowledge is power, and that information is the fuel that feeds one's knowledge. And everybody knows that reading is how you get information."

David let his expression become thoughtful. "Yes.

That's very true, of course. Your uncle must be a wise man."

"He is. He's the Vicar."

"Ah. Then I'm sure he tells you, too, that you must take into account experience, as well."

"*That's* what Diana says. She says that everything isn't to be found in the pages of a book. She says that real life teaches us, as well. And that sometimes it teaches hard and strange lessons." He frowned hard. "She looks sad when she says that, though."

A rise of his former anger at mention of the woman who had given the child that terrible bruise distracted David from the boy's last statement. She'd taught the boy a hard lesson with that blow, he'd no doubt. He sat frowning in his turn, wondering how he could bring an end to the woman's persecution of this poor child without resorting to revealing his own identity. A moment later, his stomach growled.

"Oh. You're hungry, aren't you?"

David refused to lie. "Yes, rather."

"Stay here and don't let anybody see you. I'll get you something to eat." The boy wiggled down and took off running toward the house that David could barely discern through the leaves of the oaks and elms that grew around it.

David sat quietly where he was and marveled at the simplicity with which the boy had accepted him. "Looks as if we can stay, Gulliver," he told the dog. Then he got down, favoring his injured ankle, and lifted the lid on which he'd been sitting. "Time to earn our keep," he said, and finished filling the bucket the boy had dropped back into the bin with grain.

Chapter Six

Before the boy returned, the horses had nearly finished their grain and the barn was filled with the quiet sounds of their munching. Outside, since the rain had stopped, the wind had died, and the evening was still. Only the calls of the birds as they settled to their nests, and the barking of a single, faraway dog interrupted the silence of the countryside.

David sat down on the lid of the grain bin, leaned back against the rough wall behind it, and let the quiet calm of the place flow over him. Even if the boy had gone to get an adult to tell him to be on his way, he was still ahead of the game. He'd begun to gain the peace he'd left his dukedom to obtain. Feeling his muscles relax for the first time in months, he watched Gulliver staring out the barn door in the direction of the barking dog and smiled. Here in the Vicar's barn, at least, all was right with the world.

A moment later, David was inordinately pleased to see he'd had no reason to doubt the boy. His had been a genuine offer of supper! Blond head bent with the effort, the child lugged a huge basket and a heavy jug. As he came closer he called, "I hope you like roast beef."

"Very much."

"I brought some of Cook's apple tarts, too. They're good."

"I'll wager they are." David's stomach growled again in anticipation.

"And there's ale to drink." The boy hefted the jug up onto the grain bin triumphantly. "I borrowed it from Elijah's cottage. He lives over there just beyond the vicarage."

"Won't he mind you, er, 'borrowing' his ale?"

"No. He's gone to the village to have supper with his daughter and her family tonight. I'll have the jug back before he even knows it's gone." He placed the basket beside the jug and hopped up on the other end of the grain bin.

David knew he should say something about the ale being 'borrowed' without the owner's permission, but declined. Instead he asked, "Might I have your name? It seems rather odd to break bread with someone to whom one has never been introduced."

The boy burst out laughing. "My, your speech is polished for a seaman. You sound just like people talk in a drawing room."

David made a mental note to watch his speech. It would be a simple matter to mimic that which he'd heard in the forecastle of the ship he'd served on.

"I'm Jonathan," the boy was saying. "Actually Sir Jonathan Alastair Kelington, Baronet, since my papa died."

"Ah. Should I call you Sir Jonathan, then?" David offered with a smile.

"No. Please do not. That seems frightfully stuffy, don't you think?"

"Indeed I do." If there was one thing David had known from birth, it was the stuffiness of titles, his own especially.

"Now you have to tell me your name."

"Of course. I'm Michael David Lawrence . . ." He stopped, appalled at his own carelessness. He'd been about to tell the boy his real name. No doubt he'd have tagged "Ninth Duke of Smythington" on the end, too! He cleared his throat and began again. "I'm David Lawrence Smythe," he told the boy, using for a common enough surname the nickname his comrades in The Lucky Seven had given him. They'd wanted to avoid having to say "Your Grace" all the time, so they'd chopped his title short and dubbed him "Smythe."

The boy didn't seem to notice any hesitation, and David relaxed again. Jonathan handed him a loaf of bread and a long knife. As David began to slice the loaf, Jonathan asked, "What are you doing in our barn?" With great care, he spread a snowy linen napkin on the bin between them, then reached back into the basket and pulled out a sizable chunk of roast beef. "Here." Jonathan patted the napkin with his free hand. "Put the bread here, and slice us some of this."

David put down the slices of bread, accepted the roast beef, and answered the question. "Taking shelter. I hadn't planned to. I'd hoped to get farther along in my journey, but a curricle ran me off the road, and I twisted my ankle when I jumped into the ditch."

"Does it hurt?"

David grinned rather mirthlessly. In his recent adventures in the Middle East, he'd had occasion to learn what real pain felt like. Compared to whips and a hot iron, a sprained ankle was nothing. "Not very much."

"Still, you're wise to keep off it for a while. You'd better stay here. Just be careful no one sees you."

David smiled, his heart swelling. It had been a long time since, outside of Smythington Park, anyone had shown him a simple kindness, and he was deeply touched. "Thank you. I'll be careful to stay out of sight."

"You're welcome. Diana says we must be kind to the less fortunate, and I guess that's you."

David felt the spurt of anger he'd experienced before at the thought of the woman who'd brutalized the boy seated beside him. "Very good of her, I'm sure," he ground out.

"Oh, yes. Diana knows the rules. She just doesn't always obey them."

David hid his thoughts on that subject by doing as he was told, wondering what his butler would say to see him trying to slice his own roast beef neatly. He did a job that seemed to suit the two of them here on the grain bin, but he had to admit that his slices were a bit ragged. He wouldn't win any prizes for their uniformity of thickness, either. How in the world did Jessops do it? The butler's slices were always perfectly even and of a similar thickness.

"What is your journey?"

"A quest for peace."

"Peace! Do you mean peace for the world?"

David laughed. "Nothing that ambitious, lad. I doubt there'll ever be peace for this tired old world."

"Well, if not for peace for the world, what kind of peace?"

David cast a glance his way. "Why, peace for myself. Inner peace, I guess you'd say."

"Huh. That doesn't sound very exciting." He was clearly disappointed.

"That depends on how easy it is to find. I'm finding it a little difficult, myself."

"Really?"

"Really." David's mind was bent on creating a sandwich. He'd never made his own food before. In better days servants had prepared his meals for him. In his days as a slave and on the ship-o'-the-line, he'd had slop poured out for him, rather like a pig. To be fair, though, on the ship, the slop had come with a ration of rum. This was a new and fascinating experience.

There was a lovely round of cheese, and he sliced some to add to the sandwich he was so carefully putting together. He looked at the boy. "Want some?"

"No, thank you. I had my supper, you know. I'll wait for you to eat tarts with. I can always eat tarts, supper or not." Jonathan was still interested in his new friend's quest.

David finished the construction of his sandwich, took a big bite, and settled back with a sigh of contentment. Much as he hated to admit it about former enemies, the French were right. Hunger *did* make a fine sauce. The sandwich was as good as any banquet he'd ever attended.

"Well?"

"Oh, yes. Thank you for bringing me supper. It's delicious."

"I didn't mean *that*." The boy swept the basket with a scornful glance. "I meant your quest."

"My journey?"

"Yes. I want to know all about it. What are you doing exactly?"

"I'm walking through the countryside of our great land, waiting for the beauty of it to help me forget." He left it there, and hoped the boy would, too.

"Forget what?"

His hunger appeased slightly, David told the boy, "I want to forget the things I saw while I was captive of a sultan in the Middle East."

Jonathan's eyes lit up with eagerness. "Oh! How splendid! You have had a real adventure."

David took his time answering that. Somehow he had a bit of a problem looking at his captivity in just that way.

"You will tell me all about it, won't you?"

"There really isn't a great deal to tell." Not that he'd tell this innocent English boy, at any rate.

"Oh, there must be lots. How did you get captured? Was your ship sunk?"

"No, the ship didn't come into it until the end of the story."

"Then how did it begin?" Jonathan's eyes were pleading. "Please tell me. Please do. Nothing ever happens here at Smythingdale Village. The Duke and his people take too good care of us all."

"And you find that a bad thing?" David scowled down at the boy.

"No. Of course not. Just . . ." He sighed heavily, "Very dull."

David chewed his roast beef thoughtfully. While he was glad that those under his ducal protection were well cared for, he wasn't certain how he felt about having that protection described as dull.

"Please tell me how you got captured."

David relented. Talking to Carrington had seemed to help. Perhaps providing this eager child with a carefully edited version of his story would as well. "I was captured by slavers here in England."

"In England!" Jonathan was outraged. "Slavers don't operate here in *England*. Haven't for years and years." His eyes grew wide. "They don't. Do they?" Then he decided for himself, shaking his head. "No, they don't."

"Even so, my story starts in England."

Jonathan was torn between curiosity and disbelief.

"A friend and I were on our way to look at a ya . . . er, at a boat he was thinking of purchasing, when we ran into a band of men herding a line of Englishmen and -women in chains."

"Ooooh, my!" Jonathan's eyes were round, avid.

"Attempting their rescue, we were captured and added to their number."

"Didn't you even fight?"

"My friend did. He was very valiant." David saw again Mathers fighting against terrible odds while he, after firing both his pistols, was easily struck down. "I'm afraid I wasn't much help to him, however."

"Why not?"

"I never really learned how to fight until later, you see." Not until he was pitted against his fellow prisoners in hand-to-hand combat to amuse his owner's guests. This combat would have been the end of him sooner rather than later if it hadn't been for one of his fellow slaves teaching him a strange Far Eastern method of fighting.

"Oh." Jonathan looked sadly disappointed in him. "What happened then?"

"Then I was sold as a slave to a sultan in Araby." His skin crawled as he recalled the slave market. He could almost hear again the crack of the whip and the cries of the suffering slaves. He skipped quickly over the intervening memories and told the boy, "Then I was sent to work in his mines."

"Were there guards?"

"We'd not have stayed if there hadn't been." David was almost amused.

"Did they have whips?"

"Yes." David sighed. He knew where this was going.

"Did they ever hit you?"

"'Fraid so."

"That must have hurt awfully."

"Indeed," David answered dryly.

"And you have scars." It wasn't a question.

David just narrowed his eyes at the boy, waiting for it.

With a gulp for courage, Jonathan, eyes wide and eager, asked, "Can I *see* them?"

David threw back his head and laughed. "You could if I'd show them to you, but I've no intention of doing so, you little ghoul."

Jonathan laughed, too. "I *do* apologize, but it was worth a try, don't you know."

And David did know. He'd been a boy once, though it seemed a very long time ago indeed, and he remembered the burning desire to hear the goriest parts of every tale. He changed the subject. "I thought you said there were tarts for dessert."

Instantly distracted, Jonathan dived back into the basket and pulled out two napkin-wrapped apple tarts. Their smell alone was more than enough to divert Jonathan.

David was careful to have a new topic of conversation ready when they'd given Gulliver the last scrap of the roast beef and had finished their own apple tarts. "About your fencing lesson tomorrow."

"Yes?"

"Tell your cousin that the footing here in the stable yard is firmer and smoother than that in the garden." He looked up from searching the basket for more tarts. "It is, isn't it?"

"Oh, yes. There are lots of uneven spots in the garden. I live in constant fear that my clumsy old cousin will stumble over one and skewer me by accident."

David handed him a second tart. "Then you should easily be able to get her to fence here. The stable yard is smooth and, being high and well drained, will be dry. I'll watch, then tomorrow evening when you come to feed the horses, I'll be able to give you pointers on how to best her in your next match."

"Oh, that would be splendid!"

"Very good." Then he raised the glass Jonathan had brought for his ale and toasted the lad. "To your health."

And Gulliver added a bark.

The next morning, David arose from his luxurious bed of hay and performed his ablutions in the horse trough. He smiled to think of his staff's probable reaction if they could have seen him. He could almost hear Carrington clucking, "Oh, my dear boy!" and he'd absolutely no doubt that Jessops would simply keel over in a dead faint.

Briefly his expression turned grim as he wondered what their reaction would have been had they seen him filthy and stinking of sweat as he'd labored in the mines with flies crawling in the bloody whip stripes on his back. He gave a mirthless bark of a laugh, and shook the water from his hair. Jessops would probably have expired at that sight!

David whistled Gulliver to him and went back into the barn. He stopped at the ladder. "Up you go, boy. Can't have you running around down here when they arrive." He boosted the big dog up and braced him as he clawed his way up the ladder, then swung himself up into the hayloft.

Piling hay at the loft door, he formed a shield for himself so that he could see without being seen and settled down to wait. When the Dreadful Diana and young Jonathan arrived, he wanted to be certain he had a good view of their fencing practice. Tonight he'd be able to give the boy pointers that would enable him to best the beastly woman in future. The thought made him smile.

At the vicarage, Diana stood in front of the pier mirror she'd brought with her from Huntley House and stared at her reflection. Whatever had possessed her to wear *the* dress? She hadn't the faintest idea. It had seemed a compulsion, thrust on her by the nostalgia of the night before when she'd rediscovered it in her armoire.

She looked critically at the grass stains her maid had never been able to get out of it and smiled to remember how vehemently she'd ordered the poor woman, "Don't you touch that dress!" when she'd reached for it to throw it away. An earnest apology had mended the maid's feelings, but Diana obstinately refused to let herself know why she had clung so to the gown.

Well. That was years ago. This was now. It *was* ruined, and though she would still probably never part with it, more fool she, she'd at least give herself this one more pleasure of wearing it. No one could comment adversely about her wearing a stained dress to fence in, surely.

"Diana!" Jonathan burst into her room. "Oh. You're ready."

"Rather a good thing for you, wouldn't you say?"

"How so?"

"Wouldn't it have embarrassed you if I'd still been in my nightgown?"

The boy cocked his head. "I suppose it would have. I'll remember to knock in the future." He hung his head, gave a great sigh, and made the admission she was tapping her slender foot waiting for. "As I should have this time."

"Thank you."

Eager to change the subject, he told her, "The foils are downstairs in the study."

"Yes, I know. I put them there."

"Shouldn't have thought Uncle would have. He's not much given to military things, is he?"

"Does that trouble you?"

"No." He considered carefully. "Not much anyway. He is a vicar, after all. And men of the cloth are supposed to be men of peace, not war."

"Yes, that's true." Diana wondered, then, why she was so drawn to men of war. Could it be because her grandfather and the men of his family had all been warriors? Or, a small voice whispered, could it be because the Duke of Smythington had gone to war? He hadn't had to go. As a peer without an heir, no one expected it, but he had gone anyway, and, oh, how she admired him for it!

Certainly, in her quest for information about his safety, she had spoken more with soldiers than with the dilettantes of the *ton*. She'd found by doing so that she much preferred them, too. They'd been patient and unfailingly kind to an anxious sixteen-year-old girl, answering all her questions. Without exception, their sometimes bluff manners had pleased her more than the fulsome compliments of the dandies and nobles who'd stayed safely home.

"I say, Diana," Jonathan interrupted her thoughts, "that dress has grass stains all over the skirt."

Well, so much for her theory that no one would comment on her wearing a ruined dress for fencing practice. She smiled enigmatically as she told him, "Not all over. Just where I spun around on my knees to see who my savior was."

"How could you get grass stains on your knees in church? And everybody knows that it was Jesus who died to save us."

"Spoken like a true nephew of the Vicar of Smythingdale." She smiled, but Jonathan sensed that it was not really at him, but at something she was thinking. "And you are quite right. I should have said 'my rescuer.' "

"Sometimes you don't make any sense, Diana."

She just smiled again. On the subject of this dress and the man who'd changed her life, she had absolutely no intention of making any sense.

David heard them before he saw them. They came down the lane from the vicarage bickering like children.

"It's drier and smoother in the stable yard, I tell you. You'll see."

"It is also full of ruts from the carriage wheels."

"No, it isn't."

"How do you know?"

"Because I checked last night after I fed the horses." He had, too, and the one rut he'd found he'd smoothed out very carefully, just as David had told him to.

"Humph."

David smiled to himself. The Dreadful Diana had evidently run out of objections. He could see them now, the boy he was coming to know and like and the detestable woman who'd left that big bruise on his small frame.

Leaves on the trees obscured the approaching figures now and again, but he was surprised to be able to make out, as they appeared and disappeared behind the greenery, that the "dreadful big bully and obnoxious ox" Jonathan had described to him was a slender young woman who moved with a grace that was a far cry from the lumbering gait of an ox.

Frowning, he tried to see her better. Certainly her voice was lovely, even if she were not. When he shifted to get a better view, he almost fell out of the loft. It was . . . it couldn't be, but it was . . . Baroness Huntley! *His* Baroness Huntley.

Astonishment gripped him. His heart threatened to pound its way out of his chest. Here was the winsome girl he'd rescued from the pack of bullies her husband had left her prey to. Here was the girl who'd filled his dreams from the first moment he'd seen her tumble, spent and gasping, out of the forest at Merlington Park.

She'd been brought to her knees by exhaustion, hunted past her endurance, but never for an instant had she considered surrendering to its tormentors the puppy she'd rescued. He thought he'd never seen anyone braver on all the battlefields of Europe.

Her eyes had captivated him. Yes, and down through the years, they'd haunted him. The memory of those eyes had filled his thoughts and his heart from the instant his own gaze had met them, and he had been more her slave than ever he'd been that of the sultan who had owned him.

Diana. Now he knew the name that he'd been careful never to learn. Careful never to possess to add to the torment of knowing she could never be his, that she was another man's wife. What little knowledge he'd had of her had been painful enough.

But what was she doing here at the vicarage? Dammit! Military habits snapped to the fore. Why wasn't he better informed? It was *his* vicarage, after all!

For an instant hope soared, and he refused the shame that sought to follow it. Hadn't Jonathan called her his *widowed cousin*? Could it be that Huntley had died?

He made a sudden movement as if he would rush back to Smythington Park right now and set Carrington to finding out all that there was to be known about Huntley. About her!

Eagerness merged with inattention, nearly causing disaster. Part of his hay shield fell from the door of the barn loft. The slither of it as it plunged down to the stable yard alerted those below. Hastily, he drew back into the shadows.

Just in time.

Diana looked up toward his hiding place. "What was that?" she asked the boy at her side.

"Rats," Jonathan answered with nimble wit and supreme confidence. "There are rats in the barn."

"Oh, dear, Jonathan." She was all concern. "They don't come near you when you feed the horses, do they?"

"No." He swaggered a little. "I'm careful never to spill any of the grain. That's what they're after, you know."

"Yes, I suppose I did know that." She put her hand on his shoulder and offered, "Would you like me to come with you to the barn when you feed the horses at night?"

David listened and heard the concern for the boy to whom she spoke. So *she* was the awful bully Jonathan had described, this lovely, caring vision who'd just offered to come to the barn with him so he would be safe from rats!

David registered this last thought with only half his mind. His attention was focused on this exquisite woman whose cherished memory had haunted him for almost five years. Had she changed from the dream that came to sustain him every night?

No. She was just as lovely. If anything, she was even more beautiful than he'd remembered. No longer a slip of a girl, wide-eyed and fearful, now she was a woman grown, and certain in her movements and her speech.

Her hair was a darker blonde, but the blue of her eyes when she'd glanced up to see why the hay had fallen was as deep as ever. They were like sapphires in the perfect oval of her face. The intelligence he had admired in them long ago was still there, as well.

He realized with a start that she was wearing the dress

she had worn the day they met. He smiled to see the grass stains still at knee level on the skirt.

Why had she kept it? His heart lurched. Had their meeting meant something to her? Could it have meant as much to her as it had to him? He shook his head. Impossible.

The male in him stirred to see that the bodice of the dress had grown tight across her breasts since their last meeting. She was more rounded at the hip, as well. His lips parted for his next breath as his blood ran more quickly through his veins. She was no longer a girl. She was a woman. A woman to be held close and caressed—to be loved.

He saw, too, that her youthful vulnerability was gone, but in its place he saw a restlessness and a worry that gave him pause. Was she still in need of rescue? And if so, from what?

Well, whatever it was, he fully intended to be the rescuer.

Tomorrow he would return to Smythington Park! There he would set in motion the plans that ran through his head—he was almost dizzied by them. He'd find out what had happened to the Baron she'd been married to.

He'd ascertain what flowers she liked best and bury her in them, and what jewels, in addition to sapphires, she fancied, and bury her in those, too.

Most of all, he'd learn what made her look as if she still needed rescue. And, as God was his witness, he'd rescue her!

He threw himself backward into the hay with a silly grin on his face. Tomorrow—for he'd promised the boy he'd be here tonight—he would return to the vicarage in all his pomp and glory and sweep her off her feet and into matrimony!

Gulliver was looking at him as if he'd taken leave of his

senses, and David's grin widened. Before the big dog could back away, His Grace, the Ninth Duke of Smything-ton, reached out and crushed him in an exuberant hug.

It took the singing slide of steel rapier blade against steel rapier blade to return him to sanity and the duty he had promised Jonathan he would perform.

Chapter Seven

That evening at the vicarage, everything was at sixes and
sevens. Oswald, Baron Runsford, had arrived late in the afternoon, with two coaches, a curricle, and an entourage of
servants. The servants had carried in two trunks and a portmanteau, then they had piled back into the second coach
and headed back into the village—taking the other traveling coach but leaving the curricle—where they were to
stay at the Smythingdale Arms.

When the bustle was over and the dust had cleared, it
appeared that Baron Runsford had brought only his valet
with him to stay, and that was in order "to help him with
his toilette for dinner." The Vicar and his meager staff were
relieved that the valet was going to stay to tend to his master, as they were certain, from the quick efficiency of his
arrival, that the task was beyond anyone in residence.

Jonathan was fascinated. He'd never met people so impressed with their own importance before. He couldn't decide which was the more haughty, man or servant. He

could decide whom he liked, however, and it was neither the Baron nor his man. He made himself scarce.

Mrs. Appleby and the Vicar both had escorted the Baron to the best bedchamber. The Baron's valet had immediately put onto the small fire the extra coal Mrs. Appleby had had Betsy put by the fireplace for later when the evening cooled. When he turned from the fireplace and ordered Mrs. Appleby to see to it that more coal was brought immediately, he sank himself with the housekeeper.

While the Baron rested after his journey, the Vicar and Mrs. Appleby vied with each other in trying to find something nice about their overbearing guests. While the Vicar had some small success, Mrs. Appleby had none. Nor, secretly, did she in the least regret it.

Through all this, Diana was conspicuous by her absence. She intended to avoid the Baron as long as she could. She dawdled in her room until Betsy came to dress her for dinner, and would have lingered longer if she could have thought of an excuse to do so. She could hardly claim she felt ill when she had clearly been quite well all day, and her father knew she never had headaches! Finally, she had to go down.

Dinner was a cumbersome affair. Diana, beautifully attired in one of the many elegant gowns she'd had made in London, ably presided over her father's table. She'd hoped her aunt would do it so that she could be seated opposite their guest instead of having him beside her. She had a good idea of the advances she'd be subjected to if she were sitting within his reach.

Diana was the highest ranking woman there in the vicarage, though, and her very proper aunt steadfastly refused to usurp her position as hostess. Diana wanted to wring her neck.

As her father's guest of honor, Baron Runsford sat right

beside her, while Diana fervently "wished him at Jericho." From his own place at the foot of the table, her father beamed at each of them in turn.

"You look exceptionally lovely tonight, Baroness Huntley." Runsford stared down at her bosom, and breathed softly so that no one else could hear, "Ravishing."

Diana pretended she didn't hear the suggestion in his voice at that last comment, smiled tightly, and said, "Thank you, Baron Runsford," just as stiffly. Glancing down the table, she tried hard not to blame her father for failing to notice the way his guest leered, or that his only daughter had resorted to stuffing a pretty piece of lace into the neckline of her gown to preserve her modesty from the Baron's rapacious gaze.

She sighed. The Vicar was, after all, such an innocent that it was only natural that he be completely unaware of their guest's avid interest in his daughter's cleavage. The Baron grinned like a wolf about to devour prey at the way her breasts rose when she sighed.

If she hadn't disliked Runsford before now, his present attitude would have given her more than enough reason to do so. It disgusted Diana that his gaze continually rested on her bodice. Hadn't the man any idea that she had a face?

Though she wouldn't admit it, she was deeply hurt that her father didn't look after her better. Why did he have to be so unaware of the baseness of some men? Surely determined ignorance must be the price of such bland innocence.

Her father's innocence had already caused her to pay a heavy price for it once. Now, however, Diana had no intention of paying a second time by being maneuvered into marriage with yet another man she couldn't love!

Her attention was commanded by the voice of the man she detested. "I hope you will show me around the village tomorrow, Diana." The Baron smiled fatuously. "I may call you 'Diana,' may I not?"

"If it pleases you." She shot a fulminating glare at her father, offended by Runsford's familiarity and angered at her father's ignoring it. Why couldn't he see that the Baron was taking liberties he had no right to take on such short acquaintance? Why couldn't he see what this man was?

A tiny voice cried deep inside her, *Why can't he protect me? Cherish me just a little? Love me just a little?* And finally, *Why can't he care?*

She was almost grateful to have her childish thoughts interrupted—until she heard what the Baron meant as well as what he said. His voice so low he almost purred, he said, "I understand the inn is quite comfortable. Perhaps we could dine and . . . pass a little time there?"

Diana wanted to slap his face. The look in his eyes told her exactly how he hoped to "pass a little time" there. With difficulty she restrained herself from making the scathing remark the cad deserved. She braced herself. She could play this particular game. She'd learned it well enough in London.

Besides, she told herself, soon she'd be gone and free. Free and safe with her Godmother. So she sat and bided her time, fighting the feeling that garden slugs were crawling over her.

Instead of her dinner companion, she concentrated on the fact that she'd already gathered her things and was ready to leave the vicarage as soon as everyone was safely asleep. There was no repeat of last night's rain to stop her, and no matter how slowly it seemed to Diana to be doing so, the dinner was ending. Soon there would be nothing left for her to do but sneak a portmanteau from the trunk room and quietly go.

She'd already ascertained that the London stage arrived

in Smythingdale Village at three in the morning. When it departed, she'd be on it. So, for the moment, and for her father's sake, she could afford to pretend to be charming.

There was actually a hint of warmth in her voice as she asked, "More wine, your lordship?"

"But of course, my dear."

Appleby stepped forward and poured the wine. When the Baron added in an oily voice, "How could I refuse anything *you* offered?" Appleby, lips tight, deliberately slopped wine on the lecher's hand.

The Baron cursed him for his clumsiness.

Appleby muttered a patently bogus apology and stepped back, looking to the Vicar to speak. Both the Vicar and Lady Kelington were shocked to silence.

The Baron noticed nothing out of the ordinary, and his eyes, and the smile he directed at Diana, told her he hoped that she would offer even more than wine once everyone else had gone to bed.

In disgust and despair, Diana realized that the Baron's assumption of her willingness to warm his bed came from her father having unwisely invited him to stay at the vicarage. Obviously the Baron thought the kindly intended invitation was nothing less than a clumsy ploy to give her an opportunity to seduce him into offering for her.

Just as she was thinking she couldn't feel any more loathing for him, she felt the pressure of his knee against her own. She tightened her grasp on the stem of her wineglass. One more touch, one more innuendo, and she would fling its contents into his leering face. She moved her knee away from his.

The insufferable cad! If he'd known how she felt about this situation, and about him, he'd have asked that every knife in the house be locked away and a guard be posted at his door!

When dinner finally ended, Diana asked if she might have a word with her father. "Aunt Mary would be delighted to show the Baron the library, I'm sure." She beamed a bright smile at her bewildered aunt and literally dragged her father to the kitchen. The task was made easier by the fact that the Baron jumped at the offer of being shown the library.

"What is this, Diana?" Her father shook his arm free from her grasp. "We cannot be rude to our guest."

"Please, Father. I beg you. Don't let this go any further. I cannot marry that man."

"Now, now, dear. The Baron is a perfectly acceptable *parti*, and I couldn't help noticing how attentive he was to you at the table." While his daughter stared at him incredulously, he went on, unperturbed, "You weren't all that eager to marry Huntley, as I recall, and look how well that worked out."

Tears of frustration gathered in Diana's eyes.

Her father patted her arm. "There, there, dear. Everything will be fine, you'll see."

"But Father—!"

I really must get back to the Baron, my dear. We can't be rude."

"Father!"

He left the kitchen, in spite of her cry, confident that all was well with the world.

Diana dashed her tears away and wondered if her father really believed Voltaire's *Candide. She* certainly didn't believe that "this was the best of all possible worlds!"

Slipping out into the kitchen garden she concentrated on regaining her composure. The kitchen cat came out and twined himself around her skirts, purring, and when she'd finished telling him all her troubles, more time had passed than she'd intended.

She was hurrying up the back stairs half-blinded by tears she told herself were only tears of frustration, when she heard voices in the hall above. Stopping because she didn't want to run into anyone just now, she overheard a snatch of their conversation.

"Did I give you long enough to find it?" It was the Baron's voice.

"Yes, my lord." A servant, obviously. The only one in the vicarage was his valet, an obsequious little man Diana had caught a glimpse of earlier. Nothing she was overhearing raised her estimation of him.

"Good. You have it safe, then?"

"Safe in the hiding place you had fashioned for it, my lord."

"Excellent, excellent." Diana could picture him rubbing his hands together. "Good man."

The servant's tone changed, becoming intimate. "And you? How did you fare with the heiress?"

"Very well." There was a swagger in his master's voice. "She's ripe for the plucking." Both men chuckled.

Diana, on the back stairs, felt her face flame and her temper rise.

The Baron added, "Good work. I must go. It won't do to keep the old fool waiting. I think he intends to offer me his daughter's hand."

The men parted, laughing.

Diana waited a while, then headed for the attic door. She'd get a portmanteau from the trunk room now. Rounding the last corner of the hall, she drew back quickly. "Blast!" she whispered to herself.

"Hello? Anybody there?" The Baron's valet, sitting on the bottom step of the attic stair to polish his master's riding boots, must have heard her vehement whisper. *Damnation!* She was careful only to think that word. She was being kept from getting the portmanteau because of the Baron's lackey. She'd have stamped her foot in frustration if she hadn't been certain he'd hear and come to investigate.

Very well. Obviously, the odious Baron hadn't arrived at the vicarage with his valet carrying an armload of clothing for him. There must be a portmanteau in his bedchamber. While he was busy with "the old fool," being offered the heiress who was "ripe for the plucking," she would just go borrow it! *If it inconveniences the Baron, so much the better,* she told herself. For she certainly had every intention of taking his bag and serve him right!

Full of righteous anger, she strode to the best bedchamber, threw open the door, and marched to the wardrobe. Flinging that door open, she snatched the empty portmanteau there out of it and slammed the door shut.

Moments later, she was packing the clothes she intended to take with her into the purloined portmanteau. Satisfaction at stealing it from the man who'd obviously taken something from her father, coupled with the knowledge that she would soon be gone, calmed her anger.

If there had been anything in the vicarage of value, she would have alerted her father to the theft perpetrated by the Baron's valet, but there was not, and at this point she didn't really care. If her father mentioned something missing later, when she was safely out of his well-meaning clutches, then would be the time to pursue the matter.

She packed her things, hid the portmanteau in the very back of the wardrobe, and called Betsy to help her undress. While the girl assisted her, she ordered, "See to it that I'm allowed to sleep late tomorrow morning, will you please, Betsy? I think I may be coming down with a cold."

"Oh, my. Did you take a chill walking down by the river?"

"Either that or fencing with Jonathan in the damp this morning, I suppose." She hated lying, but it was certainly getting easier as she acquired more practice.

Betsy warmed the bed with hot coals heaped in the ornate brass bed warmer while Diana tied the bow of her nightcap under her chin. Then the maid was gone with a cheery, "Good night, my lady. Sleep well."

Diana settled down to wait for the tall clock in the hall downstairs to chime two. She had allotted ten minutes to dress, another ten to get out of the house undetected and down the lane past the barn. She'd decided that it was safer to go the back way even though it would take longer. Then twenty minutes to get to the inn and purchase her ticket, and she'd be on her way at three.

London. She couldn't wait.

Chapter Eight

David slept peacefully under his old campaign cloak, burrowed deep in the Vicar's hay, his dreams of Diana causing him to smile. Gulliver lay close at his side, his feet twitching every now and then as he pursued the fat rabbit that eluded him night after night.

Suddenly, the dog lifted his head. All dreams of plump prey fled as he listened for the sound that had disturbed his slumber. After a moment, he rose and went to look out at the night. Ears strained forward, he watched the darkness that cloaked the lane that led to the vicarage. Soon every muscle in his frame vibrated with the intensity of his interest. Someone was coming!

Whirling from his lookout post, the dog bounded to where his master slept in the hay. He thrust his nose into David's cheek and whined.

"What is it, Gulliver?" David was awake instantly. Neither soldiers nor slaves slept through a friend's warning. He sat up and watched as the big dog ran back to stare down at the lane. Seeing how Gulliver's tail quivered, he moved stealthily up beside the animal. "What's got you so attentive, boy?" he whispered.

The fact that he could neither see nor sense the object that so engaged his dog's interest didn't deter him. If Gulliver said something was out there, then something was out there. He'd learned long ago to count on the special abilities of his animals.

Soon he heard a bump and a dragging sound—something slithering along on the still-damp dirt of the lane. His curiosity rampant, he leaned forward and stared hard in that direction. Finally, the clouds that had been obscuring the moon parted, and he almost fell from his vantage point in astonishment. There, coming down the lane from the vicarage pulling a portmanteau along beside her, was Diana!

"What the devil!" he muttered.

Gulliver drew breath to bark.

David clamped his hand around his muzzle. "Quiet, boy," he hissed.

Diana must have sensed she was being observed, because she threw an uneasy glance at the barn and her step faltered. Then she took a deep breath, squared her shoulders, and continued.

David could see that she was steeling herself, gathering her courage to approach the barn. He watched her beloved face and could clearly see that she was valiantly refusing to admit that she was nervous. Nevertheless, when she came near the big open door into the barn's aisle, she hurried just a bit to pass it.

David scowled fiercely. What the blazes was she doing? Running away from home? He snatched up his campaign cloak and the knapsack he'd intended for his journey—the journey that seeing Diana again had knocked completely out of his head—and hurried across the loft to the barn ladder.

Dropping his burden to the dirt floor of the barn aisle, he made short work of following it.

Gulliver barked once sharply at being left behind.

"Shhh!" David held out his arms and the dog launched himself in complete trust. The man staggered under the onslaught, and regretted not helping the big dog learn to back down the ladder as he'd intended to. Time was of the essence now, however.

David grabbed a lead line from where it hung next to the stall belonging to the handsome gelding that Jonathan had told him was Diana's. Made expert by his stint as a seaman, he bent a bowline knot that wouldn't slip to choke the dog and fashioned a leash for his companion. He had no way of knowing what was about to happen, and he'd no intention of either losing his shaggy friend nor of having him dash ahead and alert Diana to their presence.

Gulliver pulled away, trying to free himself of the rope.

"Easy, boy. I'd never hurt you. Easy."

Obviously, the dog had been mistreated while tied at some point in his brief life, for his eyes were accusing, his body tense. He gave one more yank, then stood trembling.

"There, there, boy. Good boy." David lifted the rope slightly, gently calling it to the dog's attention. "This is only for your safety. I don't know what's ahead for us, you see, and I don't want to risk losing you." He knelt and held out his hand, forcing himself to be patient against the agony of haste that consumed him. He mustn't lose sight of Diana!

After a long moment, Gulliver moved one step forward, wary, stiff-legged. Another long moment went by while David held his anxiety for his newly rediscovered beloved in check and waited for the dog's next move.

Finally, Gulliver lowered his head and licked the tips of David's outstretched fingers. He had decided to trust.

David gave the dog a big hug. "Good boy!"

Tentatively, Gulliver wagged his tail. When David rose and began to walk away, looking back over his shoulder at him, he hesitated only an instant before following. When Gulliver found that there was no pull on the rope around his neck if he followed the man closely, it seemed to put the animal's mind at ease and he walked quietly beside his friend.

David let out a sigh of relief. Until that moment, he hadn't realized how very much the great dog had come to mean to him.

Up ahead, Diana alternately carried and dragged the portmanteau she'd stolen from the Awful Oswald, as she now thought of the man to whom her father sought to marry her. It was only a little way to the village, now, and the inn was at this end of it, so she straightened as she approached, touched her hair to neaten it, and entered boldly.

The inn servant on duty at this wee hour of the morning took one startled look at her and decided the situation was beyond his ability to handle. Scrambling to his feet, he stuttered, "J-just a m-moment, your ladyship!" and ran to summon the landlord to his post early.

Mr. Little came, pulling on his vest, and stared at her as if he had not believed his lackey. "Lady Diana! Where is your maid?" He looked around as if he would conjure Betsy up by searching for her. When the maid was not to be found, he asked, "Your aunt?"

"No, Mr. Little," Diana told him firmly. "I am quite alone. I am going straight to London and will be met there by my Godmother's man of affairs, so I have no need to take Betsy from the vicarage where she is needed to help with a guest." Having started to make excuses, Diana couldn't resist embroidering them. "And, of course, my aunt is acting as hostess for my father, and can hardly be spared."

Mr. Little was frowning.

Ah, well, Diana thought, *in for a penny, in for a pound.* Smiling her most radiant smile, she told the innkeeper, "We decided it was hardly proper for me to remain there at the vicarage when there is a very eligible single male guest visiting, you see." She dropped her voice and gave him a glance that said she knew he shared her knowledge of human nature. "You know how people talk."

Behind her back, she had her fingers crossed. Not that she thought that would make her lies all right with God, but her strict Christian upbringing demanded she do *something.* Telling the truth, however, simply wasn't it under the circumstances, so the Lord was going to have to make do with her crossed fingers. She'd apologize tonight when she said her prayers, safe in the lovely room her Godmother always kept ready for her.

"What is it you would like me to do, my lady?" Mr. Little was clearly perplexed by the situation, and nervous about getting involved.

Diana could almost hear him wondering what she was doing here without her father having brought her. Wondering why she had walked to his inn. That she had done so would be clear to him by the state of the hem of her gown. The innkeeper was not used to questioning the Quality, though, and Diana's level gaze did nothing to invite more curiosity. Therefore, Mr. Little closed his lips firmly, ran his hand over the shining dome of his head, and waited for her reply.

"Why, I'd like a ticket for the stage, of course."

"Oh!" He released a gusty breath. "I was afraid you

were going to want to hire a post chaise, and the only one
we have is gone at present." He went to the tall desk that
stood at the back of the spacious foyer, rummaged in the
top drawer, and came up with the ticket she needed.
"Going to London to visit your Godmother. That will be a
jolly time for you." He beamed at her. "Like as not the
Vicar will miss you, though."

Diana felt a pang. She couldn't decide whether it was a
pang of conscience, or one of longing. How she wished she
could believe that her father *would* actually miss her! He
wouldn't, of course. She could only hope that her absence
at her Godmother's would serve him as well as would have
his plan to marry her to Baron Runsford.

In either case, she'd be out of his way. She could only
pray he'd accept her solution. She was *not* going to be
married to another man she couldn't love!

". . . or would you like to wait in the private parlor
here?"

Diana recovered her wits and realized the innkeeper had
moved a short way off and opened the door to a little parlor where ladies often waited for the coach. "Oh. Yes, that
would be lovely."

The innkeeper bowed her into the little chintz and
china–decorated room. It was warmed by a tiny fire in its
small fireplace. The whole room seemed to say "Welcome," and Diana was a little tired after her struggle from
the vicarage with the Baron's portmanteau. With a heartfelt
"Thank you," she settled in a wing chair at the fireside,
grateful to be out of sight of anyone who might alert her
father to her solitary presence in the inn.

Outside in the darkness, David arrived at the inn and stood,
quiet, just out of the circle of light that spilled from the

lanterns on either side of the front door. Placing his hand on the head of the dog, he held him silent and still, as well.

Watching Diana, he was puzzled. Why was his beloved standing there with her fingers crossed behind her back? He heard her ask for a ticket to London and was aghast. What the blazes was Diana thinking? If she took the stage as she obviously intended to do, she would arrive in London in the early afternoon, in a part of town that demanded that ladies be accompanied by an escort!

The first of many dangers lay in the fact that madames from the town brothels often met stages. They hoped to lure young girls arriving fresh and innocent from the country, or for that matter, any attractive young female with no one to look after her, into their clutches with bright promises of interesting employment. Without an escort or a traveling companion, no one would be the wiser when the girl disappeared to become the sordid plaything of a long series of lustful men.

Not only that, but dandies who had nothing better to do and bored young Corinthian bucks harassed the incoming passengers when it pleased them, as well. What match would Diana be against such perils? Obviously, he would have to serve as her escort, though it would have to be clandestinely, of course.

Stooping, he took Gulliver's face in his hands and whispered, "Steady now, boy. I'll only be gone a few minutes." Then he slipped the end of the lead line he was using for a leash into the ring of a horse tie and made it fast.

Gulliver yanked back.

"No," David told him in the sharpest whisper he could muster. Pressing the dog's hindquarters firmly down, he added, "Sit, Gulliver. Stay."

"Who's out there!" The innkeeper was coming to the door to see.

David left Gulliver chewing the lead line and entered the inn hoping he could conclude his business before the dog gnawed through the rope and ran off. "Two tickets for the London stage, innkeeper."

His voice was the commanding one of the Duke, not that of a lowly seaman. As a result, the innkeeper was already on his way to the drawer of his desk in which he kept the tickets before he realized the type of traveler for whom he was getting them. His hand pressed firmly against the drawer's front, he demanded, "I'll see the color of your money first, if you please."

David was amused. "I trust the color gold will do?"

The innkeeper stared at the sovrans tossed carelessly on the desk top and fought down his surprise. "Very well. Two, you say?"

"Right." David watched for the man's expression as he said, "One for me and one for my dog."

"What?"

"I said, one f—"

"I heard what you said. You can't mean you intend to take a dog on the stage." He frowned mightily.

David was not intimidated. He was too busy savoring the experience of being interrupted. As the Duke of Smythington he had never been interrupted. He couldn't remember having been interrupted as a slave or as a sailor, either. The experience was unique. He turned it over in his mind once or twice, trying to be fair about it. He didn't think he liked it. Good manners dictated that he answer courteously anyway, though, so he told the innkeeper, "I have no one to leave him with. He is a friend, and I won't abandon him."

"Huh. Little chance you'll get a dog on Hank Sturgeon's coach."

David remained silent a moment. It was useless to argue

with the innkeeper. Time enough to decide the matter when he faced the coachman. He appreciated the warning, however.

"Thank you," he said, and the voice again held the tone of a Duke as he swept up his tickets and went out to his friend.

He'd hardly gotten back to Gulliver when the clarion call from the coach's "yard of tin" sliced through the silence of the village night. Close upon the sound came that of the rumble of coach wheels and the pounding of the team's hooves.

Gulliver fought his leash to be free to run, but David threw an arm around the big dog and held him close, speaking soothingly to him. When the ostlers dashed out of the stable yard leading a fresh team, Gulliver cowered against David.

"It's all right boy. Trust me."

Gulliver buried his face in David's side and shivered as the chaos of passengers alighting to attend to personal matters hurried past them.

David held the dog close and watched. Diana, as lovely as moonrise, appeared at the door of the inn. She surveyed the scene before her and made her way to the coach. A quiet word to the coachman, and she was settled inside, facing the horses. When the others who'd been riding in the interior of the coach returned, Hank Sturgeon, as David had learned he was called from the innkeeper, caught a youth by the arm and informed him, "You'll be riding on top the rest of the way."

That was David's chance. When the coachman turned his back on the outraged young man, David approached him and said, "A spot of revenge if you'll assist me."

The youth looked at him, startled.

"I need to get my dog to London, and you, if I'm not

mistaken, would like to get even with the coachman for his having put you out of the coach. Am I correct?"

"You don't talk like a sailor, sir." The young man was more perplexed by David's cultured accent than by his words.

David grinned. "That's because I wasn't one for long enough to learn how. Will you help me, or not?"

"I will." The boy grinned back. "What must I do?"

"Get aboard, and hold Gulliver's lead when I toss him up."

The boy eyed the huge dog, then looked the dog's master up and down. "*You* are going to toss him up?" Clearly, he thought David's small frame unequal to the task.

David laughed. "If I do not, then you will have no task to do—nor any revenge on the driver for ordering you outside."

"True!" With that the youth scrambled quickly to the top of the coach. David waited till the coachman was out of sight and tossed Gulliver up to the roof of the coach. "Stay," he commanded.

At the sound of his voice, the coachman spun around. "Hey! You can't take no dog on Hank Sturgeon's coach!"

David held out his two tickets. "I have purchased a ticket for the animal. He takes up less space than a human, and I have only a knapsack for my baggage."

"That don't make no never mind wif me, sailor. Off he comes."

David looked pointedly at the boy secretly holding Gulliver's lead and told the man looming over him, "As you wish."

"Well?" the driver demanded.

"Well what?" David answered mildly.

"Get the blasted dog down!"

"Oh, but I have no wish to get him down. I want him to

travel to London with me. That is why I bought him a ticket. I'm afraid that if *you* don't want to drive him there you must get him down yourself."

"You get that mutt down." The driver pointed his whip toward David.

Immediately Gulliver snarled and slavered menacingly from just over his head. Spittle flew and fell on the coachman's sleeve.

"You get your damn dog offen my coach roof!" the driver shouted.

David refused the driver's command with a quiet "No."

The coachman had fallen back a step when Gulliver snarled. Everyone watching could see that he wasn't going to be the one to get that animal down from the top of his vehicle.

The sailor stood at ease, his arms crossed over his chest. The giant coachman dwarfed him.

Just then, the door to the coach opened, and Diana called to the angry man, "If the dog has a ticket, driver, then let us be gone." She spoke in her most imperious voice. "The animal is bothering no one there on the roof, and our delay is certainly bothering me." And it was. Every moment spent in Smythingdale Village made discovery more of a threat to her.

The coachman heard the other passengers take up the pretty lady's argument. To stand any longer would make him late to London, as well. Balancing tardiness against his dislike of driving an animal anywhere, he decided his reputation for punctuality was the more important matter. Scowling at David, he clambered quickly to his box, snatched up the driving lines, and whipped up his team.

Only David's recent experience at climbing ratlines at sea made it possible for him to get aboard. As Diana watched him, frowningly trying to recall who the sailor's firm voice and quiet manner reminded her of, David leapt for the coach, grabbed the rail that ran around the edge of the roof, and swung himself lithely to the top of the vehicle.

Gulliver greeted the arrival of his master with a glad bark. In his exuberance, he almost knocked him back down off the coach roof.

Laughing, the youth David had just befriended steadied them both.

"My thanks to you," David told him.

"Indeed, sir, it is I who should thank you." And they laughed together, relishing the driver's defeat.

Below them in the coach, Diana remembered another day and another dog and another quiet man. A dear, gentle man who, because of his bulk, could never have leapt to the roof of the coach if his dear life had depended on it. No matter, he had rescued her in spite of his corpulence, and she would never forget it. She closed her eyes at the sweet pain of that remembrance, and a tear escaped to run down her cheek.

The overdressed woman opposite her brightened at the sight of the tear. When they arrived in London, perhaps she could offer to help the pretty young lady. That was the least she could do for a poor, sad lady traveling all by herself. She nodded firmly. It would be an act of Christian kindness. A star in her crown.

And if the beautiful little dear accepted her assistance, she'd make a fortune off her!

Chapter Nine

By the time the coach had rocked, jolted, and slewed its way to the smoother turnpike approaching London, Diana was heartily sick of the idea of traveling by public transportation. Obviously, she had not sufficiently appreciated the comfort and ease that traveling—in well-sprung luxuriously cushioned coaches—had always been before.

She gave a disgusted little snort to admit that she actually had discovered one thing about her life with her late husband that she could appreciate. Instantly the woman whose knees touched her own leaned forward. "Are you all right, dearie?" she asked.

Diana's chin flew up and she looked down her nose at the person. Surely, the overpainted creature didn't think she failed to recognize her for what she was? Heaven knew she had seen enough of her kind in the company of her late husband and his friends! Nevertheless, the woman was trying to be kind, so she answered her. "I'm fine."

Ignoring the shortness of Diana's answer and the forbidding look that accompanied it, the procuress said, "Well, I'm glad to hear it. I was afraid you was feeling poorly." The hardness in her eyes belied her verbal concern, and Diana watched that hardness give way to sly avarice as the woman made her next comment. "I have me husband and his brother meeting me when we gets to London. We'd be happy, I'm sure, to take you wherever you wanted to go when we reach Town."

"I think not," Diana told her, and turned her head away to look out the window. She decided she would stick close to the formidable coachman when the stage stopped in London and she disembarked. At least she would until this harridan and the two male companions the woman was expecting had gone off. She suppressed a shudder. There was little doubt in her mind what would happen to her if she accepted the woman's invitation. Indeed, she didn't think she'd better even chance getting within grabbing distance of the men the woman had spoken of either.

For the first time, Diana began to have doubts about the wisdom of her solo flight. Perhaps she should have made Betsy come with her. She hadn't even given that thought any real consideration, though, fearing Betsy would find a way to stop her from leaving the vicarage without her father's permission. Now she regretted that caution.

She took a deep breath and told herself to think, not panic. She had trained to fight, hadn't she? She wasn't completely helpless. She just wasn't certain that she would be able to overcome three assailants at once.

She thanked the Lord that she had learned enough about the seamier side of life from Huntley and his disreputable friends to enable her to correctly assess the woman across the coach from her. If she hadn't, she might have fallen victim to the woman's obvious intent to add *her* to a brothel—and judging by the woman's crude accent, not even an elegant one!

Diana recognized the danger of the situation. It saddened her to realize that that was because she'd lost the shining innocence she'd had when she'd married. And innocence, once gone, was never to be recovered, she knew. That admission so discouraged her that she put her head back and pretended to sleep.

The journey ended, they swept into the traffic of London. Drays loaded with huge barrels rumbled along the cobblestones, pulled by heavy draft horses in thick leather harnesses, darkened by their sweat. High perch phaetons drawn by nervous bits of blood in fine, silver decorated harness sped in and out of the stream of vehicles as young bucks urged their teams on with varying degrees of skill and no consideration for safety—for themselves or for others. Diana felt the noise of Town like a physical presence, familiar but unloved, and couldn't wait to get to the sanctuary of her Godmother's elegant townhouse in quiet Mayfair.

The coachman had to thread his way through the streets with care, but finally they arrived at their destination. By the time they reached the coaching inn, everyone aboard was most heartily eager to leave the stagecoach.

On its roof, Gulliver was so agitated by the unaccustomed sight of so many people and animals in one place that he was beside himself. He lunged from one edge of the coach's roof to the other, barking frenziedly. David's new acquaintance sat on the rope to hold the dog and both he and David attempted to calm him.

Below them in the inn yard, Diana was careful to go stand at the coachman's side, pretending to be waiting for her portmanteau to be found in the boot at the back of the coach. From the corner of her eye, she watched the woman who had attempted to "befriend" her and saw her in earnest conversation with two men. All three of them were looking Diana's way. The hair rose on the nape of her neck. She moved even closer to the stage driver.

Just then, David, not certain he could catch and hold the big dog if he climbed down off the roof and signaled the animal to jump as he had in the Vicar's barn, took Gulliver up in his arms and slid down the heavy canvas flap that covered the luggage in the boot of the coach.

"'Ere, now!" The coachman strode toward them. "Ya can't go sliding down the boot cover that way!"

David gave him his mildest look and said innocently, "But I thought you wanted my dog down."

Purple-faced, the coachman, shouted, "I wanted him off before we ever got started!"

"Oh." David was all innocence. "It's rather late for that, isn't it?"

Diana, amused and distracted by this byplay, didn't notice that her "friend" and her two male accomplices had taken up positions surrounding her. When she became aware of their presence, a little flutter of panic rose in her. Her voice was tight with it as she demanded, "My portmanteau, driver, if you please."

The driver turned from David and looked at her as if he wished she'd disappear. He'd obviously rather teach the cheeky sailor a lesson than wait on her, but he recognized that she was Quality, and however reluctantly, threw the boot cover back and dug out her portmanteau. "'Ere ye be, miss."

As he handed it to her, one of the men who stood too close intercepted it. "I'll take that, driver. She's going with us."

Diana bristled and tugged at the handle of the portmanteau. "Indeed I am *not* going with you!"

"Now, dearie . . ." The woman stepped forward to hide the fact that the second man had taken a grip on Diana's other arm. "Don't be 'ard on yer Uncle Alfie. 'E's only trying to 'elp." To the coachman she said, "Our niece is hexcitable, driver, but we'll take good care of 'er."

Seeing her dilemma, David said, "The devil you will," very softly. Then he spoke a single additional word to Gulliver and let go his lead.

Gulliver plowed into the little group struggling over Diana's bag. Snarling at the two men, he charged to stand against Diana's legs, daring anyone to approach her. "Good dog!" Diana cried, catching his rope to keep him near her.

The men backed off. "Not going up against that monster, Lettie, not even for you," one said. The other shook his head in disgusted agreement and turned away. The woman called Lettie tried for the last word. "We was only trying to be 'elpful, Miss High and Mighty," she told Diana.

"I don't need your help. No decent woman would!"

"Well, I never!" The procuress stomped off in a huff.

Diana turned to the quiet man to whom the dog seemed to belong. Holding the lead line out to him, she said, "Thank you for sending your dog to the rescue."

The sailor bowed graciously, his warm brown eyes smiling, and reached to accept Gulliver's rope from her. "I'm glad to have been of service, your ladyship." Then their fingers touched and his eyes widened. It was exactly as it had been five years ago when he had touched her fingers as he accepted the puppy from her. There was that current again, and stronger even than when he'd settled her in that long-ago boat on that long-ago lake at Merlington Park. Because so much time had passed, and because he had recalled it so many times, he was surprised at the strength of this current that passed between them now. What a fool he was, to think it might have diminished when nothing else he felt for her had.

David was glad he had spoken before their fingers met, because, now, he found himself oddly out of breath. He simply stood and stared into Diana's eyes.

Diana was used to causing some disarray in the thoughts of men meeting her for the first time, but she couldn't understand why she, too, was having an instant of breathlessness. Surely it was from relief. Relief that she was rid of the threesome that had threatened to kidnap her.

She frowned slightly, finding something about the slender man that tantalized her memory. Something about him touched a chord of memory. His eyes? His voice? She shook her head, puzzled.

There was no more to be said, though, and after a moment, she turned away. She hadn't time to be confused by a stranger that bore no resemblance to the man she constantly sought. She must keep her mind busy with running away from her father and his marriage plans for her. Tarrying to stare at this kind sailor could easily result in her getting caught before she could escape to safety with her Godmother.

Dragging her portmanteau, she hurried to the first of three carriages-for-hire waiting for a fare just outside the inn yard.

David wasted no time engaging the next one, determined to see her safely to her destination. Having learned his lesson well from the purchasing of his stagecoach ticket, he tossed the driver a coin before he got in with Gulliver.

The driver looked as if he were going to protest the big dog's presence. Then he glanced again at the gold coin in his hand and held his peace.

"Follow that hackney." David pointed toward the vehicle Diana had hired, then closed the door and settled back on the worn leather of the seat. His nose wrinkled at the musty smell. Like Diana, he couldn't help comparing this mode of travel with that to which he'd been accustomed.

Then he grinned wryly. Of course, he'd been transported tightly packed in a cage with other human merchandise since, so he didn't find it as bad an experience as he once might have.

When they arrived at Diana's destination, David saw they were in Mayfair. His driver halted his carriage halfway down the square from Diana's. David and Gulliver got out. "Better wait, I may need you again," David told his driver as Diana's hired carriage pulled away.

The man touched the brim of his hat, and muttered under his breath to his horse, "That man might look to be nothing but a seaman by the clothes of 'im, but I ain't no fool, Bess. 'E's got the manner and the kind o' speaking that tell me 'e be some'un a lot more important." He dug out of his pocket and stared at the coin David had tossed him. "There ain't nothing wrong with 'is coin, neither, that's fer sure. 'Tis more'un we make in a week o' good days, Bess." The cabbie nodded. He was content to wait.

Assured the driver intended to stay, David took Gulliver to the fence surrounding the square's pretty central park, and stood in the shadow of a tree, hoping that Diana wouldn't notice them. He could see well, and was surprised to discover that there was no knocker on the door of the house to which Diana had gone. "Uh oh, boy," he told the dog softly. "Looks as if whomever she's come to visit is not in residence."

He'd no sooner uttered those words than they were echoed by a young footman with a haughty air who opened the door to Diana's knock. "Lady Bradford is not in residence," he told her frostily.

"Then I'll just come in and rest while I decide what to do next." Diana seemed almost to be talking to herself. When she would have moved forward, the young man blocked her way.

"Step aside!" Impatience was strong in her voice.

"I'm afraid I can't do that, miss."

Diana fought down irritation. After all, it wasn't his fault. She had failed to identify herself. No wonder he was confused. Striving for calm, she informed him, "I am Baroness Huntley, Lady Bradford's Goddaughter."

The footman leaned out the door, still blocking it to Diana, and looked up and down the street with elaborate interest. "Oh," he said, "and just where are your carriage, your maid, and your luggage?"

"I am alone, just as I wish to be," she told the impossible young man, "and I am tired after my journey, so go tell Jeffers that I am here."

"Lady Bradford took her butler with her as an escort to her son-in-law's." He looked at Diana pointedly as he added, "Her secretary's ill, and *ladies* do not go about unescorted."

While Diana gasped at his effrontery, the footman closed the door in her face.

Diana was outraged! The insolent young jackanapes had as good as called her a liar. Indeed, by his actions he had clearly told her he didn't believe she was who she said she was. If he had, he would never have refused her entrance, much less have been so rude and high-handed while he did.

For just an instant she considered banging on the door and demanding to know what servants were still in the house who might identify her. Then she decided she wouldn't give that young jackass a second chance to insult her.

She'd teach the footman the lesson of his life once she had her Godmother in tow. When she finished with him, he'd be grateful that she let him keep his position. Yes, and he'd thank his lucky stars she didn't have him demoted to boot boy!

Seething with righteous indignation, Diana turned away and looked for her cab. "Oh, dear," she said at last, weary enough to be talking to herself, "I shouldn't have dismissed him, for now I must hurry back to the inn and find out how to get to the Grange. Oh, why didn't I pay more attention to where Lord Tony's home was? Though I know Lady Bradford is there, I don't know if I'm bound for Exeter or Appledore!"

Her shoulders sagged. For the first time, she doubted herself. She felt so alone. And so blasted helpless. She was accustomed to the first feeling. She'd had it ever since the death of her mother, and *should* be quite used to it. Somehow, it seemed to press down on her now as it had not done in years.

"This won't do!" She said the words out loud with a great deal of firmness. She needed to be firm, it was too late to be anything else. Giving in to her fears now and running back to her father meant marriage to the Awful Oswald, Baron Runsford.

David, startled by her outburst and seeing her distress, moved quickly back to his cab. Peering up at the driver's box, he made up his mind. "Here, driver! The lady is going to want you in a minute, and that's all right with me. I don't intend to be marooned here in Mayfair, however."

The driver was perplexed. "That there lady ain't gonna share a carriage, I can tell you, sor."

David laughed softly. "No, but she won't know I'm aboard if you let my dog and me share your box."

The driver looked dubious.

"There'll be another sovran for your trouble."

The driver held out his hands to help the dog up. David lifted Gulliver to him with a grin. "Good man!"

Gulliver settled under the seat at his master's command, and David squeezed to the bottom of the box, glad for the first time that he was not a large man like so many of his friends. The fleeting mental image of Adam Stone, the giant of The Lucky Seven, fitting himself into the space at the driver's feet caused him to chuckle.

"Shhh!" the driver hissed as he dropped his lap robe unceremoniously over the exalted Duke of Smythington.

David sneezed once and was still.

Gulliver licked his chin. He heard Diana hail the driver, heard the driver say, "The White Lion. Yes, miss." Then the vehicle barely rocked under her weight as Diana got in, and with a "Giddiyap, Bess," and a flap of the driving lines they were on their way back to the coaching inn.

Chapter Ten

Hiding in the driver's box under his lap robe, David strained to catch every sound. When the bustle of the streets changed to the lesser noise of the inn yard at the White Lion, he rose cautiously, pushing aside the robe the driver had so thoughtfully tossed over him. Gulliver slithered out from under the seat and shoved his head next to his master's as if he, too, was eager to see what Diana was up to.

David assumed she was going to take another stab at coaching in order to follow her Godmother to wherever she had gone. He knew the danger of assumptions, however, and was certainly not going to leave anything to chance when it came to his lovely but unpredictable Diana.

"She's gone inside the inn, sor." The driver bent down toward David to share in the conspiracy.

"Thank you," David told him and climbed down from the box on the side opposite the inn.

"And very welcome you be" was the answer, as the

driver accepted the promised second gold coin from his unusual fare. "This 'ere's a good dog." He helped Gulliver clamber down into David's waiting arms.

David smiled and ruffled the hair on the dog's neck. "Yes, he is, isn't he?" Ridiculously pleased at having his four-footed friend praised, he gave the driver a cheerful salute, turned away, and headed for the inn door, Gulliver at his heels.

Arriving there, he stepped to the side where he would escape discovery and paused a moment for his eyes to adjust to the dimness of the inn interior. Diana was there, slim and straight, talking to the innkeeper. The mere sight of her brought a smile to his face.

His smile disappeared instantly, however.

Diana was in trouble. He could tell by the set of her shoulders. Eavesdropping shamelessly, he heard her tell the stern innkeeper, "I have almost enough." She looked down at the coins in her hand.

"I wish I could help you, miss, but 'almost enough' just won't do, you see. Think what a state the coaching companies would be in if everybody rode after paying 'almost enough.'"

David thrust his hand into his pocket and started toward them to make up the difference for her. He was cut off by a gentleman who tipped his hat and offered, "Permit me to give you the money you need, pretty lady."

At the utterance of "pretty lady," David revised his previous estimate of gentleman to *man* in gentleman's clothing. He was trying to decide whether to step forward himself or to send Gulliver to the rescue again when Diana took matters into her own hands.

"Innkeeper, please inform this *person*"—she raked the man with the same degree of contempt in her eyes as she had infused into her voice—"that I have no idea who he is and that I would prefer not to be addressed by a complete stranger."

The town beau stepped back a step, spread his hands and persisted, "Come now. You don't expect me to be deterred by a display of haughtiness, do you? A lady does not travel alone." His smile became a leer. "Take my offer like a good girl. We'll see if we can't find some way for you to repay me."

David balled his fists. He had an excellent idea of how to repay the cad. Before he moved, though, another well-dressed man stepped out of the shadows just inside the door. Perhaps he would assist Diana. Surely she would prefer that to the interference of a mere seaman.

"Here, now, Thackerson," the second dandy said. "Keeping this pretty morsel all to yourself, are you?" He stood close to Diana and smiled appreciatively down at her.

Diana was furious. "I'll have you know that I'm the Baroness . . ." She shut her mouth with a snap. How very foolish it would be to give out her identity. And evidently pointless, too, she concluded as both men went into whoops of laughter.

"No need to puff yourself up, precious. False titles aren't needed. They would only be gilding the lily, for you are quite delectable enough without the slightest embellishment."

Cold anger rose in David. It was shameful that any Englishwoman should be treated in this fashion. That it was his own cherished Diana, only made it worse. What was he to do? At this point, the objections of a simple British tar were not going to carry any weight with these "gentlemen," and he could hardly step forward and declare himself the Duke of Smythington. They'd laugh themselves sick, and *he* would lose something that had suddenly become extremely important to him—his anonymity.

Yes! He realized it in a flash. More than anything right now the Duke wanted Diana to go on believing him a lowly seaman. If he could befriend her, and win her in that guise, then he would never have to wonder whether it was *him* she loved. Far too many of the fair sex had fallen in love with his titles and wealth already. If he could just get Diana to love him for himself alone, then everything he'd ever longed for would be within his grasp. He could spend the rest of his days in the loving company of this woman he adored. . . .

As David stood there dreaming of a rosy future, Diana was being surrounded by even more leering dandies. Bored, no doubt, with ogling the lady shoppers in Bond Street, they'd come to the White Lion seeking sport teasing arrivals from the country. They'd found more than they had dared wish for in the tall, beautiful blonde so improperly traveling alone.

Diana started to push through them to gain the inn yard, but they blocked her way. She stopped and glared at them. "Permit me to pass at once."

"Oh, come, my pretty. Surely you will have a little wine with us before you go."

"I most assuredly will not!"

The man on her left took hold of her portmanteau, the one on her right, her arm.

"Unhand me!" Diana attempted to pull away.

David had started to her aid when he realized that there was very little to be gained by bloodying a few noses and ending up jailed for the pleasure of it. Fine lot of good he'd be to Diana if he was arrested. No. He'd have to find a more clever method of rescue.

Suddenly inspiration came and he cried, "My lady!" He

pretended to be short of breath. "There you are! I was afraid I had missed you!"

Diana stared at him, obviously startled.

"Your family sent me," David informed her.

For an instant, she panicked. Her father must have learned of her escape almost as soon as she had left the vicarage! Then common sense came to the fore. That couldn't be. The sailor had been with her all along. She brought her spinning mind to bear on the situation and watched the handsome seaman for a clue.

"Your mother and three of your brothers are on their way, my lady. They asked me to tell you that they've suffered a slight accident just down the road—a broken wheel—and will be along as quickly as they can get here." He added to his story with relish. "Lady Hepzibah, your good mother, is in hysterics and they could not leave her, so they prevailed on me to come and see you safe until they arrive."

Diana was struck dumb. What on earth was he saying? Then she saw him wink and understood. He had neither mistaken her nor had he gone mad. He was gallantly making up a tale to get her out of the silly pickle in which she found herself.

Hardly missing a beat, she threw herself into his make-believe. "Ah, Jeremiah!" she christened him without a blush. "You have finally returned from the sea, then. And just in time, it would seem." She glared at the men around her. "How fortuitous that your path happened to cross that of my family."

David was stunned in his turn. He'd no idea that sweet Diana had grown so adept at fabrication in the years they'd been apart. He wondered if he liked the idea. "Ah, er, yes. Ship arrived yesterday, and I'm, er, on my way home."

"And of course my brothers could not leave dear

Mother. Her heart is so very bad, poor darling. Come!" She swept through the astonished group of young men who had been plaguing her, the portmanteau she carried bumping shins and scarring boots left and right as she came. "Quickly, Jeremiah. You must take me to my poor mother at once!"

"Yes, my lady!" David cried weakly but still game, while Gulliver jumped and strained at his improvised leash in the excitement. "At once!" He snatched the portmanteau from her and started out into the inn yard before the dandies that had been pestering Diana knew what he was doing. "This way," he told her, pulling her along by the simple expedient of refusing to relinquish her luggage as Diana tried to regain control of it and of the situation.

As soon as they were out of sight and earshot of the inn doorway she commanded, "Stop this instant!"

David obliged, and she nearly ran into him. Striving to reclaim her lost dignity, Diana announced, "I am extremely grateful for your dramatic rescue, sir, but you must know that I have no more intention of following you to some fantasy coach that exists only in your head than I had of accompanying the three people your dog saved me from earlier."

As the sailor stood quietly in front of her, fondling his dog's ears, Diana realized just how ungrateful she sounded. "Oh, dear. I do sound a perfect ingrate, don't I?"

David just kept on petting Gulliver.

"I don't mean to, you know. It is just that all my plans seem to have gone awry."

David looked sympathetic.

"It's all very well for you to be full of sympathy. In fact, it is most kind of you, but it doesn't help my dilemma one bit."

David raised an eyebrow in inquiry.

Diana felt compelled to answer his unspoken query. "Well, you see, I was running away to my Godmother's, and she is not at home here in London."

"Then perhaps you should return to the vicarage." David's tone was calm, his voice infused with all the common sense he could put into it.

"Return to the vicarage? Never! To do that would be to encourage my father to marry me to an *odious* man."

"Hmmm, I see." And he did see. If she was running from an unwanted fiancé, then he would surely do all that lay in his power to help her. He had just found her again, after all. He had absolutely no intention of letting her escape him.

No. If the fair Diana was going to be wed to someone or other again, it was jolly well going to be to him. But how to bring her around to that idea? Especially since he was determined to do it incognito!

"I don't see . . ." She broke off with a startled gasp. "How did you know that I came from a vicarage?" she demanded.

"That's easily explained," David reassured her. "I know you fled from a vicarage because I followed you from one."

"Followed me?" Her voice was thready.

"Yes. From Smythingdale Vicarage to be exact." He raised a hand to forestall the flood of words Diana was marshaling, and went on. "I had taken shelter there a night or two ago, and had made the acquaintance of young Master Kelington. So, when I heard you passing the barn in the wee hours of the morning, I felt honor-bound to see to it that you were safe on your, er, journey."

"How preposterous!"

David was stung. "Gallantry ignored notwithstanding, that was and remains my purpose. It is impossible for a lady to travel alone. That has been amply demonstrated to you today. So suppose you stop glaring at me and tell me exactly what you plan to do next."

It was only by making a great effort that Diana got her mouth closed.

Chapter Eleven

"Walk?" David *was* flabbergasted. "You're going to *walk?"* All pretense at calm reasoning dropped away. *"Are you out of your mind?* That's more than a hundred miles!"

Diana looked mulish. "Well, it *could* be less, actually. I'm not precisely certain that my Godmother's son-in-law's estate is *at* Appledore. It might lie closer. Nearer Bath, perhaps."

"Are you telling me you don't have any idea where it is we are planning to walk *to?"*

Diana's temper was slipping. It had been a very difficult day, and she had had no sleep the night preceding it, after all, and she wasn't even certain where it was her dear, dear Godmother had gone. All she remembered clearly was that Jessica, Lady Bradford's only child, had married a charming young lord from somewhere west of London. She deeply regretted the fact that she didn't know just where.

Oh, if only she'd paid more attention to his direction when her Godmother had discussed it with her and a group of Jessica's friends two years ago. It had been a hazy, euphoric time, and, luxuriating in her unexpected respite from her husband—for Huntley hated weddings and had refused to come—Diana had simply forgotten to keep proper notes.

In that joyous period just before the wedding, when everyone had been so busy, the precise location of dear Jessica's husband-to-be's estate hadn't seemed terribly important. Certainly not so important as were the wedding preparations and the bridal clothes that had had them all in a dither.

Now, though, with this seaman person looking at her as if he could cheerfully sic his dog on her, Lord Anthony's precise address took on all the importance it deserved. Now it was dreadfully important to know the actual location of the Grange, as the young lord whom Jessica had married called his home. If only Diana could remember.

Well, she told herself, right now she was so exhausted and confused it was hardly to be expected that she should recall the location of the Grange. Tomorrow, after a good night's rest, she would remember.

"Why must you walk?" the irritating man asked.

"Because, as I have already explained, I do not have sufficient money with me for the fare on the stage."

"How the dev—er, how do you know you don't if you don't know where it is you are trying to go?" His eyes held a rather wild look that Diana wasn't sure she trusted.

"As I told you . . ." she began, finding it very hard to be patient with this person. After all, what she did or did not do was absolutely none of his business! "I know that The Grange is somewhere on the other side of Bath, and possibly as far past it as Appledore." She ignored his groan. "I have only to get to the approximate region, and then the most casual inquiry will suffice to make everything plain." With difficulty she refrained from adding, "Even to you!"

David groaned again and, with an effort, kept from pulling his hair out. Where was the sweet, adorable girl with whom he was so hopelessly in love? She had been so reasonable. So *biddable!* How well he remembered the absolute trust in her eyes as he'd told her to get into the boat on Merlington Park's ornamental lake.

Where was that trust now? He looked yearningly into her still-beautiful blue eyes and saw a very stubborn woman looking back at him from them.

"Why won't you . . ." he started to ask.

"*You* don't have to come with me, you know." She frowned mightily at him. "In fact, I have yet to discover a reason for you to. Nor, for that matter, any reason for me to permit you to accompany me."

"Well, if that doesn't beat all." David rammed fisted hands onto his hips. His voice had become as heated as hers, all lordly manners forgotten.

Gulliver lay down with a plop and looked from one of them to the other. He was careful to keep some distance between himself and the woman's portmanteau, however.

David went on. "As if you didn't almost get dragged off to a brothel the first minute you spent in London! Then you got yourself turned away from the very house in which you sought sanctuary, and when you returned to the inn . . ."

"When I returned to the inn"—she talked over him—"I admit that I was accosted by some men who were no better than . . . than rough seamen," she finally managed.

David stiffened. He supposed she had designed that comment to put him in his place, the little minx. It might even have worked if he'd *been* a seaman.

A crushing reply was forming in his mind when Diana

forestalled it by adding, "And 'brothel' is not a word a gentleman uses to a lady!"

David was speechless. So she realized, on some level at any rate, that he was a gentleman. So much for her scathing pronouncement about seamen.

The thought that she did recognize that he was of gentle birth brought an odd sort of comfort. It explained why she had accompanied him away from the inn to go to meet her stranded, imaginary family.

After a moment, David said, "Lady Diana, I am sorry if I was rude, and I apologize for the improper use of a word no gentleman would use to a lady. I am concerned, however—deeply concerned—for your safety. Therefore, I am determined to claim the privilege of serving as your escort to wherever it is that *we* are going."

The subtle emphasis he had placed on the word "we" seemed to be Diana's undoing. The instant his assertion was out of his mouth, David saw Diana break. Tears welled up in her lovely blue eyes, and she turned her back on him in an attempt to hide them.

Where argument had failed, kindness had prevailed. Diana, his beloved Diana, had dropped her defenses.

Gently he took her by the shoulders and turned her back around to face him. Seeing a tear trickle down her cheek, he cursed himself for being a bully. "Don't cry, little one. Please, don't cry."

Beyond anything he'd ever wanted, he wanted to enfold her in his arms—to hold her until she was all right again, but he knew he couldn't. If he offered anything more than the light touch he'd just used to turn her to face him, he would have crossed the line. That line of behavior that existed invisibly between them because of the stations in life that they currently seemed to occupy was no less formidable than an actual tall stone wall would be.

She was a baroness. If he were standing there before her as some duke of her acquaintance, he might have offered her a shoulder to cry on, but as the lowly seaman he now appeared, he'd been daringly forward to touch her at all.

She sniffed. "It isn't my fault that the servant who was left in charge of my Godmother's townhouse was someone who didn't recognize me." Diana cried quietly as she spoke. "He refused to let me in."

"Of course it's not your fault, milady." He was careful to use the form of address that clearly relegated him to a servant's status, wanting to keep her mind at ease.

He also wanted to keep his disguise intact. If he addressed her as an equal too often, she'd soon suspect he wasn't what he seemed and then all his hopes for winning her for *himself,* not for an exalted duke, would be dashed. "It's not your fault at all. Undoubtedly, that servant must have been a rude upstart to treat you that way."

"Yes, he was. If he hadn't been so awful, I could have gone up to my room and had a lovely bath and . . . and I'm so tired and hungry." She looked at him earnestly, "That's why I can't go back and spend the last of my money on the stagecoach. We shall need it for food and lodging as we go to find my aunt Bradford."

David's heart leapt at the "we," for it meant that the biggest battle had been won. She was going to accept his escort to her Godmother.

"Well, then, I must find us food and a place to rest."

Diana looked up at the sky. "It is beginning to stay light longer now. If you could but find us some supper, we might still make a few miles before we have to rest." Fear that her father might even now be in pursuit goaded her. Putting as much distance between them and the coaching inn where she was certain she would be remembered was the best course of action, she was sure. She picked up the portmanteau.

Gulliver gave it a menacing look and walked on the other side of his friend. He wasn't going to get near that thing.

David started to remind Diana that she had said she was tired, but realized that her exhaustion was emotional, as well as physical, even as he opened his mouth to speak. He'd find them supper, then encourage her to talk as they walked on their way afterwards. Confiding in someone might just be the tonic she needed right now.

"Here, give me your portmanteau," he ordered.

Diana looked as if she might refuse, then yielded it gladly. "Thank you. It has grown rather heavy." She laughed. "I think I was hanging on to it exactly like an infant refusing to turn loose its favorite blanket."

David chuckled, amused by her perception and gladdened by her laughter. As they walked, he charted a course in his mind that would take them to Bath. The Bath Road was a good one, but unless he was mistaken, there wouldn't be a great many places along the way for them to find good, hot food at the intervals that walking would set. The post houses and inns were at distances set for coaches, not pedestrians. Better find supper before they got too far from London.

"There's an inn up ahead. The Bell." David gestured toward the curve they were approaching. "Shall it be bread and cheese brought out to you to eat beside the road, or do you fancy a meal in a private parlor?"

"Neither." She smiled at him, thankful for the casual attitude he'd adopted. "I think a meal in the Bell's public room will do fine. We shouldn't spend the extra money to procure a private parlor, but a good meal will fortify us for the trip ahead."

"Wisely said. The public room it will be."

They walked along in companionable silence, enjoying the birdsong that had begun as soon as they'd gotten a little way from the hub-bub of the City. Then the rattle of a fast-moving vehicle broke the quiet of their afternoon.

"Watch out!" David snatched her up and whirled her off the high road into the bushes next to it.

"Oh, dear!" Diana gasped. "Oh damn!"

David was shocked into using drawing room manners. "I *beg* your pardon!"

"It's him!"

"Him who?"

"Baron Runsford and that dreadful servant of his."

"So?"

Diana turned on him impatiently. "Don't you see?" she demanded.

"Obviously not. Why the devil should a gentlewoman curse like a sailor to see a gentleman of her acquaintance drive by?"

Diana glared at him. "Now who's cursing?"

"I *am* a sailor!" He took temporary refuge in his disguise.

Diana stamped her foot at him. "Oh, won't you see? He's the one I'm running from. I don't want to marry him, and my father is determined that I shall. That is why I'm running away to my Godmother, Lady Bradford." In a tight little voice that fought for control she murmured, "And now he has found me."

David dragged her deeper into the bushes. "Not yet he hasn't."

They stopped in a small clearing and Diana stared, hope dawning in her eyes. "Then you'll help me escape him?"

David pledged, "My oath on it, Lady Diana." Damn straight he was going to help her avoid the man. Diana was his! He was more set on marrying her than that man could ever be. She wasn't going to fall into the clutches of any *other* male determined to marry her. Not while he had blood in his veins!

"Stay here," he commanded, shoving her deeper into the bushes. To the big dog he said, "Guard her."

Gulliver obediently took up a position between Diana and the road and watched David leave them with half an eye. Most of his attention, though, was fixed on the portmanteau his master had left at Diana's feet.

Chapter Twelve

David stole through the copse of young trees that stretched away from the bushes in which he had hidden Diana and Gulliver. If possible, he wanted to hear what the over-dressed man in the flashy curricle was saying to his servant.

". . . said she was walking with a seaman who told her her family was stranded on the road. Damn his eyes for not saying *which* road!"

"We'll find her, never fear." The servant spoke with more familiarity than David would have expected in such a pair. "You just be calm. There's more'n a few roads outta Lunnon, you know."

"Yes, blast you, I know."

"Keep in mind that she's walking. In your curricle, we can gallop all the roads to farther than a mort can walk, easy."

"Don't use thieves' cant to speak of my future wife." The gentleman almost snarled with displeasure.

David watched in astonishment as the servant laughed.

"Very well, milord. Farther than *a lady* can walk," the lackey corrected. Then he added, chuckling, "Though it's useful for you I know more about thievin' than just the language, I'd say."

The men had stopped in the yard of the Bell. A groom came running to take the curricle. The Baron told him harshly, "No, don't take it anywhere. Just hold it here. I'll want it again in just a few minutes." With that he turned and started toward the inn, thought better of it, and turned back to question the groom at length.

As they seemed determined to wrest information he didn't have from the unfortunate young groom, David took the opportunity to hurry to the kitchen door, frowning his puzzlement over the exchange he'd just witnessed.

Arriving there unobserved, he breathed in the heavenly smells of roasting beef and baking bread. He stood there quietly until he was noticed. Nothing in his ducal expertise had taught him how to enter a kitchen. In fact, he couldn't recall ever being in one before.

Finally one of the maids looked up and saw him. "Oh!" She tapped the broad back of a woman tending several pots over the cheerful blaze in the cavernous cooking fireplace. "Cook, we 'ave company."

David hastened to reassure them, "I've only come to ask if I may purchase bread and cheese for me and my . . ." It wouldn't do to call attention to the fact that he was traveling with Diana, so he quickly amended his statement to: ". . . father."

He was getting very good at lying. He frowned slightly, not certain he approved of this newfound skill.

The cook craned to look beyond him. "Your father? Why don't you bring the old body in to the table here?"

"I wasn't certain that would be acceptable. Besides, he was tired and I left him a little way back to rest." He gestured vaguely out the door in a direction opposite that in which he'd left Diana and Gulliver hidden. "I came on to purchase bread, cheese, and ale." He smiled winningly, and added, "And now that I have smelled it, I'm hoping to add a bit of that tantalizing roast beef you have there."

"Cook makes the best roast beef in three shires," a male voice announced.

The comment startled David. As he was standing just out of the doorway in the full sun, his eyes hadn't adjusted enough to the interior dimness to discern the speaker in the shadowed part of the kitchen. Now he stepped inside, and immediately saw the figure of the slender older man in dark clothes on the far side of the table there.

"I'll wager from the smell of it that she does," he agreed about the cook's ability; then added softly, "And I've truly missed good English beef."

"Have ye now?" The man arose and came to where David stood. "And just why is that?"

"Why, I've been away." David added after a pause in which scenes of his captivity shot through his mind, "At sea."

"Ah. And ye've got on the comfortable garb to prove it." The old man pointed with the stem of his pipe. "Used to do me gardening in clothes like them—when I still had 'em left over from me sailing days. Missed 'em bad since they wore out. Not just for the comfort, neither. Always put me in mind of me days on the ole HMS *Audacious*. That they did." He stuck his pipe back in his mouth and stared out the door into his own past, his eyes dreamy. "I miss 'em still, them canvas culottes."

Suddenly, David had an inspiration. He looked care-

fully at the man. He was much older, and once probably
had been of larger stature, but the years had taken their toll,
and now he was almost of a size with him. The man's dark
vest and pants were of good quality—his shirt immaculate. David guessed him to be a waiter taking a rest before
the crowd arrived in the inn for the evening meal. "Could
I speak with you a moment outside, sir?"

"Surely." The man looked puzzled, but was too curious
to refuse even had it been his inclination.

"Cook," David asked, tossing a coin on the table,
"would you make me up a package of a hearty meal for my
father and me? And I'd appreciate it if you could find a jug
you could spare for a good bit of ale? Walking is thirsty
work."

His smile won the cook as much as his gold. "I'll be that
glad to," she assured him.

When David finally returned to pick up the package the
cook had prepared for him, the handsome sailor was no
more. Instead, he was soberly clad in the clothes of the old
gentleman who'd been smoking the pipe.

"Larksamercy!" the cook screeched as she threw up her
hands. "What ha' ye done with the master's da?"

"Peace, Marnie!" the older man called out as he stepped
into the kitchen. "Here I be." He pirouetted like a girl with
her first ball gown. "Just ye look. Got me some gardening
clothes I can bend down in to me vegetables and flowers
again, and a nice bit of blunt to go with 'em." He showed
her the golden sovran David had paid him to exchange
garments with him.

"Your son ain't gonna feel so happy about it, Abner. He
just got you them other clothes the day 'fore yesterday."

"Ah, but I've enough to pay him back for 'em. Or better yet, to go out right now and buy some more just like
'em, if I'd a mind to." He did a hornpipe over to her. His

sailor dance was little rusty but gay all the same, and he kissed her on the cheek.

"I ain't seen ye so happy in a long time." The cook had a fond smile on her face as she watched him. She turned to David. "Memories mean a lot to older gentlemen, sir. While it do seem a little strange, still 'twas kind of ye, whatever your reasons."

"My reason for wanting to exchange clothes is simple. I'm escorting my, er, my father inland." The lie grated on David. "It just seemed a good idea to trade. Sailors tend to look more and more peculiar as they get farther from the sea.

The man wearing the culottes had started into the inn proper, but bustled back to them. "There be a curricle in the inn yard. Some swell talking Jamie' s ear off. He might want service. I'll go see."

That was David's cue to leave. Scooping up the jug of ale and the neat bundle of food the cook had made for him he smiled his thanks.

"'Ere now! You wait just a minute."

David turned back, hiding his impatience.

"Ye be forgettin' ye've money coming back to ye. Ye gave me far too much." The cook grabbed his wrist, turned his hand palm up, and spilled several coins into it. "There. Now we be even." She closed his fingers around the coins.

David started to tell her he'd wanted her to keep the coins for her trouble. Then he realized that that would be out of character for a traveler who had been, until just a moment ago, a mere seaman. "Thank you," he told her instead.

Just then, he heard the voice of Baron Runsford in the inn foyer shouting for the landlord. David saluted the cook and left quickly.

She bustled off toward the angry voice in the inn. Nobody was going to talk to the innkeeper's old father that way if she could help it!

While David was making his slow, careful way back through the trees to the bushes in which he'd left Diana, there was an angry shout from the doorway of the Bell. Standing where he was hidden, he parted the bushes and watched as the large gentleman he knew to be Diana's pursuer burst out of the inn and headed back toward the boy tending his curricle.

"Seaman they told us! They said she'd left the White Lion with a seaman! Blast their eyes. That old gaffer in there is not the person Diana was seen with. They said the sailor with Lady Diana was young and handsome. We've been sent on a wild goose chase!"

"Well, good sirs," the older gentleman with whom David had exchanged clothing told them from the doorway, "I do be the onliest seaman here in this place." He was clearly agitated. Evidently the Baron and his man had displeased the old gentleman. "Ye can ask Cook, here."

The large woman who had charge of the inn's kitchen appeared in the doorway behind him. Sensing her friend's mood, and resenting the rudeness shown him, she scowled at the two who were hastily settling themselves in their light vehicle, and cried, "Why, ye should be glad you got to see old Da." She scowled harder. "Huh!" she snorted scornfully. "Imagine two grown men being silly enough to be lookin' for a seaman so far from the sea."

Furious, the Baron threw himself into his curricle. With a string of curses aimed at the inn staff, Runsford turned his horses, whipped them up, and galloped back toward London.

The sailor and the cook looked at each other a moment,

then burst into whoops of laughter. They laughed so hard at the unpleasant nobleman's frustration that they had to pound each other on the back. After their merriment had died down a bit, they linked arms in mutual satisfaction and returned to their warm places in the inn kitchen.

Chapter Thirteen

The noise of the departing curricle had died by the time David reached the tiny clearing in the midst of the bushes. The sight he saw there made him gasp as his heart twisted in his chest. Diana, his cherished Diana, was huddled down beside Gulliver in a tight ball. She had knelt and put her arms around the big dog and was holding to him as if he were a lifeline. Eyes squeezed shut, she was hugging the huge dog fiercely as tears ran down her cheeks.

David was transfixed by emotions that hit him like an avalanche. Diana wasn't the strong, intrepid woman she pretended to be. It wasn't as he feared. She hadn't completely abolished all evidence of the young girl with whom he'd fallen in love. That brave girl was still there under the veneer of worldliness that time and unhappiness had given Diana, and his heart leapt to find her again.

Dropping his parcel, he set down the jug of ale and went to her. Kneeling beside her, he transferred her arms from the dog's neck to his own and drew her to him. Tenderness almost overcame him when Diana came as willingly as a child seeking comfort—for a split second. Then she shoved away from him. "I'm quite all right," she assured him untruthfully.

He sat back on his heels. "Then why are you in tears?"

She dashed them away with the back of her hand, raised her chin, and declared, "I was having a moment of weakness."

David wisely concealed his smile.

"For just an instant, I thought, 'He's going to catch me. I know he is.' but I don't think so now."

"Oh?"

"No. He won't. I have you to help me, and he has gone off in the wrong direction. I'm safe."

David wished he could agree with her, but he shared the mind of the servant accompanying Diana's pursuer. They could cover far more ground in a curricle than he and Diana were going to be able to walk.

"Why are you looking like that?"

"Like what?" David hedged.

"You look as if you think they *will* catch us," she accused.

"Only if we are not sufficiently careful."

Diana frowned at him. "But they're following a false scent. We are on the road to Bath, and they are off on some other."

"Yes, but they can easily gallop the other routes out of London for a distance equal to what we could have walked in the time since we left the coaching inn and still return to search for us farther along this road."

Diana grasped his arm, horrified. "Then we must get off this road!"

"I agree." He thought hard for a moment. "I seem to remember that my tu . . ." He stopped himself just in time and deftly substituted, "*Someone* told me that the old King's Road runs parallel to the Bath Road for several miles—at least as far as Kensington. Perhaps it does the whole way, but I really don't remember that being part of the information I was given, so I simply don't know. We could look for it, though, and use it instead of this one."

"Oh, that's a capital idea." Diana was relieved. "I'd have had no idea how to go if we'd had to take to open country."

David frowned. "Neither, I'm afraid, would I." The thought was irritating. All his several coachmen knew their way about the entire country, off road or on, yet he did not. Being a rich, pampered duke had a debilitating side, he concluded. In the future, he'd prepare better for real life.

David cleared his throat.

Diana looked at him. "Yes?"

"What are you afraid of, Diana?"

"I told you! Baron Runsford. He's going to catch me and take me back to my father."

"Would being with your family again be so bad?"

"You'd never understand."

"Try me."

"It's my father."

"Is he a cruel parent?"

"No! Of course not." Diana sighed heavily.

"Then tell me what the problem is."

"The problem is me." She tapped her chest. "I'm . . . I'm *inconvenient!*"

"I beg your pardon?" David was puzzled. How could anyone as charming and beautiful as Diana be an inconvenience? Unless he was grossly misinformed—and he made it a point never to be misinformed in matters as important as the spiritual welfare of the people in his care—

his vicar was a kind and gentle man of God. Surely he hadn't turned into an ogre in David's absence.

"Inconvenient," Diana repeated with a hint of irritation. "The word needs no defining."

David could hear the frustration and pain in her voice. He was wise enough to wait for her to explain. Now, no doubt, he'd learn her reason for pursuing her Godmother across the English countryside instead of returning to the peaceful safety of the vicarage.

Diana took a steadying breath and told him, "My father is a very scholarly, peaceful man, and I disturb his peace." She wiped a single tear defiantly. "Therefore, I am unwelcome." Her lips quivered and her head almost drooped, but she caught it and thrust her chin up again. "Unwanted." Her eyes dared him to disagree.

David looked at her, incredulous. How could this beautiful young woman, whose very nearness had the power to turn his bones to water, ever be unwanted? Still, he held his tongue.

Diana relented and said more softly, "You don't know what it's like to be given away to a grandparent because your father doesn't want you when your mother is no longer . . ." Diana swallowed painfully, then finished, ". . . there."

That was true. When his parents had been killed in that carriage accident, Carrington had been there for him. He'd felt bereft, missing them terribly, but he'd never felt alone, as Diana obviously had.

Diana went on, "Then I lost my grandfather after I'd learned to love him more than anything in the world. And again I had to be *disposed* of. I was barely sixteen and I was married off—to a brute—so that I wouldn't *disturb* people!" She said "disturb" in a voice accented by pain and frustration.

That voice all but broke David's heart.

He couldn't help it. " 'Disturb' people? I'm afraid I don't understand. In what way?"

"I ask questions, I express opinions. That's really enough, you know. People don't like to be questioned, and they certainly don't want to listen to opinions, particularly when they are strongly expressed."

She shot him a sidelong glance. "Oh! And I answer people truthfully when they ask me for advice." She sighed. "Sometimes I think that's the worse mistake of all. People don't want advice, you see, they just want to be told they're fine as they are."

"And that's all?"

For an instant she avoided his gaze, her tear-damp lashes hiding her eyes from him. Then the corners of her mouth twitched, her lips formed a smile, and she gave him a mischievous little grin.

David was hit with such a wave of pure desire it was all he could do to control it. He'd give half his fortune to be able to draw her close and kiss those lips. He went warm all over. His whole being shouted for him to snatch her to him, hold her hard against his heart, and crush her mouth with his own.

He clenched his teeth with the effort he had to make to keep her from seeing how much she affected him. A muscle jumped in his jaw. Still, his face flamed.

Diana didn't notice. She confessed, "I let people know what I thought they should do when they asked me, and when they didn't take my advice, I scolded a little."

That broke the spell! David threw back his head and laughed.

"Well, I did." She scowled at him, her winged brows drawn down in a severe V over her lovely blue eyes. Then she smiled in spite of herself and admitted, "Well, maybe I scolded a lot." Then she informed him defensively, "But it always struck me as pointless to ask advice only to ignore it!"

David considered his reply and let a moment pass before making it. "Perhaps asking advice was the only way the person had of getting you to listen to their troubles."

Diana's face fell, her irritation forgotten. "Oh, dear." She was clearly distressed. "Do you really suppose that could be true?"

"Indeed I do."

"That's awful."

She looked so dejected that David wished he hadn't spoken.

"If that's the truth," Diana murmured, "then I have been excessively cruel."

David couldn't help it; he had to tell her, "I honestly don't think that would be possible, Diana."

"Oh, yes it would. I was always telling people to pull themselves together and make a greater effort to overcome the things that they complained of."

"Hmmm."

"What do you mean, 'hmmm'?" Diana was a little belligerent.

"Well . . ." David took time answering. "Haven't you ever noticed that that sort of advice is always being given to people who are incapable of doing it?"

Diana sighed and turned her face away. "I'm aware of it now that you've pointed it out to me. Thank you." Her tone was cool, but even so, her voice was infinitely sad.

David wanted to cut his tongue out.

Funny, he'd been rather firmly against such a mutilation when the Sultan had threatened to have it done. It was different now. Now his words had wounded Diana. He shook his head. Being in love was certainly a strange and uncomfortable state.

Diana shook out her skirts. "There's daylight yet. We can walk a few miles before dark, can't we?"

"Yes, but if we depart this inn and leave the road for the old one, once we are through Hyde Park and on past Kensington, we will be far from anywhere we can be sure of procuring a comfortable night's lodging."

"Then we shall just have to sleep in a hedge or a haystack as I'm told the soldiers returning from the war with Napoleon frequently did."

Having done that more than a few times in his own military career, David was fairly certain Diana had no idea how uncomfortable it could be. However, he had some serious doubts about turning up back at the inn with a *lady* instead of the *father* he'd claimed to be escorting, so he picked up all their paraphernalia, whistled Gulliver to heel, and followed Diana.

Chapter Fourteen

Diana and David hadn't gone far before the swirl of traffic had Diana spinning around every moment to see if the Baron's curricle was coming up on them. Sensing Diana's uneasiness, Gulliver pressed close to David to avoid the noise and danger from the wheels flashing past. Mud from the recent rain splashed up and on them when they passed low places in the street.

Finally, David had had enough. Diana's firm pronouncement that they had to save every penny notwithstanding, he hailed a passing hackney.

"No, we can't," Diana protested, "We can't afford such an extravagance. We have a long way to go."

"Aye," David acknowledged, lapsing into the language he'd been forced to use for the last few months. "And I for one am not willing to walk so much of that 'long way' that I'm caught here in this part of London when night falls. We came into the north of the city. In the interest of safety and dispatch, I intend to ride to the end nearest Bath, thank you."

Diana opened her mouth to protest, saw the determination on her escort's face, and closed it again. Reluctantly, she permitted him to bundle her, their dinner, Gulliver, his knapsack, and her portmanteau into the hackney, but when she heard him tell the driver, "My mistress won't let me ride inside with her," as he swung up to join the driver on his seat, she wanted to explode.

Since there was no one else to take her exasperation out on, she turned to the only other occupant of the carriage. Speaking as if she knew he understood, she told the dog, "Gulliver, I'm really not certain this arrangement is going to work out. Your master is a little too high-handed to suit me, I'm afraid."

Gulliver cocked his head and whined.

Diana threw herself back against the seat. Dust flew from the ancient squabs, and her planned pout turned into a sneeze.

Gulliver gave one sharp bark and sneezed, too. After that he regarded Diana with something very like reproach until she laughed and gave him a hug, mud and all.

On the box, David was taking full advantage of the driver's knowledge of the city. He'd seated himself there in order to question the driver. He knew he certainly needed a great deal more information than he presently possessed if he was going to escort Diana safely and reliably to . . . wherever the blazes it was she was trying to go!

In answer to his questions, the old gentleman told him, "Ye can get the coach to Bath at the Gloucester Coffee Tavern in Piccadilly, ye know. Fast she is, too. The Bath Road being better'n most, don't ye see. That is, once the coach gets free of all the traffic hurrying to get into Lunnon afore nightfall. Then it really moves out."

"When does open country begin?"

"I'd say 'bout four mile past Hyde Park. After Kensington Village a little way."

"And the King's Roads? My mistress is a great walker and intends to make a walking tour of her trip to Bath."

"Why, bless ye, sir, the King's New Road an' his Old Road, too, feed back into the turnpike to Bath shortly past Hyde Park. Right after the Hogsmire Lane Tollgate." He calculated swiftly and added, "That be about mile and a half down the pike." He looked at David earnestly. "If'n she wants to walk the King's Roads, either one of them, then ye want me to let ye down at Hyde Park Corner, where they begins."

David scowled. So much for his plan to walk the old roads to escape detection. "And you say that open country doesn't start till four miles out of London?"

"Weel, there's country afore Counters Bridge, where the pike narrows, but 'tain't till ye git beyond that bridge, over Stamford Brook it is, that I calls it *open* country."

"And the last safe inn?" David said a prayer of thanks that the driver they'd gotten was so helpful. He could just imagine how much help the driver of the stagecoach from earlier today would have been.

"The Bell and Anchor's the place most people stop coming into or outta the City. That's not quite to th' three-mile marker, though."

"Nevertheless," David decided and declared mendaciously, "that's where my mistress wishes to go." And Diana was going to go there whether she liked the idea or not.

Though this kind, garrulous man was well informed about the turnpike, David doubted that a London cabbie could tell him much about the open country beyond. Having learned during his years of army service on the Continent the danger of being without maps in strange territory, he knew he needed to be much better prepared to find his way about the English countryside than he presently was. He needed a lot more information, because he fully intended to be knowledgeable before he'd be willing to go along with Diana's harebrained notion of striking off across country on foot instead of traveling on the Bath stagecoach!

Besides, spending the night at the inn would provide much-needed comforts as well as rest. A hot bath and some attention to the mud their clothes had been splashed with wouldn't be unwelcome. Gulliver, especially, needed care in that area.

He sighed. Taking over the care of the girl and the dog was proving more wearisome than any previous undertaking. Could that be because no one he'd tried to take care of had ever actively opposed him before? The matter gave him fuel for thought.

"There be tollgates," the driver was saying, "and I'll have to pay both comin' and goin', you know."

"Aye." David gave the man more money than he'd need. "Just set us down safely at the Bell and Anchor."

"Consider it done, sir. But, I give ye a word of warning, Hounslow is at the nine-mile stone, an' Hounslow Heath is an evil place for travelers. Many a thieving highwayman still lurks there, don' care what they likes to tell ye about all of 'em being gone. So take care how ye pass it."

"I appreciate your warning." He clapped the driver on the shoulder. "Rest assured, I'll escort my lady well clear of Hounslow Heath."

Gratified by David's comradely gesture, the driver gestured to his right with his whip. "That be the Gloucester Coffee Tavern over there. A bit quiet right now, but ye jist wait till the evening coaches start rollin' in. Excitement aplenty then. The stagecoaches leave right on the minute they say they do, and it makes for a mighty confusion, I can tell ye. 'Tis a sight to behold."

David turned to look sharply at the place the driver had indicated. The tavern seemed to have enough going on as it was. The yard was crowded with stagecoaches, and private traveling coaches, a post chaise, and several drays delivering hogsheads of ale and casks of wine. It took him a minute to be sure that there was no curricle driven by a large and intemperate baron in the inn yard.

"Here we be at Hyde Park Corner, and that be the milestone the road to Bath figures from." The driver pointed to their left. "There be St. George's Hospital, and here be the first tollgate."

David watched the driver pay the toll and did swift mental calculations to be sure he'd given the man money enough and to spare. Satisfied that he had, he settled back to watch the sights.

Not ever having ridden on the box of any of his traveling coaches, David had never had such a splendid view of the road. He found he was enjoying this adventure even more than he'd expected to. The "balm for his soul" that he'd been so melodramatically seeking when he'd started out from Smythington Park must have arrived and slathered itself over him, for he felt a quiet peace beneath the watchfulness this odd adventure called for.

They passed the second tollgate and the barracks of the Kensington Palace guards in less than a mile. Then they were proceeding at a sedate pace through the village of Kensington. David's heart gave a bound midway to the tollgate at the end of the village. He realized that he'd barely flinched as a passing Corinthian cracked his whip over the backs of his fine pair of matched grays.

Taking that as a good sign he was on the road to recovery, he settled back with a grin. Now if he could just get through the rest of the trip without having any nightmares. . . .

In the carriage, Diana had shifted her portmanteau and the rest of their baggage to make things more comfortable. Now suddenly, she was attempting to appease some sort of doggie nightmare.

Gulliver, exhausted by the excitement of all the strange sights and sounds of the city, had curled up and fallen asleep almost as soon as they'd gotten into the carriage. Now he'd awakened with wide, staring eyes and a vicious snarl.

"Gulliver! What is it?"

His eyes fixed on the portmanteau she'd just moved, the big dog growled and arched his heavy neck.

"Great heavens, dog!" Diana was reluctant to touch him in his present mood. "What *is* the matter?"

Gulliver continued to regard her luggage with a malevolent stare.

Puzzled, she watched the dog. "Is it my portmanteau?" She tried to make her tone soft in spite of the need to have it carry over the rattle of wheels and the constant creaking of the carriage.

Gulliver calmed down a bit at the sound of her soothing voice.

"Gulliver"—Diana smiled at him gently—"it's only a piece of luggage. And while I dislike intensely the man to whom it belonged, that is all it is."

Gulliver shot her a glance and stopped his growling.

"See," Diana told him as she reached out to touch the offending object, "it's only . . ."

Gulliver lunged into her, knocking her back against the

seat and pressing her there with his large frame as they passed through yet another turnpike tollgate.

Diana shoved the dog away from her. "Oh, for pity's sake, Gulliver! All this fuss about a simple portmanteau. Here. Let me show you."

When Diana brought the portmanteau onto the bench beside them, Gulliver leapt to the opposite one, bumping her in his haste.

"Honestly!" Diana was getting annoyed. She blew a strand of hair out of her eyes and opened the fastenings on the dreaded object. "Look!" she ordered the dog.

Gulliver looked at the mouth of the portmanteau his friend held open for him. Then he threw back his head and howled.

Immediately, the horse drawing the hackney broke into a gallop.

Diana was thrown to the floor. "Well!" She picked herself up and braced herself in her seat. "They could at least have given us some warning!"

Gulliver, already braced before the horse galloped off, just glared at the portmanteau.

"Now listen, dog." Diana glared at *him*. "I have had quite enough of your foolishness." Grasping her much maligned piece of luggage, she plunged her hand into it.

Gulliver's eyes rolled.

Outside, the driver called, "Whoa, whoa there, Nelly!" and turned to laugh at David. "The old girl don' never git to stretch out like this in Town. Guess she can't pass up the chance."

David grinned back at him and held on for dear life. He could see a humpbacked bridge coming up fast.

Inside, Diana ordered sternly, "Look! Look, you silly animal," and brought out a handful of frilly underthings. "See! They are just clothes."

David shouted a warning. "Hang on, Diana!"

Diana didn't hear it as she firmly reiterated, "Clothes!" She threw the first handful down and brought out a dress. "See? A dress. My dress. Nothing to be so upset about."

Gulliver's glare had become baleful. It never left the portmanteau.

"Dresses!" She took out and shook two more at the belligerent dog.

Then they hit the bridge, and everything went flying. Diana landed on the floor again. Her clothing was all over the interior of the carriage. And her lovely, lacy underthings were draped all over *her*.

The coach slowed to a halt.

Diana heard David calling to her, as he jumped down from the box. "Diana! Diana, are you all right?" Then his hand was on the carriage door handle.

David, impatient to see for himself that Diana was all right after the fearful bump, opened the carriage door. The sight that met his eyes was one he'd never forget.

Gulliver was braced in one corner of the coach, staring at the opposite corner where Diana's portmanteau, open and gaping empty, had landed. Clothing that had once been neatly packed into it was scattered everywhere, and Diana, his precious Diana, was on the floor of the hackney.

Her hair in glorious disarray, she glared up at him from under the lacy ribbons of a chemise that had somehow come to rest on her head. The ribbons were blue. A lovely blue just like the blue of her eyes.

David stood stock still, enchanted. Until he saw the look in those eyes.

"You could have warned me," she accused.

"But I did!"

"You most certainly did not!"

"Diana," he said stiffly, "I never lie, or at least I didn't until recently, and I did call down a warning the instant that I saw the bridge."

"Well," she said grudgingly, "I didn't hear you."

He wondered if it was safe to offer to help her up, decided that it wasn't yet, and instead inquired again, "Are you all right?"

"I'm fine." The mischief he had come to love peeped at him from the back of her eyes. "Nothing hurts but my dignity."

A smile pulled at the corner of his mouth, but he fought it down. At school, he remembered, the headmaster had sometimes referred to the caned bottoms of the students as their "dignity," when assuring them that he intended to make it difficult for them to sit on same.

Diana's eyes lit with understanding. He was thinking exactly what her grandfather had called her bottom when she was in need of a spanking, she *knew* he was. The light of understanding became the light of irritation. Her eyebrows snapped down in a V again. How dare he?

David thought it was high time for a distraction. "Did the bump throw open your portmanteau?"

The irritation gave place to real aggravation. "No," Diana answered shortly.

"Then why . . ." He could hardly ask his goddess why she was wearing a chemise as a bonnet—even though it made a very becoming bonnet. He couldn't help himself. He stared at it admiringly.

Diana blew a ribbon up out of her eye, realized that her sailor-escort was staring at . . . her . . . her *intimate apparel* like a mooncalf, and snatched the article in question off her head. "This is all your dog's fault."

"I beg your pardon?" He looked stunned.

"Yes, your dog's fault. He's been staring and growling at my portmanteau ever since he met it . . ."

David didn't correct her in that one did not actually *meet* luggage.

". . . and I thought that if I showed him it was only a bag for clothes, he would calm down about it."

David had the picture now. "And so you brought your things out to show him there was nothing, er, danger-ous . . . in your portmanteau?"

"Exactly!" She was stuffing the lacy things back into the object in question. Those packed, she snatched up the three dresses scattered about and began putting them in to cover up the intimate apparel.

Suddenly, David was arrested by the sight of a yellow dress that had obviously seen better days. He knew that dress!

Why had Diana brought it? That dress, he was certain, was the same one she had worn the day they'd met so long ago in Merlington Park. He'd recognized it before at the vicarage barn when she'd worn it to fence with her cousin Jonathan. Recognized it and had thought, while wishing he was wrong, that she'd worn it to save other clothes that she cared about more.

But why had she brought it now?

His heart pounded. His mind tumbled into chaos. Could it be that the dress had special meaning for her? Meaning as special as it had for him?

He reached out to touch it . . . to caress its pale fabric.

And Diana yanked it away from his hand.

Her gesture sobered him like a dash of cold water thrown in his face. This wasn't Merlington Park and he wasn't the lofty Duke of Smythington. This was the dusty turnpike in front of the Bell and Anchor—and he was a lowly seaman. A common seaman who was tolerated as an escort by a woman whom he knew wouldn't put up with him were she not running away from something she could bear even less than she could bear his company.

To make matters worse, he was a man sailing under false colors. A man hoping that the time with her he gained by doing so would enable him to win her love.

A dream. A simpleminded fool's dream.

He watched Diana fold and put away the yellow dress, and his sad heart was gladdened by the tenderness with which she handled the garment.

Thank God the larger problem of explaining who he was and why he'd deceived her was far in the future. He could push it aside for now, but someday he was going to have to decide how he was going to tell her that he not only knew that the yellow dress had meaning for her, but that it meant much to him as well.

And how, for the love of God, could he? Would he dare tell her that he remembered as if it were this very morning the day she had worn it? And last and far from least of all, that he had given her his heart that day?

Dear Lord, how could he ever tell her it was her dear memory that had gotten him through the last horror-filled year of his life? No, that he could never share, though he loved her all the more for it. As he helped her to descend from the carriage and picked up all their belongings, he kept his face turned away from her so she wouldn't see the raw emotion that ravaged it.

Following her toward the inn, he walked behind her like the proper servant he was pretending to be. As he did, he wondered if he'd ever be able to tell her how he hoped beyond hoping that she had understood all that transpired in the final glance that had passed between them that fateful day.

Chapter Fifteen

Diana led the way toward the inn, David, laden with their belongings, trailing behind her, and Gulliver bringing up the rear. Short of the doorway, she turned and asked in a whisper, "Which side will we go around?"

David stared an instant, then caught her meaning. "We aren't going around. We're going in."

"In? You can't be serious."

"Oh, but I am serious. Just look at what a mess we are." He gestured at her gown. The jug of ale he'd procured for them sloshed as he did so. Inspiration came. "We can save by eating this dinner I've already paid for . . ." He saw her about to comment on that expenditure and headed it off by saying, ". . . by exchanging clothes with the man who wanted to remember his days before the mast."

Diana looked doubtful. Then Gulliver shook himself mightily and pelted her with half-dried specks of mud. "Very well," she capitulated. "I'll bespeak two rooms for us."

David chuckled. "No need."

Diana looked shocked. "What do you mean, 'No need'?"

"Surely you don't imagine an inn of the caliber of the Bell and Anchor would allow a dog inside? No, I assure you Gulliver will be sent to the stables, and I"—he bowed low—"your humble servant, will be sent to keep him company."

Diana was indignant. "I wouldn't think of putting you in the stable!"

"Ah, but I would. Gulliver, you see, would not know where we were or why we had deserted him. There is no way I would permit the suffering that would cause him."

Diana's eyes widened, but she wasn't seeing David. She seemed to be looking far away, into some other place. And she was, into a memory. In her mind's eye she saw again the distant past, and another man who cared about a dog.

Her heart melted a little toward this high-handed "servant" she'd somehow acquired. His spirit was similar to that of her lost love. Turning to look at him, she told him, "I shall arrange for a bath for you, at least."

"My thanks, milady." Again he bowed, his smile a little mocking.

Diana shook her head in exasperation. Next he'd be pulling his forelock like a peasant! She turned away and preceded him into the inn.

"May I help you?" The innkeeper was having trouble deciding how to address the bedraggled pair. His doubts were put to flight when Diana lifted her chin and commanded, "Two rooms, innkeeper, one for me and one for my servant. And baths for all of us, including my dog."

David watched with interest to see how this was going to go. Diana might have the air of a queen, but the innkeeper was looking at her entourage with a decidedly jaundiced eye. He stepped forward. "I shall stay with your dog, milady, wherever our host appoints us."

The innkeeper was visibly relieved. Tuning to the maid standing nearby, he told her, "Show milady to the bed-chamber overlooking the back garden, Alice, while I show this man where he and the dog are to stay."

David gave Diana's portmanteau to the maidservant, then turned back to the innkeeper as Diana and the girl started up the stairs. "Come along," the innkeeper told him. "We'll just cut through the kitchen so I can order baths for the three of you." He chuckled. "You'll have to be the one to help Master Dog with his, however."

David laughed. "Then may I suggest that you prepare *his* bath first?"

An hour later, when David and Gulliver were clean, David dressed in a white shirt and a pair of knee britches from his knapsack. Putting Gulliver in a stall from which he couldn't escape, and leaving his knapsack with the whin-ing dog as a pledge of his soon return, he took up the par-cel of food and the jug of ale and left him. Going back to the kitchen of the inn, where he had had the dubious plea-sure of bathing behind a sheet stretched across a corner for privacy disturbed now and again by the peeking of a bold-eyed serving maid, he looked in.

"Oooh," the same maid flirted, "back again so soon, are we?"

David grinned at her. He'd never been treated as an equal by a serving maid before. He found it a pleasant nov-elty. "Why, I came to see how my clothes are faring in your care, sweet Rose."

"Faring very well they are, good sir. Laundry maid 'as your shirt and stockings, and old Boggs is seeing to the sponging off of all the mud from the rest." She fluttered her eyelashes at him. "Is there maybe sumpin' *more* that ye wanted?"

"Ah, sweet Rose," he said with a smile, understanding her well. "I've no time for what I might want, though I thank you kindly. I must be taking these to my mistress." He lifted his jug and parcel for her to see. "She's a strange one and will only eat what she has had prepared for her by her own cook." He added hastily, "Except for breakfasts." No need to begin their trek on empty stomachs.

"Ah, well. If ye must, ye must." She smiled broadly. "If ye want anything later, though . . ." She let the provocative turn of her shoulder speak her invitation and left the sentence unfinished.

David gave a great shout of laughter, caught her to him hard with his free arm, and planted a quick kiss on her lips. Just as quickly he released her. Leaving her staring after him wide-eyed and with her fingers gently pressed to her smiling mouth, he went in search of Diana.

As he took the stairs two steps at a time, he marveled at the fact that the formerly sedate, sober, respectable Duke of Smythington was evidently becoming a libertine as well as a champion liar. And, his conscience accused in an acid voice, rather enjoying it.

Diana was sitting at the dressing table in the spacious bedchamber the landlord had given her. She stared into the mirror, more worried about finding her Godmother than doing anything attractive with her freshly washed hair. Finally giving up any idea of a style, she tried simply to make order of it. She was tying the heavy mass back with a ribbon when there was a tap at the door.

Startled, she went to it and called, "Who's there?"

"Your supper, milady."

Pulling open the door she started to tell him to stop

being silly. When she saw him, the words died in her throat.

He stood there with his arms spread wide, a parcel in one hand and a jug of something in the other. The stance opened his shirt more deeply down his chest than just around the bronzed column of his throat. Because he'd probably not been offered towels, as she'd been, he must have been damp when he pulled his shirt on, and it clung to his broad shoulders and well-muscled chest like the dampened muslin worn by some of the more daring women of the *ton*.

It was his eyes that caught and held her attention more than anything else about him, though. Sherry brown and full of mischief, they reminded her of a pair of eyes she longed to see again. Eyes that had looked on her with kindness and understanding five years ago when she had been a lost and awkward sixteen-year-old catapulted into a hostile world full of slights, hurts, and actual pain.

He lifted the jug he carried toward her and quirked an eyebrow, and suddenly, Diana realized that she was seeing this man for the first time. Really seeing him. She saw that his hair, wet and out of its sailor's queue, hung loose to his shoulders and that the smile on the freshly scrubbed face it framed was dazzling.

In her haste to escape pursuit, she'd never really paid him any attention. She was paying it now, as attested to by the shaky feeling in the pit of her stomach.

Oh, dear. This man wasn't just a mild annoyance that had attached itself to her, nor merely a convenience to help her run away. He was a man. He was all man. A handsome, virile creature that radiated confidence in his every move or gesture. A man sure of himself and his abilities, who met the world head on. He radiated the assurance that he could defend her against any danger—in spite of the fact that he wasn't very tall.

Suddenly, with a blazing clarity that equaled a flash of lightning, Diana knew she was in trouble. Deep trouble.

How in heaven's name was she going to explain this person to her Godmother?

Chapter Sixteen

Diana, stunned momentarily by the realization, shook her head in bewilderment and stammered, "I . . . I don't even know your name."

David laughed. "You'll feel better after we eat." He shouldered his way into the room and put his package down on the high four-poster bed. Pulling a chair over from the fireplace, he gestured Diana to sit.

"My name is David." He cut the string on the package and spread the paper out flat, chatting easily to help Diana over her embarrassment. "Michael David, actually, but my mother called me David, and you may, too."

Diana approached the chair and stared at him.

"Michael David . . ." He grinned and used the name that had come to him when he'd nearly introduced himself to her cousin Jonathan by his full name and title: ". . . Smythe."

Diana said, "How do you do. I am Lady Diana, Baroness Huntley." She sat because David was holding the chair, and it seemed the thing to do, but she had the strong feeling that she was losing control of the situation.

"There's bread and cheese and good English roast beef. And ale to wash it down with."

Ignoring the food, Diana looked at the jug of ale as if it were something offensive.

David frowned. "Would you rather I went down and got you wine?"

"No." She shook her head, still looking at the jug. "It's just that I . . . have an aversion to spirits of any kind."

"Mild English ale can hardly be termed spirits, Lady Diana. At least not when spoken of in the tone of voice you just used." His expression sobered. "What is it? What troubles you?"

Diana saw that kindness in his eyes again and some of the apprehension brought on by being alone with him in a bedchamber vanished. "Some men are brutes when they drink to excess. My hus . . ." She stopped there and refused to go on. It wasn't this man's business that her late husband had abused her when he was drunk.

David sat down on the edge of the bed next to their picnic. He considered her quietly for a long moment before telling her softly, "Lady Diana, you have no need to worry where I'm concerned."

Diana's gaze locked with his. She seemed to be holding her breath.

"Getting drunk is a habit I've always found repugnant," David told her. "And at the risk of sounding even more stuffy, I'll tell you that when a man drinks to a point at which his behavior changes and he ceases to be himself, it gives me a disgust of him."

His earlier laughter and this last quiet statement had their desired effect. Diana relaxed in her chair.

David regarded her with a carefully pleasant expression

while in his heart he raged against the man who had caused that touch of fear he'd seen in her eyes.

He waved his hand over their picnic. "Would you like a sandwich or . . . ?"

"A sandwich will be fine."

David wished he could make a neater job of it, but after all, he'd only just learned to make a sandwich the other night in the vicarage barn. When he'd finished making hers, he congratulated himself that it looked much better than his first attempt had and made a second one for himself.

As he did, Diana watched him carefully. Truth to tell, the fact was finally dawning on her that she had run off with this man, this stranger, without any thought at all, and now she was wondering if she'd made a mistake. Certainly, she told herself, it had hardly been a prudent thing to do. For all she knew, he might be a felon fleeing justice!

Somehow his escorting her had seemingly happened without her volition, but, again somehow, she wasn't sorry. He made her feel safe, though she couldn't have told why if she'd had to.

David produced two glasses and poured ale from the jug into both.

Diana threw him an assessing glance. The anxiety reappeared in her eyes.

To David she looked like a frightened child trying to decide whether or not to trust a parent's promise. He forced a laugh. He didn't feel the least bit like truly laughing because he'd seen that faint glimmer of fear return to the back of her eyes.

His dear love had obviously been given good reason to be afraid of a man who lingered too long over his brandy—he had no doubt of it. He sought again to reassure her. "My dear," he said in a voice that rumbled in his chest, "you have no need to be afraid that I will ever drink to excess. I give you my word that I never do."

He tried to lighten the mood then by adding with a smile, "If I should, you have my leave to shoot me."

Diana sprang from her chair and took a rapid turn around the room. Half laughing, half accusing, she said, "That's a vain permission, for you are perfectly safe in making it as I have no weapon."

"Hmmm. I shall have to remedy that, I suppose."

"Oh, don't be foolish." She came and sat down again. "Eat your supper," she commanded like a queen.

Perhaps if she were lofty enough, she could reestablish their odd relationship of mistress and servant. Glancing surreptitiously at David's warm brown eyes—eyes that kept reminding her of another pair of kind brown eyes— she knew she wouldn't feel completely comfortable until she had.

Downstairs, two men conferred with the innkeeper about the pair who had arrived earlier with the big mongrel dog. "You say you're looking for a woman, a sailor, and his dog?" The landlord shook his head. "No, I've not seen that."

"You seem unsure."

"No sailor's been here at the Bell and Anchor for many a day."

The taller of the two men sensed some hesitancy in the innkeeper's manner. He seemed to be the spokesman for the pair. "But?"

"Well, there was a lady, her manservant, and *her* dog. They got in late this afternoon."

The spokesman stepped toward him eagerly. "Was the lady a rare beauty with long golden hair?"

"Aye."

"And the man, was he a little fellow no taller than my friend here?" He gestured to his short, sturdy companion.

The innkeeper frowned. "Maybe a mite taller, but not much."

The two inquisitors exchanged triumphant glances.

"And where are they now?"

Something in the questioner's voice bothered the landlord. "Why do you ask?"

The tall man caught the guarded tone in the host's voice.

"Aw," he answered with elaborate boredom, "we'd just noticed them earlier in London and wondered if they'd gotten this far along the road." His eyes shifted, then his gaze returned to the innkeeper's eyes with an unnatural steadiness. "Er, my friend here took a fancy to the sailor's dog, and would have made him an offer for it if we'd caught up with him, that's all."

The landlord hadn't spent thirty years keeping the Bell and Anchor without learning to know a liar when he saw one. He regarded the two steadily for a minute.

The short one ran his finger around his neck inside his poorly tied cravat. The spokesman shifted his weight from one foot to the other.

That was all the innkeeper needed to confirm his assessment of the pair. He wasn't going to help these two. "Well, I'm afraid you're out of luck," he lied easily. "They were here briefly, but decided to see if they couldn't get farther along before dark. You might try to catch them."

The two men exchanged glances.

The innkeeper lent them impetus. "She said something about trying to get closer to the nine-mile marker, so when they started out again in bright of day they'd have nothing to fear from the thieving varmints that still pop up now and then from Hounslow Heath." Watching the false affability that the two had worn when they first arrived fade, he decided that another lie might serve to remove them more quickly from the vicinity of the Bell and Anchor Tavern. "Seems the lady was eager to see Google Goose Green. Seems a great uncle of hers had teased her with the name once, and she's never forgotten it. Wants to put a face with it, if you see what I mean."

"Google Goose Green?" It was obvious the man thought he was being sent on a wild chase after a bird of the same name. Both men looked decidedly unpleasant now.

"Aye. Down past Paddingwyck Park, right there at the four-mile stone it is."

The men were staring at him with suspicion.

The innkeeper laughed. "Cross my heart." He performed the childish gesture. "'Tis called Google Goose Green." He looked past them into the inn yard. "And that's the best I can do for you, for here comes the stage."

Dust, whinnies, and shouts from the driver and the ostlers convinced the inquisitors that it was time to move on. They'd never be heard over the stamp of hooves and the jingle of harness anyway.

The landlord watched them go even as he ordered a tray of liquid refreshment to be brought out to cut the dust the passengers on the stage had swallowed. With a sigh of relief, he returned to his business. He'd no need of the sort of trouble he thought those two represented.

For a moment, he wondered if he should warn the lady's servant about them. He shrugged. It really wasn't any of his concern. He stood still, the chaos the stagecoach always caused swirling around him, thinking of the lovely blonde lady and her clear-eyed escort. He recalled the man's considerate treatment of the big dog. That decided him. He would warn him if the opportunity arose.

Chapter Seventeen

When David left Diana and headed out to the stables, the innkeeper intercepted him. "I say. Have you got a moment?"

David stopped and turned back. "Of course. How may I be of service?"

"No. That's not the way of it." The innkeeper frowned. "'Tis the other way around. There's something I think you should know. Maybe it's nothing to do with you, and maybe you won't care if it is, but I'll feel better telling you just the same."

"What is it?" David was frowning now, too.

"There were two men here twenty or so minutes ago. They left when the stage that was passing by from London stopped in." He smiled and explained, "Driver always wants something to wet his whistle and take the dust out of his passengers' throats, you see. Dusty between here and Piccadilly except for the stretches with the granite pavers."

"Yes, it certainly is." David was trying hard to control his impatience.

"Well, the two men were looking for a beautiful blonde lady, a sailor, and a dog."

David regarded him steadily, willing him to say more. Were they betrayed so soon, or did he still have a chance of getting Diana away safely?

"Anyway," the landlord came to the point at last, "I didn't like the looks of 'em after I'd told them about you. They were rough sorts and they stopped looking mildly curious and started looking as if they were the sly cats who'd emptied the canary cage. Too blasted triumphant by half."

"And?"

"And"—the innkeeper blew out a great breath and ran a hand through his hair—"so I told them you'd left." The first lie off his conscience, he grinned and added the next one. "Told 'em that the lady wanted to get down closer to Hounslow so as to wake up in the morning and be able to pass it in broad daylight."

"And they accepted that?" David was still tense.

"Well, yes, but they were still a bit suspicious. And by that time I had the sneaking feeling they weren't up to any good." He chuckled. "So I told 'em another lie to move them on."

David smiled a tight smile. They weren't out of the woods yet.

"I told 'em your lady had wanted to see Google Goose Green since she was a small child. When I convinced 'em that there really was such a place, they finally believed me." He spread his hands in a broad gesture. "After all, who'd make up a story with a name like that in it?"

David laughed, then. He clapped the innkeeper on the shoulder. "Many thanks! I appreciate your protecting us. I can't tell you if the two men had anything to do with my lady and her dog, for I honestly don't know, but it feels more than good to have been saved from finding out."

The innkeeper looked a little disappointed that David didn't know for sure the men were after his fair employer.

"I'll tell my lady about it in the morning. I know she'll be grateful to you."

That perked up the landlord's spirits. "Will you be needing anything—sleeping out there with the dog?"

"No. Your stables are a lot more comfortable than many places I slept on the Peninsula, thank you."

The two shook hands, smiling like old friends, and parted.

The landlord went back into the inn glad he'd warned the man. He had a soft spot for ex-soldiers. He'd lost a younger brother to Napoleon's armies.

All the rest of the short way to the stables, David was thoughtful. When he reached the stall in which he'd imprisoned Gulliver, he praised the dog lavishly for having remained there all alone and smiled as the big animal nearly turned himself inside out in his glad antics to see his master again. Then, when Gulliver had calmed down, David upended an empty water bucket and sat down for a council of war.

"Gulliver," he announced, smiling to see the dog cock his head and prick his ears as if he were interested in every word, "we have a problem."

The dog whined.

"Thank you. I think it's serious, too." He stroked the animal's broad head as he thought aloud. "I think the two rough-looking men our host warned me about were indeed after Lady Diana. So what to do? I can hardly share her room to see to her safety; she'd be scandalized." He cocked his own head. "Perhaps . . ."

Gulliver barked sharply.

"Yes, I'll get on with it. Perhaps the only thing to do is to take advantage of that turn in the hallway and the alcove her bedchamber door is set in and mount guard."

This time Gulliver barked excitedly.

David smiled broadly. "Sometimes, Gulliver, I almost think you understand every word." He rose, caught up his knapsack, and told Gulliver, "All right, boy, to heel."

Together they left the stables and made their way through the twilight to the inn.

The next morning the maid, coming to awaken Diana as requested, almost shrieked at the sight that met her eyes. Then she smiled instead at such devotion. The handsome young man lay across the threshold of his mistress's door, his head on his battered knapsack, and a heavy, dark blue cloak over him for covers. His lashes, now that she saw them resting on his cheeks, were thicker and longer than a girl's.

Good thing she hadn't sent one of the younger maids serving under her to awaken the Lady Diana, as she was certain none of them could have resisted that soft look his firm lips had as he slept. She'd have been tempted to steal a kiss from such a handsome serving man, herself, a few years ago.

An instant later, the sleeper was aroused by the sudden alertness of the dog and sat up. "Ah," he said, completely awake, "have you come to awaken Lady Diana?"

"Yes, sir." So much for a stolen kiss to tease the other maids with later in the kitchen.

He rose in a single fluid motion, smiling as he did. "No need to tell her Gulliver and I played guard, is there?"

"Not if you ask me not to, I won't." She beamed at him as if she enjoyed a conspiracy.

The big dog sniffed at her hand, and she patted him on the head a bit warily.

David slung his cloak around his shoulders, while she watched in appreciation, and picked up his knapsack. "I do ask it."

She started, then giggled as he pecked her on the cheek. Then he smiled one last time and was gone.

As he turned the bend in the hall that had made his vigil safe from the eyes of other guests, he heard her sigh and murmur, "And I always thought I only liked big men."

Downstairs, David found the innkeeper. "Breakfast for my lady in a private parlor in twenty minutes, please, landlord." He handed the man a golden sovran and told him, "This should cover our shot."

"'Tis more than enough for your bill and then some."

"Any remainder is for you, sir. A small token of my lady's gratitude for telling me of the two men who came by last evening."

"Breakfast in twenty minutes it is, then." He grinned. "For both of you." He opened the door to the parlor under discussion and turned a blind eye as Gulliver walked into it.

When he left, David went to the window and stared out, assessing the weather. It might be spring, but only the afternoons were warm as yet. Morning brought bright, cool dew, and evening sometimes still arrived wrapped in chill mists. It worried him.

There was no doubt that they must strike out across country now that the two men had shown up in pursuit of his lovely Diana. How, though, was he to keep her safe from the blessed weather? This was England, not Spain, and sleeping under the stars was pleasant only when the climate was warm.

He supposed . . . His supposition was interrupted by Diana's entrance.

While David marveled at the fact that she could appear even more beautiful every time he saw her, Diana took a deep breath to scold, "What extravagance is this? I thought I made it perfectly clear that we cannot afford to be spendthrifts on our journey!" She closed the door firmly behind her, not wanting anyone to overhear their conversation.

"I thought it safer to breakfast hidden," he told her quietly, "in the light of a new development."

The anger Diana had been working up ever since the inn's maidservant had told her she'd come to escort her to a private parlor for breakfast evaporated. Instead, apprehension filled her eyes. "What new development?" Her question was whispered. Her hand was at her throat.

David went to where she stood at the door. Looking deeply into her eyes he said very softly, "Trust me, Diana. I swear on my oath that I will keep you safe."

Diana's knees seemed to turn traitor. She leaned back against the door for its support. Those eyes, those sherry-colored eyes. Why did they have such power over her?

If they had been the other pair of the same hue, the pair belonging to the portly Duke she idolized in a private shrine in her heart of hearts, she would understand—but these were only the eyes of a slender, common sailor who had somehow insinuated his way into her life.

David offered her his arm and led her to her place at the table. For one wild moment, when he felt the trembling warmth of her hand on his sleeve, he wanted to confess to her his true identity, tell her that he'd been in love with her since the moment he first saw her. He wanted to offer her the protection of his exalted name and lofty station.

But he didn't. Hoping she would, by some miracle, one day be free, he'd dreamed for five years of winning her for himself alone. To hear her say "I love you," and know she meant that she loved him, the man, not the title he'd been born to or the fabulous riches that went with it. Him.

There was no way he was going to give up that objective at this point.

Diana might be fearful, but she was in no real danger. Not while he was there to keep her safe at all costs.

"There is nothing to be alarmed about," he reassured her. "Two new men came asking for us, but the innkeeper sent them on a wild goose chase."

"Why in the world did he do that?" She looked at him, astonished.

David chuckled. "He didn't like their looks."

"Are we safe then?"

"They'll be watching for us to hurry past Hounslow Heath in the middle of the morning sometime. I plan for us to cut off the road right after you've eaten breakfast and strike out across country, however."

Diana sat, lost in thought.

David served her plate for her. He did it very well simply by remembering how he had watched his butler Jessops expertly serve and present his own for years. He was rather proud of the feat.

Diana barely noticed.

"You must eat," he told her gently. When she didn't respond, he reminded her, "You plan to walk many a mile today, don't you?"

"Yes," Diana rallied. "Yes, of course I do."

"And you do trust me to look after you, don't you?"

"Yes. . . ." The reply was hesitant.

David was piqued. "You don't seem certain."

Diana's eyes lit with mischief. "Well, as escorts and guards go, you aren't a very impressive figure, after all."

David scowled at his love, visibly insulted. He'd never

been called insignificant before. This was yet another new experience, and this time he knew damned well he didn't like it.

Diana laughed at him. "Well, you aren't much bigger than I am, you know."

"I can assure you, madam, that size is not always on the side of the victor."

Diana would have regretted upsetting him, but his calm confidence that he would prevail against a larger opponent irritated her. "I suppose you could vanquish both our pursuers without the slightest effort."

David looked up from his plate sharply. His level gaze challenged her. "Two unarmed men would present little difficulty for me."

She dropped her fork, flabbergasted. "Of all the overconfident, cocky . . ."

"I assure you, Diana, I am never overconfident. I'm merely aware of what I'm capable of."

"Good heavens! You talk with all the authority of some self-centered duke."

David's face flamed, and he was silent.

"Oh, dear. I haven't hurt your feelings, have I?"

"No, not at all." And she hadn't. Not really. She had simply, all unaware, neatly tagged him as that which he had been for so much of his pampered life.

They were both quiet for the rest of the meal.

Chapter Eighteen

Just as Diana and David were finishing their breakfast, the innkeeper brought Diana's portmanteau and placed it next to David's knapsack just inside the door of the parlor. Then he closed the door gently and left again without disturbing the two who sat at the table.

Gulliver rose from where he'd been lying in front of the fireplace and put himself between his humans and the object that bothered him. He sat watching Diana's portmanteau with the same intense interest he'd use to watch a poisonous snake.

David frowned slightly at the dog's odd behavior, and made a mental note to see if he could discover the cause for it later. Right now, Diana was his main concern. "My lady, do you have any idea why these other men are following us?"

"No." Diana looked a little apprehensive. "My father wouldn't send them, I know he wouldn't. If he sent someone to find me it would be someone like Mrs. Appleby and her husband. A genteel couple—friends as well as people who work for him at the vicarage."

"You're certain." David made it a statement, because he was as sure as Diana. The Vicar wouldn't send men like the rough individuals the innkeeper had described after his beautiful daughter. Who then?

"Yes, of course I'm certain. Father is not really that interested."

"Diana!" David's shock at her words caused him to forget that he was not, in his disguise, her equal. "You know that isn't the truth."

Diana blushed. "You're right. Father would care that I am safe. But I left him a note, and he'll be positive that I'm safely with my Godmother by now. If he remembers, he'll even check to be sure." She added miserably, "In a day or two."

David was hard put to control his outrage. "You can't mean that he will wait that long! Knowing you are wandering about the countryside unaccompanied and unescorted? Why, that's scandalous! Even more scandalous than your harebrained flight!"

Diana's mouth opened in shock. "How dare you!"

"How dare I *which?*"

Diana was so angry she was almost sputtering. "How dare you cast aspersions on my father."

"Simple." His temper flared. "He's neglectful of you!"

Diana stood up so abruptly that her chair went over backwards and crashed to the floor. "He is not neglectful. He's . . . he's scholarly. And forgetful."

"And neglectful," David insisted, his eyes hot with righteous anger.

"He is not! He's a busy man. He can't watch out for everyone. He has a large parish to consider."

"And he neglects the most important person in it! The greatest gift God has given him, his beautiful only child."

At the end of her emotional tether, Diana burst into tears.

David's chair went over this time as he rose to catch her in his arms. "I'm sorry. Oh, God. I'm sorry, Diana. Forgive me!"

He held her close, his head reeling with the sensations her nearness sent through him. To hold her at last was heaven, but to hold her while she wept was hell, and he was torn by both.

"Please, Diana, don't cry. I'm sorry I said that. I'm sorry I said anything! Just don't cry. Forgive me."

Diana pushed herself out of his arms and stared up at him through tear-drenched lashes. "No."

David died a little.

Then she went on. "No, I won't cry anymore."

David breathed again.

Diana dashed tears away. "Crying is a foolish weakness and I never do it," she stated firmly in spite of David's lifted eyebrow. "No doubt it's the strain of having run away and finding my sanctuary closed to me. Once I locate my Godmother, these silly feelings will pass." She sniffled.

David handed her his handkerchief, mentally thanking his valet for having put several in his knapsack.

"And of course I forgive you." She turned her back on him and blew her nose gently. "You have a right to an opinion, and I'm sure that it does look . . ." She struggled to select the right words: ". . . rather unusual that my father, ah, hasn't expressed a great deal of . . . of concern about my whereabouts."

David's heart twisted in his chest when she turned to face him. She looked so blasted proud, and so calm. She was so pitifully confident that what she was saying would make him see her point. But he would never agree with her. Never. Not in this life or the next.

Diana was so beautiful. So vulnerable. A precious treasure to be cherished. And her father was so careless of her, when *he* knew he'd give his life to keep her safe. Hadn't he vowed it years ago?

He'd hazarded it once already in the duel he'd finally fought back then with Calverson over his treatment of Diana at Merlington Park. So what did it matter if he told yet another lie in this matrix of lies in which he found himself enmeshed? He'd do anything to keep Diana from fretting over his bad opinion of her father.

David took a deep breath, and lied again. "Of course I understand."

Diana's smile was dazzling. "Oh, I'm so glad, so very glad that you do."

And that single smile made him stop regretting the lies. Diana was his responsibility, his love, and whatever he had to do to keep her safe and happy, he would do.

David was a little less uneasy about their trek when they finally left the turnpike three miles later at Cut Throat Lane. Waiting to depart there had gotten them across the Grand Junction Canal, at least, and he didn't have that to worry about.

Feeling acutely the responsibility of getting Diana safely away from the two men the innkeeper had warned him about, he had given a lot of thought to strategy. His intention was twofold. First, of course, he wanted to be certain they avoided being discovered on the turnpike by a returning and predictably irate Baron Runsford or the two strangers who'd been asking about them. Second, he wanted to travel far enough down it to convince anybody watching from the inn that they were indeed heading down the turnpike. That way, if they helpfully supplied that information to anyone inquiring for them, they would throw them off the track.

He kept looking behind them, making sure they weren't being followed. The look that the innkeeper had given him told David a great deal more than his words when he'd warned him. The admission that he'd "not liked the looks" of the men asking about a blonde beauty with a dog and a sailor had spoken volumes. The fact that he'd deliberately misled the two strangers said even more. David wasn't taking any chances.

He'd have to do something about being the pack mule for the three of them, however. Encumbered with the knapsack and Diana's clumsy portmanteau, he'd hardly be ready to fight at the drop of a hat—even if the effort of carrying them didn't wear him down to a thread after a few hours.

The knapsack hadn't been any trouble, resting as it did high on his back, but the portmanteau was deucedly inconvenient to carry any distance. He wished he could simply drag the dratted thing.

Diana looked over at him and saw him scowling down at it. "Are you getting tired?"

"No. Just irritated that this object"—he lifted the portmanteau toward her—"is so clumsy to manage."

"Would you like me to carry it for a while?"

David didn't dignify that with an answer.

"It would be nice if we had a cart, wouldn't it?"

He shook his head. "We couldn't go across country with a cart. But you've given me an idea."

Diana looked a trifle alarmed. "Does it mean spending money?"

"Don't be such a nip-farthing, Diana. We have to do

something to make our way easier. And I don't propose to procure a knapsack for you to carry your things in."

Diana lifted her chin. Her expression was haughty. "Well, I suppose I should thank you for that, at least." Then she changed her mind. "I *could* carry one, you know," she told him a little belligerently. "I've been training myself to be ready for difficulties."

"So your cousin Jonathan told me."

She shot him a suspicious glance. He'd used a very dry tone for that last comment. She didn't like it, but she decided to let it go.

They walked along in silence for a while, the green of the countryside rolling away into the distance before them. After a while, they saw a farm. It wasn't a very prosperous farm by the looks of it. The fences were in sad repair and the barn roof was sagging badly in the middle. David said quietly, "There. That is just what I'm looking for."

"What?"

"That donkey."

Diana looked where he indicated, and saw a tiny donkey whose every rib showed. "Oh, dear, the poor thing is pitiful."

"Then I shall rescue it. Wait here." He gave her an excuse to keep her out of the business he intended to do: "I don't want the poor beast frightened by Gulliver."

Diana nodded and took a firm grip on Gulliver's collar.

Gulliver, who had been walking perfectly obediently without such a precaution, shot her a resentful look.

"I'm sorry, Gulliver," David heard her say to the dog as he left them, "it's just for a few minutes." It came as a relief to him to know that he wasn't the only one talking to animals. He grinned whimsically as he wondered what they'd be saying to the donkey soon.

The door to the dilapidated cottage was opened by a burly man in a dirty smock. "Whaddaya want?"

David ignored the surliness, and told him, "I want to buy your donkey."

"You must be daft. That donkey's little enough good, but I need her in case there's a heavy load to be carried to market."

David held out another of the supply of golden sovrans Carrington had insisted he take with him from Smythington Park and silently blessed his old friend for his foresight. Helping Diana without her realizing it was getting to be a rather expensive proposition.

The man's eyes filled with greed. Snatching the coin from David, he tested it with his teeth. Satisfied, he said, "Take her, then, and good riddance."

"Hold fast. I'll want a packsaddle and her bridle as well."

"In the barn." The man waved an arm in the general direction of the building in question without taking his eye off the coin. "Get 'em yerself. Y' can take her headcollar, too. Wif 'er gone, I'll not 'ave any need fer it."

David didn't waste a thank-you on the brute, and when he got close to the little donkey, he was glad he hadn't. It was obvious the poor beast had been badly mistreated. He was especially careful to move slowly as he approached her. Even so, she flinched away when he reached toward her with the halter the man had said he could take in addition to her bridle and the packsaddle.

Talking soothingly and quietly, he got the halter on and the buckle fastened. The packsaddle he decided to carry himself until he got her away from the deep, stinking mire of the small paddock in which she was imprisoned.

Murmuring encouragement to the poor beast, he started back to the road. Halfway there, she balked. David looked up to see why and saw Diana and Gulliver coming to meet them.

"What have you done? You' re not stealing that donkey, are you?"

"Of course not!"

"Then you must tell me how much you paid for it, so that I may reimburse you." Diana was looking her most mulish. "I will not have you spend *your* money on *my* flight."

"Very well." David knew better than to argue when there was no hope of winning. "We shall settle accounts when I have delivered you safely to your Godmother."

He had been stroking the donkey as he spoke, and now the little creature let out a sigh that was almost human and dropped her head against him.

Diana stepped closer and exclaimed, "Oh! Look at the marks on her poor back. Someone has beaten her."

"It's over now. The man in the cottage said he had no more use for her, so she is safe with us."

Diana was lightly touching the welts on the skinny animal's ribs. "I wish I had a stick and the chance to beat the man who did this."

"I think a better plan would be to find something to pad the packsaddle so that it doesn't discomfort her, and get on our way."

"You're not going to make her carry anything, are you? You can't." Diana's eyes accused him.

"Oh, yes, I can. I think she wouldn't feel right unless she was working a little." He cocked his head and considered the donkey. "If we don't show her what we require of her from the beginning, she will only dread that it may be something much more difficult than what she's used to."

"You're mad!" Diana was scowling again. "You can't possibly know what this beast is thinking."

David sighed as deeply as their newly acquired donkey had. Where was the lovely, compliant young thing he'd fallen in love with? This Diana was a bit different from that dream he remembered. Time was not always kind, it appeared.

"Wait here," he told his love. "I see just the thing we need to pad her back." With that, he walked briskly back to the tumbledown cottage and to the clothesline behind it, and yanked off it a comforter belonging to the donkey's former owner. Coming back to Diana and the donkey, he began to fold it to fit the donkey's back.

"You can't just *take* that!"

"Why not?"

"David. It's stealing."

"I shall just think that . . ." He stared pensively at the donkey. "Esmerelda here earned this comforter by the sweat of her brow. After all, the sores on her back are from work done for the owner . . . the former owner . . . of the comforter and of Esmerelda, so it is only fitting that the comforter now be hers, er, to comfort it."

Diana gurgled with laughter. "That is the most illogical bit of reasoning I have ever heard, but I am so enchanted by your name for our noble beast that I'm incapable of censuring you."

David fastened the packsaddle in place over the pad he'd made carefully, then loaded it with the awkward portmanteau and his knapsack. When Esmerelda turned her head to look back at it, then at him, as if to ask "Is that all?" David added his heavy blue campaign cloak.

Donkey and man stood looking at each other for a long minute, then David turned and tugged at her lead line. One last look behind her and Esmerelda decided to follow her rescuer. Glancing up at the sky to gauge the weather, he led his little procession westward, toward Bath.

Behind them, the man from the cottage changed to his best clothes and started the long walk over to the turnpike to celebrate his good fortune in the sale of a worn-out donkey for a great price, with a pint or two of gin. Arriving at the Bell and Anchor, he sat down at a table and pounded on it for service.

The innkeeper was about to throw him out when the cottager showed him his gold. "Ye can't turn me away. I be a payin' customer. 'Sides," he reminded, "I've always been a good customer."

"Too frequent a customer, more like," the innkeeper muttered darkly as he went to get the man his gin.

By lunchtime, the man who'd sold David the donkey had had more than a few pints of gin. He was feeling quite convivial by the time he was joined in the public room by two men covered in dust and eager to quench their thirst. "Buy ye a drink, I will," he offered.

The two men moved from the bar to the cottager's table. "That's a mighty nice offer. We're so dry we could spit straw and we'll surely accept yer invitation."

All the while the innkeeper watched, polishing glasses.

"Well, come ahead. Good fortune I've 'ad this mornin', and I've a mind to share."

"Ah?" The taller of the two removed his hat and ran his hand over his damp hair to tidy it. He wasn't interested in the man's story, but he was getting a free drink out of the bumpkin, after all. "What was yer bit o' luck, then?"

They pulled out chairs and plopped down into them. "I'm Jem, 'at there's Gilly."

"Skaggs is my name. And my good fortune is that some folks bought me donkey for a whole sovran." He grinned at the strangers over his glass of gin. "Old worn-out beastie wasn't worth tuppence." He threw back his head and laughed. "Properly gulled the man, I did."

The shorter man, Gilly, asked, "Howdya get 'im to pay that much for an old donkey?"

"Weren't no trouble a-tall. He just upped and offered me it for 'er, can you believe."

"Not hardly." He picked up the tankard of ale the innkeeper had brought and took a long drink.

Jem said, "Ye're luckier'n us. We been looking for a mort and her dog and man all morning, and ain't see'd hide ner hair of um."

The cottager sat forward eagerly. "This man had a lady and a dog wif 'im. I saw 'em when they went on down the road."

"Cor." Gully forgot his ale. "Ye means we ain't lost 'em complete?"

Jem laughed, stood and clapped the man called Skaggs on the back. "No, I thinks not. Not if our new friend can tell us what road he saw the man lead his donkey down!"

Chapter Nineteen

The evening was getting cooler, and David looked for a place to camp as they walked along. He searched for a place where he could keep Diana warm and safe from the evening damp he felt certain was on its way up from the river. Also, a place where the donkey could graze as she rested.

Gulliver was ranging a little ahead of them, investigating various rocks and chasing the odd squirrel, when he stopped suddenly and reversed his position. Staring back along the road behind them, he gave a sharp bark.

"Come on!" David grabbed Diana by the arm and all but catapulted her into the thick bushes growing beside the road. Pulling the donkey even further into them, he placed a gentle hand over her muzzle to keep her from making a sound.

"What is it?" Diana shook his hand off her arm, and stamped her foot. "Why are you perpetually dragging me into the bushes!"

"Be quiet."

"What?" she hissed. "And deprive you of the chance to muzzle *me?*" But she said it in a whisper.

David wondered where she'd learned to be so blasted sarcastic.

"Gulliver." He used a tone of voice he knew wouldn't carry far, but the big dog heard and dashed over to him. "Good boy. Sit. Quiet."

Checking first that the donkey stood with her side with the knapsack nearest them, the dog settled near his humans. The hated portmanteau was safely on the other side of the packsaddle.

Soon they heard what Gulliver had warned them about. Two horses were approaching at a trot. David watched them with narrowed eyes as they came. The taller one looked crafty and sly, and was obviously in charge. His companion was stouter, his face noncommittal, in fact almost vacant. David decided the second man was a follower—a man who would do what he was told, and very little more, to save himself the trouble of thinking.

David listened carefully to their conversation.

"They can't be far along 'ere," the sly-looking man said. "That farmer told us his donkey was on its last legs."

The second man grunted, shifting uncomfortably in his saddle.

"I wish I knowed what it was Lord High and Mighty wanted so bad with that damned portmanteau. Was it me, I'd be wanting the lady what's carrying it."

Diana moved closer to David.

"Uh," the stout man contributed.

"Well, we'll catch up to 'em soon. Just hang on."

That was the last thing the two in the bushes could hear, as their pursuers rode out of earshot, but it was enough. David and Diana looked at each other for a long moment.

Finally David broke the silence. "So it's Runsford who sent them."

"And not for me — for the portmanteau. That's a relief." She cocked her head. "Though I don't know whether to be relieved or insulted."

David chuckled. "Be relieved. I'll have my hands full keeping that blasted portmanteau safe if those two get reinforcements. It's good to know I don't have you to worry about as well."

"Why on earth bother to try to keep the silly portmanteau safe? Let them have it!"

David's back stiffened and he shot her a look that was almost a glare. Then he relaxed again. "Yes, I suppose that is the sensible thing to do."

"Of course it is." She ran a hand over her hair to smooth the damage their precipitous rush into the bushes had done it. "I can't believe you were ready to fight two men to keep possession of this unattractive . . . *thing.*" Diana waved a hand at her luggage.

David grinned sheepishly. "It's become difficult for me to let someone take anything from me by force lately."

Diana ignored the grin. There was something grim behind the statement in spite of it. She stared at him for a long moment, then asked in a quiet voice fraught with solemnity, "Why?"

David realized she wasn't going to be put off with a glib explanation. The humor died out of his face and he turned his back on her. How could he explain to this sheltered English girl what it was like to be a naked slave with every possession stripped from you?

Finally he managed to say, "It's a male attribute, milady. We don't like to give anything up to another man without a fight."

Diana put her hand on his shoulder. Her voice was gentle as she said, "That's not really all, is it?"

David's whole frame stiffened, but he didn't reply.

"Someday you must tell me," she said softly, and let it go.

David moved abruptly away. He brushed through the bushes in which they'd hidden and stood looking up the road. The dust the two riders had raised was settled, and there was no sign of their return. "All clear. Come on out."

Gulliver responded with a joyous bound.

Diana and the donkey came out more carefully.

"I think we'll leave the road now. As best as I can think, we'll be cutting south toward the Thames"—he sighed in exasperation—"or maybe the Crane. I don't know the countryside, so I don't know which of the rivers it is. But we must go southwest toward Bath."

Diana tried to be cheerful. "At least we'll have the sun out of our eyes for a little while."

"Going south, anyway."

"I'll just be glad to get off this road."

David looked at her inquisitively.

"Well?" Diana looked at him as if she thought him a little dim. Then she supplied her reason, hoping to dispel the somber mood her earlier question had brought down on them. "The name of this particular road is Cut Throat Lane. Didn't you see the little road sign as we left the turnpike?"

David laughed. "Yes, I did, but I was hoping that you did not." His eyes lit with a hint of mischief. "Would it make you feel any better to learn that it also runs along the edge of the notorious Hounslow Heath?"

"I'd swoon with fright for you, David, but I don't believe a highwayman would look at us twice. Clearly we've nothing of value."

David couldn't agree with her. He had the most valuable thing in the world with him. Diana. He was confident, however, that the danger to her had just ridden past. Nevertheless, he'd be constantly on the lookout for the men's return. By stopping to camp before true darkness arrived, he knew he'd also avoid the famous robbers of Hounslow Heath.

From then on, he watched Diana carefully for signs of fatigue. When he saw her begin to flag, he searched the landscape for a suitable place to camp. Finding one, he used their new four-legged friend as his excuse to stop for the night.

"Esmerelda is getting tired, Diana. We must call a halt."

Diana merely nodded.

Possibly she was more fatigued than he'd suspected. David called himself several unpleasant names under his breath for not realizing it.

Stepping over the ditch and waiting patiently for Esmerelda to decide to follow them, he led the little group to a gate which opened into a lush meadow. He took them through it and another, to the meadow beyond in which they could hear the soft sounds of a river nearby. On the far side of this second meadow, there were several haystacks standing.

Esmerelda perked up immediately.

Gulliver bounded down to the river's edge for a drink, while David relieved their little donkey of her packsaddle. Then he went to one of the haystacks and began to dig enough hay out of the side of it to make a small cave for sleeping in.

Diana watched with interest as he carefully bound it into bundles, which he placed to one side.

Feeling her gaze on him, David looked up from his task

and explained. "I shall have to put it back neatly in the morning, you know."

Diana was really too tired to think why, but she felt the oddest warmth rush through her when he smiled at her as if she were a co-conspirator in his endeavor. Was it because he was treating her like a friend? Whatever the reason, it was a lovely feeling, and she had no intention of pulling it to shreds to discover its meaning.

Diana reveled in a peace and contentment she had not felt a very long time. She didn't want to spoil it by recalling the rules and warnings she'd been taught all her life. Right now, it was enough that David was there with her, and that he had gotten a funny little donkey for them and that he was helping her run away from something she didn't want to do.

She yawned mightily, not even covering her mouth as she did. She was more relaxed and happy than she had been in years. And if she had ruined herself by being out here alone with a common seaman, what did it matter? She never wanted to marry again, so society's good opinion didn't weigh with her. She wouldn't trade the feeling she had at this moment for all the approval she might gain from the *ton* in a lifetime.

She probably ought to do something about the way David was behaving as if he were her equal, but she didn't think that mattered either. At least it didn't when she was so tired.

She felt as if her brain were wrapped in a bit of the mist that was rising from the river and creeping over the meadow to where they stood.

She'd sleep now. Then tomorrow she'd worry about reestablishing proper distance from David.

She went over and sat close beside the haystack, threw her arm around Gulliver when he came and sat down beside her, and, as he leaned against her, she slumped against the hay and slept.

When David had finished the cave to his satisfaction, he took the little donkey down to the river for a drink. When she'd drunk her fill, he cleaned each tiny hoof to be certain that nothing remained of the foul mire she had been stabled in, then let her go to graze.

Returning to the haystack that was their lodging for the night, he stood for a long time just looking down at his beloved Diana. Pride in her ran warmly through him. It had been a long day, and he had pushed hard, wanting to distance them from the dangers that pursued. Never once had his gallant darling complained. Never once asked to rest.

Love for her flowed through him like a tangible force.

Gulliver tried to leave her to come to David, and Diana clutched the big dog tightly. In answer to the animal's plight, David knelt and removed her arms from Gulliver's neck and placed them about his own. A wild desire to kiss her half-open lips surged through him as he rose with her in his arms.

Diana's head fell back, and the silken spill of her hair fanned across his arm. Her throat, smooth and white in the light of the new-risen moon, was open to his kisses. There was no one to stop him if he decided to unleash his longing.

No one but himself and the deep love he'd had for her since the moment of their meeting. But that love was enough, and it stood sentinel to guard her, even from him, as he lifted her higher and bore her into their cave in the haystack.

Tenderly placing her on the bed of hay he had made for her, he lay down beside her and covered them with his campaign cloak. When she moved closer to him for warmth, and twined her arms around his neck, he had all he could do not to kiss her awake and tell her of his deep and abiding love.

Sweet love, sweet torture.

There was no sleep for David that night. The dream he'd dreamed through years of war and months of slavery — the dream that he'd been denied for five long years was here beside him. His lovely Diana lay sleeping in his arms at last, and while it was not as his wife, that possibility at last existed for him and sleep, long a friend, now became an enemy he was determined to hold at bay.

Chapter Twenty

Diana awoke slowly and sleepily felt beside her for the lovely source of warmth that had made her sleep pleasant, but seemed to have disappeared. Sitting up and stretching, she yawned and smiled.

Suddenly, her eyes flew wide. She was sleeping in a haystack! The only warmth she could have had would have been from the body of the man who had taken over her life. She couldn't even convince herself that it had been Gulliver she'd been snuggled up against, for the extent of the comfort she'd enjoyed was beyond what a mere dog was capable of giving.

She wanted to die of embarrassment. Could she really have spent the night in the arms of a . . . of a . . . of a *common sailor?*

Preferring pretended outrage to genuine embarrassment, she threw off his campaign cloak and rushed from the cave he'd made in the haystack. She'd find him and give him a piece of her mind for taking such liberties with her person!

Blinking outside in the sunshine that was rapidly burning off the morning mist, she looked around for her victim. Hearing a splash and a happy bark from the direction of the river, she marched off toward it.

When she got near the river, she heard David. "Fetch, Gulliver." There was the sound of something whizzing through the air, then there was another splash, a lesser one than the one that must have been David's dive into the river.

Approaching the sounds, Diana came upon the neatly folded pile of David's clothes. The discovery stopped Diana in her tracks. He'd be nude, of course. She hesitated. Then she spoke to herself sharply. "Don't be a henwit, Diana. He'll be in the water." She continued toward the river.

Abruptly she stopped. The mist that concealed her and had muffled her comment had lifted from the space where David and the dog played. In the still-weak morning sun, she could see David's back clearly. It was crisscrossed with scars. With cruel whip marks!

Diana fled, nauseated by the thought of the pain he had suffered, weeping angrily that he'd been treated so. She ran all the way back to her cave in the haystack, threw herself down, pulled the cloak—his cloak—carefully around her, and pretended to be asleep.

Before long, David came and knelt, just looking at her. After a moment, he leaned down and kissed her on the forehead. Diana started. Quickly she turned her response into a long sigh and turned over, her back to him.

It wouldn't do to let him see the tears of empathy that threatened to escape between her lashes.

David left the cave then, and she could hear him catching up Esmerelda. She heard him whistling softly to the little donkey exactly as the grooms in her grandfather's stables had whistled to the horses there as he placed the packsaddle on her back and loaded it. Then he called Gulliver from where the great dog was drying in the sun. "Go wake Diana, boy," he ordered, and Diana was relieved that he hadn't come himself.

David had risen early specifically to keep Diana from feeling embarrassment at having slept in the same bed of hay with him. As a result, he couldn't understand why she wouldn't meet his eyes as they exchanged good-mornings.

Diana needed time to come to grips with the odd warring of emotions she was experiencing. On her way to the river to perform her morning ablutions, she tried to straighten them out. Somehow she was being assailed with a feeling of disloyalty to the memory of a certain duke, and that was absurd. The Duke of Smythington, in spite of his great kindness to her, had no doubt forgotten her very existence. And her sympathy for this man who was taking her safely to her Godmother didn't in any way detract from her secret devotion to her cherished memory of the Duke. Certainly it did not.

"Take a grasp on yourself, Diana!" she muttered darkly, as she returned to their little camp.

David, while she had been down at the river, had set out the cheese and bread he'd brought with them from the Bell and Anchor. "It's not much, but it will break our fast." He smiled at her. "And it will keep you from fainting on the road before we can find a place to get you a hot meal."

"I don't need a hot meal." She hated the grumpy tone in her voice, but she really didn't have money to burn. Not *with* her, at any rate. And she didn't like the idea that this poor seaman might be spending his hard-earned savings on her flight.

They munched contentedly on the day-old bread and the excellent cheese. Somehow, David had contrived to build a small fire and warm water over it for the tea that he had in his bundle. It was lukewarm, because, as he said, "I've only the mug from the ale to warm the water in, and I fear if I get it too hot it may burst. I know nothing of such things unfortunately." Grinning, he asked her, "Do you know about pottery jugs?"

"I know they have to be fired to *be* jugs." She frowned. "Whether or not one can cook in them after that, I simply don't know."

He laughed then, and Diana liked the sound of it. What she didn't like was that she noticed that he had beautiful white teeth, and that he was indeed a handsome man. She knew better than to notice such things when she was with a strange man. She was no green girl. Doing that sort of thing usually preceded forming a *tendre* for the person in question. And that simply could not be allowed to happen.

The last thing she needed was to be attracted to a man so far beneath her social station. She was going to be deep enough into the soup trying to explain his presence to her Godmother without also having to explain that she wasn't attracted to him as a man. She sighed. Which, she admitted reluctantly as the sun picked auburn highlights out of his dark brown hair, could very well turn out to be a lie.

David laughed again. "Don't you like your breakfast?"

Diana gave her full attention to the bread and cheese. "Yes, I rather do. It is certainly a far cry from the hot breakfast on the buffet at home, but for some reason, it is absolutely delicious."

"I wager it's the fresh air." He turned his head and

looked away toward the river. Softly he added, "And the fact that it is eaten in freedom."

"I beg your pardon?" As he'd intended, Diana hadn't heard.

"I said, 'It must be the company.'"

Diana raised an eyebrow.

He gestured, "Gulliver and Esmerelda, of course."

Diana made a face at him and they both laughed.

David placed the bundles he'd made of the hay he'd taken out of it to make their sleeping quarters back into the haystack. Poking it back into place with the long staff he'd fashioned from one of the numerous saplings down by the river, he soon had the haystack looking as if it had never been disturbed.

"Ready?" he asked Diana, and looked around for the donkey.

Diana gave one final look at the first place she had ever slept out-of-doors and nodded. Her cheeks heated as she silently acknowledged that it was also the first place she had slept in the arms of a man not her husband. And, a tiny voice told her, the first time she had slept well and willingly in any man's embrace. At that her face really flamed, and she drew in her breath sharply.

David turned back to her at the sound.

To cover her confusion she asked, "That is a new staff, isn't it?" *New indeed. And where was his old one, ninny?* the small voice said. "I mean, you have a staff now," she inanely stated the obvious, mentally chastising her inner voice.

David looked at her oddly. "Er, yes. I thought one might come in handy." Still looking at her with a tiny frown, he went to collect the donkey from the far corner of the meadow to which she'd trotted to graze.

While David caught up Esmerelda's lead rope from

where it trailed in the grass as she grazed, Gulliver made short work of the leftovers of their simple breakfast and of the last scraps of roast beef.

They walked out of their meadow and through the next to the road, closing both gates carefully behind them. Gulliver came gamboling back to them from where David had sent him to see if the road was clear, and they were on their way again.

They'd walked almost a mile in companionable silence when Diana finally broke it. "It's lovely, isn't it?"

David smiled across Esmerelda at her. "Yes, this stretch of England has always been. The fact that it is all rolling meadows and estates makes it, I'm told, the garden spot of the realm."

Diana smiled back. "I rather like the part I grew up in. I suppose we all do."

"Yes," her companion answered vaguely. David's smile had faded and he was frowning. His eyes narrowed as he peered ahead. He'd seen that Gulliver's ears were quivering, and he didn't know why. Even so, he began looking around for some cover for them to hide in.

"What is it?" Diana caught his concern.

There was no time to tell her, and no need. Over the slight rise ahead boiled a cloud of dust and the riders who'd stirred it were upon them.

It was the two men who had been asking about Diana at the Bell and Anchor. They'd been reinforced by another pair of ruffians since their last appearance. And these two were bigger, stronger, and more menacing men than the bumbling first pair.

Instinctively, Diana drew nearer David.

David, with every nerve stretched for a move from the ruffians who sat their horses blocking the road, led his little party to its very edge. He was far from feeling the nonchalance he pretended as he looked up at the one who moved his mount to further block his and Diana's way.

Chapter Twenty-one

David's voice was as deceptive as his nonchalant pose as he asked mildly, "May we pass?"

The man on the horse was the largest and the roughest looking of the foursome. His sneer did nothing to convince Diana that he intended to let them get by him, and he laughed gratingly as he told David, "Not now, not never, me pretty little gamecock."

David stood looking up at him innocently, but Diana saw his hand tighten on his staff. She wished with all her heart that she had asked him to cut one for her as well.

"What is it you want? As you can plainly see, we are poor people walking with this worthless donkey to our destination. Surely, there are better pickings for men of your number and stature over on Hounslow Heath where the mails pass and there are gentry in carriages."

"Oh-'o, listen at the little cock. 'E talks like a swell in spite of 'is 'alf-dead donkey and 'is scruffy dog."

Gulliver bared his teeth.

David dropped Esmerelda's lead line and placed his hand on the great dog's head.

Esmerelda wandered off to the opposite side of the road where she'd decided the grass was greener and began to graze.

"We want that there portmanteau the lady be carrying." The tall man who'd been the spokesman before stated.

"Take it and welcome."

Diana scowled. "Those are *my* things, and I shall keep them, thank you!" Her belligerence was obvious.

David wondered where her sense had gone. Indeed, he wondered if she'd ever *had* any!

The biggest man stepped down and walked toward Esmerelda.

Diana moved to block his way.

David sighed and went over to stand beside his precious nitwit. "Couldn't we just take her clothing out of the bag and let you have it?"

The large aggressor stopped and looked toward the obvious leader. That man frowned. After a moment's thought, he said, "Naw. I think we'd better take everything. We don't know what it is 'is nibs is after."

Diana looked mulish and dropped into her idea of a fighting stance.

The large man smiled. "Maybe we need ta take the mort, too. She's a feisty little beauty."

David sighed again. Then he brought his staff up swiftly. It caught the leering man under the chin and rendered him incapable of further insult.

The stout man they'd seen before piled off his horse and hurled himself on David, shouting, "I'll do for ya, ya little bastard!"

David seized him by the wrist of the fisted hand he threw at his chin, and assisted him on his way into the ditch beside the road. Carried by his own furious momentum, he slammed into the bank. A smart rap from David's staff insured his continued presence there.

Then the other new addition to the group leapt from his horse and rushed toward him. David thrust his newly hewn staff into the solar plexus of this third attacker. As the man doubled over around the pain of that thrust, David struck him on the back of his neck with the side of his open hand, and the man dropped as if he'd been poleaxed.

Diana danced about in excitement. She'd never seen anything like this! In spite of his small size, David was amazing!

Hoping the tall slender man would dismount so that she could test some of the skills she had worked so hard to gain, she approached him eagerly. Fists doubled, jaw clenched, and the light of battle in her eyes, she arrived at his stirrup.

The man stared down into her lovely face, incredulous. One hand groped for the pistol in his saddle holster.

Gulliver chose that instant to enter the fray. Snapping at the leader's horse's legs, he barked so ferociously that the animal reared and unseated his rider. The man fell heavily to the hard surface of the lane, and the pistol he had finally managed to draw discharged harmlessly.

Diana hesitated only a second before picking up a rock. As the dazed man lifted himself onto his elbow, she smacked him in the back of the head with it, and down he went, no longer a threat to her clothing—or to anything else!

Triumphant, she turned to face David. "Two against four," she told him exultantly. "And we the victors!" Excitement pulsed through her and radiated from her.

David was doubly excited. More than the fight had raised his senses to fever pitch. He was dizzied by the forces that rioted through him in response to his Diana. Seeing the light in her eyes and the flush of battle on her face, he thought he'd never seen anything more beautiful in his life.

It took all his willpower not to sweep her into his arms and crush those parted lips with his own. His body burned to hold her, to force her body tight against the yearning length of his.

Fighting with difficulty the aroused beast that lurked just under the surface, he took a long, careful breath. When he could finally speak, he agreed. "Yes. We are the victors." He looked around them at the four vanquished foes. "But they won't be unconscious for long. Grab a horse."

Diana caught the chestnut mare that the smaller of their new assailants had been riding, and mounted.

"Get Esmerelda," David ordered. As she went to do so, he swung himself into the saddle of the horse the first attacker had ridden, and gathered the reins of the two inferior mounts belonging to their original pursuers. Checking to see that Diana had the donkey, and was comfortable riding astride, he allowed himself one admiring glance at the lovely calves his beloved was displaying and led the way down the road.

Slowing when they had gone a few miles, David cast a concerned eye at their donkey. "How's Esmerelda?"

Diana looked the donkey over carefully. "I think that run took a great deal out of her."

"Then we shall have to proceed at a gentler pace."

"Good." She looked him over thoughtfully. "You ride very well for a seaman," she told him, more than a hint of suspicion in her voice.

David looked back at her frankly. "I was not always at sea." That was certainly the truth. His stint as an able-bodied seaman in His Majesty's Royal Navy had only lasted a few months. It wouldn't have lasted that long if the blasted captain hadn't thought him a liar when he proclaimed his identity!

"Obviously not," Diana observed coolly. Then, "What shall we do now?"

"Now we will let these two spare horses go," he told her, suiting his actions to his words. "Gulliver!" He pointed to a meadow with the gate invitingly open.

Gulliver herded the two confused horses into the meadow. Their instinct to stay with their fellows was immediately overcome by their desire to sample the tender new grass of the meadow.

David watched until he was certain they would not follow, then moved his party quietly on. Half a mile later, they left the road and cut southwest across open country.

The day was lovely. The sun lit the landscape with a golden glow and the wine-heady air was full of the sound of the singing insects who lived in the tall grass.

David kept a good eye on the donkey to be sure she was not tiring. The fact that the horses' strides were very much longer than Esmerelda's caused him to call a halt soon after they were safely out of sight of the road.

"Stay here, Diana. Esmerelda needs a breather. I'm going back to obliterate our tracks so that they won't be able to follow us."

Diana didn't have to ask who "they" were, of course. Besides, she was too busy trying to figure out when and how she had become "Diana" to someone so far beneath her social class.

Sitting there waiting for David to return, she listened to the soft whir and buzz of the insects, the calls of the birds, the gentle munching of the grass by Esmerelda—and to her heart. After fighting it with all her might, she finally admitted that the worst thing she was going to have to face when she'd been safely delivered to her Godmother, was going to be trying to discover a way to bear being parted from the man who delivered her. Already she could feel a little catch in her chest at the thought of that parting. How she was going to—

Her thoughts were mercifully interrupted.

"All clear!" David sang out as he cantered back toward her.

Diana watched him as he came, drinking in the sight of him. He rode as if he were part of the horse. Sitting straight and easy, he followed the big animal's every motion effortlessly. David and his mount were one, and she acknowledged the beauty of it.

She almost wished the horse would stumble so that she could find something imperfect about the picture David made. He was beginning to make her feel disloyal to another picture she had carried for five years in her treacherous heart. . . .

No. That wasn't true. *David had not caused anything. David had only been David. She, Diana, was the one at fault.* And fault it was, for Diana was beginning to feel disloyal to the shining memory she guarded in her heart.

Again David broke into her thoughts. "There were very few traces of our passage to eradicate. We're lucky the lane is so hard."

"That's nice."

David looked at her quickly. What the deuce had he done to offend her now? Then he smiled. She wasn't annoyed; she had been lost in some reverie, and he had disturbed it. He decided to keep silent and let her enjoy her dreams. They still had a long way to go to reach Bath—or wherever it was they were going—and as she tired, it would be harder for her to dream.

At least the horses were going to make it easier for them. Unless they were apprehended for horse theft!

They rode in silence for another half mile, then he tried to start a conversation. "We really must go through your portmanteau when we stop for the night, you know."

"You've already seen everything in it." Diana's tone was wry, her glance impish.

He grinned at the remembrance. Diana wearing some frilly, blue-beribboned thing on her head had been a most appealing picture. "Yes, but you must admit that there has to be something more in it. Perhaps secreted somehow."

The insects around them fell instantly silent.

"I can't imagine what it might be. But then, it isn't my portmanteau." She looked around her, puzzled.

The birds had stopped singing.

"Whose, then?" David reined in his horse a bit.

"Runsford's."

A capricious breeze lifted a swirl of dust and dry grass from the path just ahead of them and sent it rushing toward them. They threw up their arms to protect their faces. The horses pranced nervously.

Diana shortened her reins a bit, too. The wind was rising out of nowhere and her mare was getting fractious.

David quirked an eyebrow. "What possessed you to take his wretched portmanteau in the first place?"

"Well," she explained, "it seemed fair enough. I was fleeing my father's home because of him, and when I couldn't get into the vicarage attic to get at my own luggage because his valet was polishing boots on the stair, I just popped into his room and took his."

Esmerelda brayed and pushed closer to Diana's mount.

Leaves swirled down from the trees. Twigs pelted them.

"I say. Seems to be about to storm." David looked all around them. "Funny. It's clear to the north."

"It's clear over there, too." Diana pointed in the opposite direction. She frowned, puzzled. "How very odd."

"What rotten luck. We seem to have our own private storm."

The wind rose to a higher pitch, keening through the trees. Both horses were dancing.

Gulliver sat down, threw back his head, and howled.

David led them into the shelter of a giant oak. "Remain here while I reconnoiter."

"'Reconnoiter'?" Diana repeated the word to the dog. "That's definitely a military word, Gulliver." She shook her head. "Your master becomes more and more of a puzzle."

Gulliver just pressed closer to the bole of the great oak. Suddenly, his eyes began to shift to and fro as if he were watching something Diana couldn't see. He moved to stand in front of her horse. The hair on his neck stood up in a ruff. His posture was defensive, and his whole attitude made Diana nervous.

Rearing slightly, Diana's mare called out shrilly. Only Diana's mastery kept her in place. Even so she fidgeted, shifting her weight from hoof to hoof and champing the bit.

There was an answering whinny from close by, and David rode up out of the darkness the sudden storm had brought down on them. "Come!" He took Esmerelda's lead line from Diana, seeing she needed both hands to control her mount. "There's a vale just ahead with a cottage in it. We'll take shelter there until this has passed." He had to shout to make himself heard over the screaming wind.

Turning his horse, he rode back the way he had come. Diana had only to let her mare have her head for the animal to tear off after him. With a pitiful bray, Esmerelda fled after David.

Gulliver brought up the rear, whirling around and snapping at the wind behind them as he came.

On they thundered, the force of the wind impeding every stride of the animals. David led them on and down into relative peace once they had entered the little valley he'd told them was there.

"Thank Heaven!" Diana smoothed back the hair that had been blown loose, and shot an awed glance at the storm that roiled the sky just over the tiny valley. "How black and ugly the sky has become!"

"Yes." David's voice was grim.

The storm seemed to hesitate, turn back on itself, and boil down into the little valley.

"Quickly, now!" David had to shout. "We must get inside!"

At the door of the cottage, he lifted Diana from the saddle, knocked once, thrust open the door, and shoved her inside.

A calm voice said, "Take the animals to the shed at the back of the house. Hurry!"

David was gone in a flash, and Diana was left staring at the apparition before her. She was an old woman, her porcelain-pale face delicately lined by the years, but with a light that signaled great inner strength burning in her eyes.

Her expression was grim, as grim as David's had been.

Their impromptu hostess stood leaning lightly on a staff in no way similar to David's beyond the fact that it was a staff. Her staff was old and gnarled and hung about at intervals with strange tokens of various size and color. The hands that grasped it were competent hands. Hands that got things done.

"Come in and make yourself comfortable, milady," she

invited, crossing to the fireplace where there were three chairs drawn around it in a semicircle.

Diana wondered at the woman's placid acceptance of her own precipitous arrival.

As if in answer to a spoken question, her hostess said, "I have been expecting you all morning. Won't you sit down?"

Diana dropped onto one of the rush-seated chairs with less than her usual grace. "Th-thank you." She stared at the woman, who stood quietly, waiting for her next question. "H-how did you know we would come?"

"There are many ways to know such things, child, when you have delved into the territories I have foolishly trespassed into." She shuddered lightly. "I am only glad that finally those things I learned there will do some good."

Silenced by this strange declaration, Diana could only stare.

"You are curious, child. That is only natural." She turned back to face the door. "But here comes . . ." She hesitated as if she had decided not to say what she had begun, and changed it to ". . . your young friend."

Diana wondered how the woman could know David was coming. The wind howled so fiercely and there was so much debris being blown about outside, that it would have been impossible to hear the approach of an army!

David burst through the door as if pushed by a giant, unseen hand. Dumping his knapsack and the portmanteau he'd dragged from the shed with him, he tried to shut the door. Putting his shoulder against it, he finally managed to get it closed. Not, however, before Gulliver, barking fiercely at Diana's luggage, squeezed through.

Immediately David told their hostess, "I'm sorry about the dog. He's a friend."

The woman smiled. "Let him stay." A single gesture in

his direction and Gulliver ceased his growling at the portmanteau and went to lie at Diana's feet.

David smiled in return. "Thank you. Frankly, I'm not certain I could prevent his entering, but I would have tried."

"It's quite all right, Your Gr . . ."

The acute distress in his face stopped her. She stood looking deeply into his eyes for a long moment. Then, instead of calling him "Your Grace," as she knew he should be addressed, the woman smiled and said simply, "Welcome, Michael David."

David seemed to accept this. Diana was amazed. "Do you know David, madame?"

Their hostess exchanged glances with a very tense David. Then she smiled and asked instead, "Would you care for tea?"

The shutters she'd taken care to close against the storm just before her guests arrived rattled as if fingers tried to pry them open. She cocked her head and seemed to be listening for something the rattling might tell her. Then she smiled and told Diana, "I very seldom have guests, and I'd enjoy fixing tea for you."

"Thank you very much."

"And have you had your midday meal yet?" She smiled again as they both declined to admit they were ravenous. "Of course you haven't. There hasn't been time, has there?"

"No," David admitted very quietly, his gaze fixed on her.

She nodded. "No. Nor will there be time for food or rest until you have resolved this thing." She gestured toward the portmanteau. "So I shall prepare something that will stick to your ribs, as the country folk say."

Diana couldn't stand it any longer. "Until we have

resolved what thing?" she demanded. "And how do you know that David is . . . David?" She was too bewildered to phrase the rest of her questions.

The old woman laughed. The sound began as if her laughter had not been prompted for a very long time, then blossomed into a lovely joyous sound. "All that in good time . . ." Her eyes twinkled with mischief as she added: ". . . Baroness Huntley. All in good time."

Diana gasped and fell silent. She had never been afraid of the supernatural. Indeed, except for God's Word and the rest of the things of God, she hadn't even believed in it. Not even when her father had hinted at it in his sermons as a way of keeping certain rebel members of his little flock from dabbling in witchcraft.

And even then, she'd been certain that he merely objected to them jigging about under the full moon without any clothes on. "Skyclad," they termed it. She had always liked the word, if not the deed. Most of the parish rebels weren't attractive even with their clothes *on*.

Now, however, it seemed she had come face-to-face with something that was a great deal more real than the shenanigans of her father's parish had been. Nothing other than the genuine supernatural could explain this woman's foreknowledge of their arrival and her immediate acceptance of them!

Diana stood there staring at the elegant figure that she'd decided could only be that of a witch, her eyes wide. This woman's accurate knowledge of their identities was beyond anything she could describe as natural. It was uncanny. And in spite of the homey feeling here in the little thatched cottage, it was making the hair on the back of her neck rise.

Chapter Twenty-two

"*Now,*" *their hostess* said as she cleared the table, "I think we are ready to apply ourselves to the problem at hand." The woman Diana had mentally tagged "The Elegant Witch" got up from the table and walked toward the place just inside the door where David had dropped the portmanteau.

Outside, the wind rose to hurricane pitch, screaming around the little cottage, tearing at the thatch. A shutter at the window nearest the door burst loose and slammed back and forth against the outer wall.

"Oh, dear," Diana heard their hostess say, "this must be even more serious than I thought."

Gulliver had approached, stiff-legged, his lips drawn back in a snarl. The snarl was for the luggage, not their hostess, however.

David went forward to carry the portmanteau for the woman as he realized her intent.

"No!" she cried sharply, holding him off with her staff. "Don't touch it! Can't you see it's active now?"

David stepped back, a grim look on his face. He took a firm hold on Gulliver's collar.

The woman dragged the portmanteau to the fireplace. When she arrived there, flames leapt out toward her. "Be still," she commanded. "This is *my* house!"

The fire died back fitfully.

She turned to her startled guests. "There is great evil here." The expression in her eyes was solemn. "We must take care."

David nodded. He had seen enough that he couldn't explain in the Middle East to temper his stolid English faith.

Diana, though she was startled and more than a little leery of the odd things that were happening, was still skeptical. "Surely you don't believe there is something harmful in *that.*" She pointed to the portmanteau.

Gulliver was slavering at the object in question while he strained to be free of the hold David had on his collar.

Laughing without mirth, their new acquaintance told her, "And surely you aren't admitting that your dog is more perceptive than you are, are you, Baroness Huntley?"

David cleared his throat loudly. He wasn't interested in watching the two women make enemies of each other. "I think proper introductions are in order," he said, uttering the first thing that came to mind in an effort to distract them.

The older woman turned on him. Eyebrows raised and an expression that transcended sarcasm on her patrician face, she parroted, "*Proper* introductions?"

David's face flamed, and he fell silent. Of course he couldn't introduce himself properly. If he did, his fondest hope would be dashed. Worse yet, not only would he have lost his opportunity to attempt to get Diana to fall in love with him for himself alone, he'd have angered her beyond redemption for having tricked her into accepting him as a mere British tar.

Sensing his master's distress, Gulliver thrust a consoling muzzle into his hand.

After fixing David with a long hard stare, the witch said, "While we wait for our tea to steep, I will tell you my story." She put a brown earthenware teapot down on the table. "There is a message in it for you." She let her gaze rest on Diana for a heartbeat, and then said as if she spoke to both of them, "Long ago, I was the Countess Louisa von Thallenstein. That was before my excessive pride in my superior intellect brought me to the humble state in which you find me."

Diana was eaten alive with curiosity. So much so that she forgot the storm and the portmanteau.

Knowing this, the Countess said, "You are curious, I see. Very well." She held up a hand to stem the apologies that Diana was about to offer for her rudeness. "I was a beautiful young English girl when I married Count von Thallenstein and went to live in his castle in Bavaria. The countryside there was breathtaking, but—life is more than scenery, alas. My handsome husband was a bore, and I soon looked around for something to occupy me. An affair was out of the question, as I had no desire to sully myself with such a loathsome thing.

"Unfortunately for me, there was a hut in the woods that I frequently passed in my daily rides, and one day, when I was terribly thirsty, I stopped and asked for a drink from the well. To make a long story short, the old woman who lived there told me that *she* had *made* me thirsty because she was lonely.

"I laughed at her, of course. The very idea was ludi-

crous! But I was sorry for the poor old crone and began to
stop in to see her frequently."

She sat silent a long moment, then admitted, "Therein
was my downfall." She nodded as if agreeing, at long last,
with the truth of her statement. Then she drew a deep
breath and went on. "She warned me that the things I was
curious about were very dangerous. That the power to do
such things as she could do, and was willing to teach me to
do, came from a dark place ruled by a dark master who one
day would exact his due, but I laughed at that, too. I forgot
that 'white magic' or 'black,' the source of power was the
same."

She gave each of them a long look. "You see, I was certain that while she, a simple peasant, was no match for this
dark master of whom she spoke, I would be safe. I was
proof against such superstition. I was an educated woman,
after all. I was well grounded in the faith of holy mother
church, and I had a strong mind and will. And most of
all"—she took another long breath—"I had my overween-
ing pride to reassure and sustain me."

Diana found *she* was holding *her* breath, hanging on
every word.

"And so, no longer bored, I threw myself into learning
all that the witch could teach me. The days flew by. Boredom fled. I was utterly fascinated."

Diana breathed.

David frowned, troubled.

Gulliver just kept watching the portmanteau, unblink-
ing.

"And to put a quick finish to my tiresome tale, in the
end I became a true witch. My pride in my intellect and in
myself had been used to trap me and to lead me to my
downfall. The price of learning 'the craft' was heavy. It
cost me everything. The dark master claimed his due, and

my life was destroyed. My own arrogant pride had caused my downfall."

She turned then and looked deep into Diana's wide eyes. In a voice as somber as the black day outside, she told her, "Beware, Baroness, lest *your* pride cost *you* everything."

Diana gasped with the strength of the sense of dire warning that washed over her. The witch was telling her not to let her pride turn David away! She knew it. Though the woman kept her gaze fastened on Diana's and never for an instant let it waver to include the handsome young man beside her, Diana knew. And she writhed inside.

The picture she carried in her mind and heart of the Duke became blurred, and David's face superimposed itself over it. The features were different, but the eyes were the same soft sherry brown, and Diana wanted to weep with frustration. How could she believe, even for a moment, that she might be in love with both of them? Her emotions threatened to overwhelm her as she struggled with the problem.

The Elegant Witch, instead of offering her young guest comfort, threw back her head and laughed and laughed.

Evidently, the joke was a good one.

Diana was furious, but she could hardly insult her hostess by showing it! She was just as disinclined to stalk out the door because of the storm. Settling for a reproachful glare, she remained where she was sitting. She raised her chin, regarding the witch haughtily down the length of her nose, while her back went stiff as a poker with injured pride.

How could the woman be so delighted by the prospect of her, Diana's, anguish! Evidently becoming a witch had cost her more than she knew. Evidently it had cost her her compassion for others, too.

"Ah, my dear, forgive me for my laughter. It was inexcusably unkind of me."

Diana's back relaxed a little.

"You see, I look at life from a different perspective. I see the future sometimes and . . . and sometimes it amuses me."

Diana bristled. "I'm glad it amuses *someone*. Right now I feel as if the house is about to blow down around us. There won't be much future for any of us if it does."

"True. But the house will hold, and all will be well in the end."

Diana simply stared. She was trying hard not to glare at the woman. How could she even guess what it was that had Diana tied in knots? Just because she had known their names and had expected them to come and . . . She stopped mentally accusing the witch. After all, there was a good possibility that, having known all those things, she might also know what she was talking about.

Diana was about to apologize for being mulish and ungrateful when the woman returned to the fireplace to bring back the now drier portmanteau.

Gulliver stood and snarled.

David put a hand on the dog's head and said, "It's all right, boy. Go lie down."

Gulliver whined his disapproval of his master's suggestion even as he did lie down. On David's feet. Whatever happened, he was going to save this kind man from harm.

The self-confessed witch lifted the portmanteau to the table and proceeded to remove the clothes from the bag, one item at a time. As she did, she muttered to herself.

Diana, listening closely, was startled to hear the words of the Twenty-third Psalm! "'. . . Yea, though I walk through the valley of the shadow of death . . .'"

The wind tore the shutter it had loosened to slam open

earlier completely off the house. The howling attack spun down the chimney. Flames and ashes and embers flew from the fireplace.

"'. . . Thou are with me. Thy rod and Thy staff they comfort me,'" the witch went on in a stronger voice to be heard over the shriek of the storm.

The last of Diana's clothes were out of the portmanteau. Her intimate things were a frothy heap of lace and ribbons on the table, and the witch stopped quoting the Psalm. Fixing each of her two guests with a somber glance, she said softly, "And now we shall see."

Suddenly, the wind abated. Everything went quiet. As quiet as a graveyard.

Reaching down into the portmanteau, the witch slipped her fingers along the side and pulled at the bottom of it with all her might. With a crack, the false bottom she'd suspected was there opened and the source of all their troubles was bared.

There was a book secreted there. A dark, leather-bound tome with strange symbols embossed on it in gold seemed to glow in the darkness of the recess that had been made for it.

Without bringing the book from its hiding place, the witch stood. "We must go cautiously now."

"Are you saying that there is something dangerous in that bag?" David watched her attentively.

"Something evil. I can feel its emanations."

Diana couldn't help herself. "How absurd," she uttered. Then she looked sheepish as the others turned serious looks her way.

The witch told her, "Never underestimate the power of things you do not understand." Carefully, as if she were putting her hands into a pit of vipers, she reached down and brought out the old volume.

With a sharp intake of breath, she dropped it to the table. Her face was grim as she stared down at it. "Where did this come from?" she demanded.

Diana leaned over to see it, only to be held back by the older woman. Irritated, she still identified it. "Why, that's just an old book that my father bought one day in London."

"It is far from 'just an old book,' my dear."

"What is it?" David asked, trying to push enough of Gulliver off him so that he could rise and get a better look at it.

"It's a *grimoire,*" the woman told him. "A handbook for witches." She picked it up then, and opened it. "What did your father tell you about this book, Baroness?"

"He said that he bought it so that it wouldn't fall into the wrong hands and do harm."

"Your father is a wise man. This is a very early copy of *The Key of Solomon.* It is a particularly powerful book of spells. With it one can summon and command many demons."

"Not an especially pristine ambition," David said.

"No, it isn't. And it is a very dangerous one."

"How so, if one is in command?" Diana wanted to know.

"Because," she told them solemnly, "one commands demons only by striking bargains with them." She smiled mirthlessly. "The idea is to make a bargain that leaves you a loophole through which you can escape before you have to honor it."

"A tricky procedure at best." David stared hard at the book.

"Indeed, it is. But honesty doesn't rate highly in the occult." Suddenly she scooped up the book and thrust it back into its hiding place. Shuddering, she told the watching travelers, "You would be wise to rid yourselves of this as soon as possible."

"My father wanted to keep anyone from ever getting into trouble because of it," Diana said.

"Or into mischief with it, I'll wager," David added glumly.

"That might be accomplished if you could get it into the right hands."

"For instance?" Diana asked.

"To a really powerful witch or warlock."

"That would hardly serve my father's purpose." Diana was a little indignant.

The witch nodded. "Or to one of the bishops, preferably the Archbishop of Canterbury."

David gave the matter grave consideration. "I could ride there in a day if I rose at dawn, took both horses, and rode hard."

"And your lady could remain here with me to pray for your safety the whole time you were gone."

"Good."

Diana could feel her temper rising again. "No one has consulted me. The book is my father's. And I should be with you, David." She didn't know what she dreaded most, being left alone with the witch, or having David in possible danger without her there beside him.

David turned a grave face to her. "Diana, I shall need both horses if I am to deliver this before nightfall catches me." He cast a sheepish grin toward their hostess. "And I've no interest in spending a night on the road with this book in my possession, either."

"A wise precaution, Your G . . ." The Countess-witch stopped herself just in time and substituted: "Your good sense is to be applauded."

The apprehensive look on David's face gave way to one

of amused admiration for her quick save. Suddenly, his handsome face was split by a grin. If ever he had put a double meaning into a single phrase, he did it as he said a heartfelt "Thank you."

Chapter Twenty-three

David rose from his pallet on the floor in front of the fireplace well before dawn. His hostess was waiting quietly and whispered that she would meet him in the garden with a breakfast of bread and cheese and strong tea.

David took Gulliver with him to the stables and saddled the two horses. "You can't come with me, boy."

Gulliver barked sharply, then whined as David said nothing else.

Returning with him and the horses to the front of the cottage, David found his hostess waiting there. She motioned to him to follow her to a bench outside as neither of them wanted to risk waking Diana.

"The poor child's exhausted," the self-proclaimed witch told him. "I'll let her sleep as long as she will." She smiled at him. "Then there will be fewer hours for her to agonize over your safety."

David's eyes lit with hope. "Do you really think she will care?"

"I think she already cares far more than she's willing to admit, Your Grace." Here in the farthest corner of her pleasant garden, she used his honorific without fear that Diana might overhear and discover his true identity.

"It is my dearest wish that she may come to care for me for myself. For me as a *man,* that is to say, not as a duke." He sighed.

"Give her time. She is half in love with you as it stands. Her loyalty to your memory—the memory of you she has kept enshrined in her heart for five long years—prevents her from admitting it."

"Her memory from that day at Merlington Park?" He grinned a twisted grin. "I too have carried a memory from there. The memory of a winsome girl who has haunted and ruled my heart all this time."

The witch gave him one sparkling glance and closed her lips tightly. The gift of foreseeing the future was not always to be shared, she knew. She had learned that the hard way, and it was not an error she intended to make again. And of course, there was the matter of Diana's pride to worry about. She could see their love, but beyond that she could not see. Would that stubborn, foolish pride cost these young people their happiness in the end?

Shrugging that worry away, she lifted David's saddle-bag and told him, "I have wrapped the book in a special cloth that should keep it from doing harm, or from calling forth any demons to keep you from successfully completing your errand of its destruction. In addition, I have filled the bag around it with rosemary."

"Rosemary?"

"Rosemary wards off evil spirits."

"Rosemary wards off *djins*?"

"Ah, yes, *djins*—the Muslim word for demons. It was

while you were Haroon Al Rasqa's slave that you learned of them, I expect."

"Yes." David's face closed. "I learned many strange and unpleasant things while I was in his power."

She regarded him steadily for a long moment. "We will not speak of them," she said, her voice oddly gentle, as if she could see, even now, the pain and degradation he had suffered. "Suffice it to say that at least this bit of knowledge will stand you in good stead. Without that experience, I've no doubt you would take the everyday Englishman's usual view of the problem with which we are dealing. Such ignorance could work to your detriment." She smiled then and added, "And even though rosemary wards off evil, you must still take great care." She grasped his arm. "Though I cannot see it clearly, I fear danger awaits you."

"Rest assured, Countess. I shall be careful." He rose, eager to go now. Eager to escape the memories the talk of *djin*s had brought back. "Gulliver. You are to stay and protect."

The great dog whined and pushed his muzzle into David's hand, silently begging.

"No, boy. I truly need you to stay here."

Gulliver slinked off to lie at the door of the cottage. He dropped his head on his paws and just stared, his eyes reproachful.

David untied the reins of the horse he intended to ride, then bowed over his hostess's hand. "Thank you for all you have done, and thank you for keeping my lady." Impulsively, he stepped forward and placed a kiss on the old woman's cheek. "It's time to go."

He swung up onto his mount and turned him out to the road, catching up the second horse as he went. Fresh from their night's rest, both mounts danced with eagerness to be gone.

David managed the two with ease. Looking back at her over his shoulder, he said, "Keep her safe for me." Then he waved good-bye with the hand that held the reins of the horse he was leading, and they were on their way.

"Go with God." There were tears in her eyes as she bade him the ancient farewell. Somehow, under the present circumstances, it didn't sound a bit out of place.

The Countess had been standing in the garden for several minutes, praying earnestly for the gallant young man's safety, when a sleep-disheveled Diana rushed out the door of the cottage. "David!" she cried. "David, where are you?"

She looked around frantically and found only the silent figure of the witch. Reading the look on her face correctly, she said, "He's gone, hasn't he?"

"Yes. He's gone."

Diana burst into tears.

David rode as hard as he dared, knowing that he had to conserve the energy of both horses if he intended to make it to Canterbury before nightfall. Hours after he'd left Diana, he passed from open country to farms and, finally, saw a village just ahead.

It was noon, and he was conscious that his mounts were both almost exhausted. They needed an hour or two of rest before they could go on. He acknowledged that he needed rest, as well. Anxious as he was to get rid of the foul book he carried and get back to Diana, he knew he'd have to bow to common sense. He was only halfway to his destination.

At the far end of the single street of the village, there was an inn sign swinging gently in the breeze. The King's Head Tavern, it proclaimed. The inn yard was spacious and welcoming. David turned in, dropped from his tired mount, and told the ostler, "No grain until they are properly cooled out, and only half-rations then."

"Yessir."

"And I want them each to have a good rubdown. Then just let them rest quietly until I ask for them in about an hour."

The ostler ran a professional eye over his charges. "One hour mightn't be all they need, sir."

David nodded in weary agreement, but could only say grimly, "I'll delay as long as I dare. My business is urgent."

"Aye, sir." The ostler watched as David slung his saddlebag over his shoulder and walked toward the inn.

Just as David reached the steps into the inn, a phaeton flashed into the yard. Its driver cracked his whip with a final flourish, bringing the horses up smartly.

David couldn't help it, he flinched badly.

One of the men in the phaeton laughed. "I say, Sir Joseph! Have a care. You gave that good man over there quite a scare. He looked as if he thought you were going to hit *him!*"

David turned at the voice remembered from long ago. Calverson! Of all the rotten luck.

His cousin, Sir Joseph Ewing, was out of the phaeton now, but he'd retained his whip. As the ostlers led his team away, he cracked it again.

David was ready for it this time. Even so, he winced.

Sir Joseph approached him. "Sorry, old chap. Didn't mean to make you nervous."

David took the spurious apology for exactly what it was worth, and didn't bother to answer.

Sizing up the other three members of his cousin's little band, he knew he'd eventually be recognized so he seized the initiative. "Really, Cousin? Why is it I got the distinct impression you were enjoying yourself?"

Sir Joseph was struck dumb.

" 'Cousin'?" Calverson was instantly on the alert. "Is this—this *man* claiming to be your cousin, Ewing?"

Sir Joseph had recovered from the shock of seeing his exalted cousin garbed in dust-covered and such inexpensive clothing. "Don't you recognize him, Calverson?" He cocked his head and surveyed David contemptuously. "No, I shouldn't suppose you would. You never knew Smythington before he went away to school and became . . ." He waited an instant then finished his sentence with cruel emphasis: ". . . a *fat boy.*"

David regarded him steadily, refusing to rise to his taunt.

Sir Joseph drawled his next words, "But I should have thought that you would have known the man that put a ball into your arm in that duel. Over young Baroness Huntley's little dog, wasn't it? Seems to me I remember that my portly cousin pinked you neatly."

Calverson held his peace, but his eyes glittered with hatred for the now slender young nobleman on the steps.

David bowed slightly. The graceful movement was an expression of courtesy to a group of social inferiors. "I am sure you gentlemen will excuse me." With that he turned on his heel and entered the inn. Outwardly he appeared calm. Inwardly he was seething. Of all the people he could have met, his cousin was the last he'd have chosen.

Peace during his meal was not to be his, either. He had just decided on the innkeeper's suggestions of what to eat when Sir Joseph and his cronies entered the public room.

"The public room, Cousin?" Sir Joseph drawled in pretended shock. Then he bent and hissed, "I'd have thought the exalted Duke of Smythington would have commanded a private parlor."

David looked up at him for a moment before answering. "And you, Joseph? Are you accustomed to frequenting public rooms from preference . . ." He hesitated so that his cousin wouldn't miss the insult: ". . . or from necessity?"

Sir Joseph's face flamed at David's oblique reference to his straitened financial situation. "No, I am not! I am most certainly not." He was anything but coolly bored, now. "And I can't for the life of me figure out why *you* are sitting there clothed in those ghastly garments like some commoner."

David regarded him steadily.

"Well, answer me, dammit."

"I am sitting here in these 'ghastly garments,' as you call them, because they are far less conspicuous than the garb in which I began my quest."

"What quest? What the devil are you prating about?"

"I have undertaken a walking tour to rediscover the beauties of England, Joseph." David's eyes shone briefly with malice. "Never having left home, you probably wouldn't understand." He turned away and applied himself to the steak the landlord placed in front of him.

"Are you taunting me because I wasn't stupid enough to waste years of my life chasing after Napoleon as you did?"

"Are you feeling taunted, Cousin?" Now David spoke with elaborate boredom. "What a pity. Permit me to suggest that you remove yourself to a private parlor where you will be surrounded by your equals and safe from a 'commoner's' taunts, then."

"'Ear! 'Ear!" a man seated nearby agreed. "'Twas peaceful until ye got here. Take yerself off and let decent men eat in quiet."

Joseph Ewing choked. Looking at the farmer who'd

made that remark as if he'd never been spoken to in that manner before, he shouted, "Landlord! A private parlor!" He turned on his friends with the anger he felt for his cousin. "Don't just stand there and stare!" Then, followed by his friends, he stormed out after the innkeeper.

David raised his tankard of ale in a congratulatory salute to the farmer who'd rid him of his cousin.

The farmer raised his own back. "Gor, 'e must be 'alf-looney to call ye a dook. Anybody can see *ye* be a right sort." He shook his head in amazement and said scornfully, "Dook." He snorted. "What a jackass."

David smiled and raised his tankard again. "Jackass, indeed."

Sir Joseph fumed for ten minutes after he and his friends reached the private parlor. "Blast and damn!" He swatted the bowl of flowers off the table in the center of the parlor. It flew against the wall and shattered. "He had to come back. He just had to come back!"

"Who back from where?" the newest of his acquaintances, a fresh-faced youth, asked. "I seem to be the only one in the dark here."

"My blasted cousin. Smythington."

"Smythington? You mean the missing Duke all of England's been talking about?"

"Yes, you fool. Smythington. Probably the richest non-royal duke in the realm."

Calverson laughed.

"Damn you, Calverson!" Sir Joseph flared.

Calverson said, "Carefully, Ewing. I might take offense."

Sir Joseph colored, and turned his back. Everyone knew Calverson was a dangerous man.

"Thank you. I accept your apology," Calverson drawled.

"I didn't offer one," Ewing said, but his tone was subdued.

"So I noticed. But I forgive you for the sake of our friendship." His voice dripped malice. "I know what a terrible strain your cousin's reappearance has put you under." He watched his friend squirm for a moment, then turned and addressed the bewildered young man. "Sir Joseph, here, would have been the next Duke of Smythington if His Grace had stayed missing."

"Really!"

"Oh, yes." Calverson crooked a finger at the waiter the landlord had sent to them and made a gesture as if pouring wine. The waiter nodded and left to bring it. "Our friend Sir Joseph's creditors have been very generous about letting him run up his accounts, with the understanding that he would soon be able to pay. With Smythington safely back in England, however . . ." He shrugged elaborately and let the young man figure it out for himself.

He did. "Then they'll want him to pay up!"

"Exactly."

"But if he doesn't inherit, he won't be able to. . . ."

"Enough, dammit!" Ewing looked apoplectic. "Must we discuss my personal business?" With a visible effort, he pulled himself together and tried to change the subject.

"Tollerson," the oldest member of the party addressed the youngest, "I wonder if you would be so good as to go bespeak dinners for all of us."

"But the waiter can—"

"Tollerson!" The man's tone was sharp.

"Yes. Yes, of course. I'll be glad to." Puzzled as to why he'd been sent from the parlor, he frowned his way to the public room to find the innkeeper and order their food.

The man who'd rid them of him wasted no time. "Am I to understand that Smythington is tramping the country-side alone and incognito?"

"You heard him." Sir Joseph Ewing kicked viciously at a log in the cold fireplace.

"Ah."

Ewing turned back to his friends, scowling. "Ah, what?" he demanded.

"Oh, nothing." The speaker looked carefully at the finger-nails of his right hand. "I was just thinking that it would be a very great pity if he were to meet with an accident while he is so far from home and unescorted as he is." He looked at Calverson and Ewing with great innocence. "So sad if the accident should prove to be . . . fatal?"

"My God, Runsford! No wonder you sent that weak-kneed ninny Tollerson out of the room. You're nothing short of diabolical!"

"Quickly," Runsford told them, sitting forward in his chair. "We must make our plans."

When young Tollerson returned from ordering their meal, he found them all laughing. Clearly bewildered by the turnabout in their demeanor, he asked, "What's so amusing?"

Chapter Twenty-four

Frantic, Diana paced the floor. She'd long ago given up any pretense of calm. It didn't matter that her hostess was watching her twisting her hands as if she made a practice of it, as if she were incapable of stopping. Diana pressed her fingers to lips that trembled. How could she have let him go without her? His danger was hers. She should be sharing his plight.

"Sit, my dear," the witch said. "You will wear yourself out."

Diana glanced at her in clear defiance and kept pacing. "I can't bear to sit still when David may be in danger."

"I have taken precautions," her new friend insisted.

"Precautions!" Diana was almost angry. "Against evil spells? Do you think me a complete fool? I might not have believed in their power before, but I remember that storm. David had done no more than say that we were going to investigate my portmanteau, and the gates of hell were opened. That book of spells attacked us to prevent us from even discovering its presence, and the resulting storm nearly tore your cottage apart! You are far from safe, yourself. Why should I believe poor David won't be in mortal danger?"

Suddenly, she stopped dead in her tracks. With a clarity that shocked her, she experienced the true depth of her feelings for the man. Just the remembrance of him stirred her heart. Abruptly, she realized that there was nothing she wouldn't do to keep him safe. Nothing at all.

She paced slowly to the end of the room, stunned by the realization. For a long moment she stared out the window as she came to grips with her new self-knowledge. David. She was in love with David. As the admission settled in her heart, she became even more determined to protect him.

She turned away from the window, lifted her chin defiantly, and said, "My father owned that book, and he told me he had looked through it. That was why he bought it. Seeing what it was, he wanted to keep it out of the wrong hands. Why wasn't *he* harmed?"

Her hostess cocked her head and considered Diana quietly. "You know, for a vicar's child you don't seem to know much about the battle between good and evil." She looked critically at the embroidery she was doing to help pass the time.

Diana started to argue, but realized that defending herself wouldn't lead to learning anything. "What do you mean?" she asked instead.

"I should have thought your father would have taught you something you could fall back on in a situation like this." She plucked out and reset an embroidery stitch that displeased her.

Diana came to the table where her hostess sat and perched on the edge of a chair. "Yes. Yes, of course! No one in my late husband's world ever spoke of the things of

God. I'd forgotten in the years I've spent away from my father. God is the single most powerful force in our universe! And He has invested some of that power in those who earnestly believe in Him."

"That's right, too," the witch said. Tears formed and trickled down her cheeks.

Diana didn't see her new friend's tears. She smiled. "I haven't thought of that for years, more's the pity." Now, the knowledge flooded her spirit. "Yes," she declared triumphantly. "I know that is so."

Then she grasped the witch's hands and started to speak. The sight of her new friend's tears stopped her. "Oh, my dear, what is it? What is the matter? You're crying!"

The witch bowed her head and was silent.

Diana dropped to her knees so that she could look up into the older woman's face. Gently she insisted, "What is it?"

"We must pray for David."

"Yes, of course we must. But first, tell me why you're crying."

Her eyes bleak, the witch regarded Diana for a long moment. Finally she whispered, "I am not certain that there is any hope for my prayers after what I have done. Remember how God feels about witchcraft."

"But you've repented of all that, I know you have. You even speak of it in the past tense, now. And when we were examining the portmanteau, I heard you reciting the Twenty-third Psalm."

"That was only my feeble attempt to protect myself from the *grimoire* and its demons."

"But you were quoting the Word of God." She reached out and caressed the woman's lined cheek. "If I heard you, surely you know that the Lord did." Her eyes serious, she told her, "I should think that if God thought you were still a wholehearted witch, you'd have choked on those words, but you didn't. Surely that's a sign that you're forgiven."

Diana frowned in concentration and added, "I don't recall the exact passage, but didn't He promise that He wouldn't break a bruised reed? And you are terribly bruised. I know it."

A timid hope dawned in the witch's eyes. Still she said, "The dark master will fight not to lose me, you know."

Diana made a little sound of disgust. "Just let him try to keep you away from *Our* Mighty God!"

The embroidery fell unheeded from the older woman's lap as she took both of Diana's hands. Her tears fell freely now. "Then I shall try hard to believe you, and to pray that even with all I've done to offend Him, there is hope for me."

Diana smiled through her own tears. "And I promise I shall pray for you always."

The witch sighed. As she straightened, she looked as if the weight of the world had been lifted from her shoulders.

Diana rose from her knees and sat again on the edge of her chair. "Now, we must pray for David."

Joining hands again, they bowed their heads and fervently prayed.

In response to that prayer, a tree fell across a distant road.

Dusk was stealing across the land and David was riding as hard as he dared again. He knew better than to push the horses too hard. He still had miles to go, and they had been at it with little respite since shortly after dawn.

Fervently thanking the Lord that these two mounts were of superior quality, he wondered if he, himself, was up to the challenge at hand. Every bone in his body ached, and muscles that he hadn't used for riding in years had long since been screaming.

When they pounded around a curve in the road, David saw that a tree had fallen across it. He hoped he still had the strength to stay on when the horse under him cleared it.

"Steady, boy," he said as much to himself as to his mount as he checked it to gather it for the jump. Then *he* went flying.

The horse took off to clear the tree, the saddle girth flew apart, and David, saddle and all, crashed to the ground. As he fell, he heard a sharp crack. Blazing pain seared through his left arm.

He lay where he had fallen, momentarily stunned. Both horses bolted, and David cursed himself for not having kept hold of their reins. He started to rise.

Blood puddling under his left arm caught his attention. Blast and damn! It hadn't been a muscle pull that had caused that exquisite pain. He'd been shot!

Grimacing at his own stupidity, he lay still. Any of the others of The Lucky Seven would have known they'd been shot, for they'd all had that unpleasant experience in the war with Napoleon. He'd been the only one unscathed. Till now.

Lying there with his arm on fire, he decided that he'd failed to show his wounded comrades sufficient sympathy.

Staying absolutely still, he waited to see what would happen next. Had some lad out hunting shot him by mischance? Or was there something more sinister involved?

The vague thought that there might, indeed, be something more sinister afoot galvanized him to action. Lying there waiting for the *coup de grâce* would prove exceptionally foolish should some enemy knowingly have shot him.

He wanted to shake his head to clear it faster. Some instinct warned him that complete immobility was all that was keeping him safe. The fact dawned on him that, had the horse not been rising to clear that fallen tree, his head would have been in the general vicinity of his wounded arm. That knowledge did nothing to comfort him.

His next thought was even worse. If, he concluded, his skin crawling, he had been shot deliberately, the shooter might come to see if he had done the job. And to finish him off if he hadn't.

His blood ran cold at the thought of having someone walk up and put period to him here in the dust of the road. There was no cover to run to and hide in, and he had no weapon. Whoever had shot him could just walk up and put a bullet in his brain. Not a comforting thought.

Bullet in his brain! He could manage to feign that himself. Well enough, at any rate, to draw the bastard out of hiding and cause him to feel safe enough to step too close.

Trying not to move at all, David managed to smear blood from his arm over his temple and down the side of his face.

Then he waited.

Chapter Twenty-five

David lay as still as the death he pretended. His ears were stretched to the breaking point. Soon, he heard the creak of a saddle and the heavy thump of a big man dismounting. It seemed forever before the man's legs appeared in David's field of vision.

An instant later, the man had stepped too close. David's legs shot out and scissored his assailant's, crashing him to the ground.

Atop the man, the flat of his hand pressing against the would-be murderer's throat, David gasped, "Calverson! My God, man, has our quarrel come to cold-blooded murder?"

Calverson struggled to move David's iron hand as he ground out, "No, imbecile. Though I've no particular objection to seeing you dead, it took a sizable bribe to send me after you. I've been promised that bay hunter of Ewing's I always coveted."

Anger filled David. "You bastard! You'd kill me for no more reason than to possess a *horse?*"

Calverson lay there and looked up at him calmly. "Why not? On the Peninsula I killed men for less."

David remembered then that Calverson had been considered a veritable killing machine until he had been seriously wounded early in the war. That memory, and others from their days together at school, slammed into him, and he absorbed them like a blow, closing his eyes a moment. It was true. In war, men killed without any reason at all except that the man they killed wore a uniform different from their own. In a twisted way, it did make more sense to attack a man in order to gain a horse.

The anger he felt toward the man beneath him evaporated.

"My cousin?"

"Who else?"

David let the man sit up, and the two of them sat there together in the dust of the road.

"Oh, come now, Smythington, don't be a complete fool. Think, man. Who wouldn't do murder to step into your shoes?"

David simply looked at him.

"Well?" Calverson sought to make the matter clear. "Ewing—and half of England, I might add—thought you were dead. When Mathers got rescued from the caves near Clifton-on-Tides, even he said that you were a goner." He shifted his position a little and removed a rock from under his hip. "You can't blame Ewing for hoping."

"No?"

"No. Nor for his creditors letting him have anything he wanted, with the dukedom seemingly within his greedy little grasp."

David frowned.

Calverson groaned in exasperation. "You are certainly living up to the expectations we all had for you from school, Smythington."

"Oh?" David was curious in spite of himself.

"Yes. We were all of the opinion that your high-mindedness would lead you to make foolish mistakes sooner or later." When David said nothing, he went on. "Well? Just look at you. Here you are, off in the middle of nowhere, without an escort, and with no one the wiser, certain that you'll be safe. You're just asking to be killed by anyone interested in being the Tenth Duke of Smythington. A cousin next in line who is as far up the river tick as Sir Joseph Ewing is might just be tempted, don't you think?"

David, lost in sober thought, rose and offered Calverson a hand up.

"There! You see?"

"See what?" David was busy brushing dust off his clothes.

"See what a ninny you are, that's what! I mean, I say! I just got through taking a potshot at you, and here you are giving me your hand to assist me to rise!"

"Well, I did knock you down." David examined the graze on his upper left arm and hissed at the pain he caused it.

"I begin to think I'm sorry about that wound, old chap. Here. Let me bind it up with my handkerchief."

"Thank you. Most kind."

"There you go again!" Calverson was greatly annoyed.

"To what are you referring?" David winced as the man who'd shot him knotted his makeshift bandage.

"To your thanking me. You should be threatening me with a hanging."

David regarded him steadily for a long moment. "Calverson," he finally said quietly, "I have known you almost all my life. You are hotheaded and heedless, yes, and sometimes even a little cruel."

"I say!" Calverson was not flattered.

"But I have always thought that there was a good man somewhere inside you, and that given time he would come out someday."

Calverson was staring, openmouthed.

"If I had not thought so, I would have killed you when we fought that duel I encouraged you to force on me several years ago. So you see, it would be foolish in the extreme to have you hanged before my judgment could be proven correct." David went to his saddle where it lay in the dust of the road, noted that the girth had been cut (just as he suspected), and removed the saddlebag.

"Encouraged me to . . ." Calverson was sputtering. "You did no such thing! I forced the quarrel on you because I . . ." Then he closed his mouth, suddenly realizing that David had the right of it. He'd been about to lead his faithful hangers-on in a plot to harass the lovely young Baroness Huntley for some reason or other that escaped his mind just now, and David had objected. So, instead of teasing Lady Diana—thanks to the man whose arm he'd just bandaged—he'd ended up in bed for three weeks being bled by an idiot surgeon every few days when he'd already lost quite enough blood on the dueling field.

"Yes, well," David was saying, "I'm glad your aim has not improved with the years. As I recall, however, you were deadly with swords." He limped toward the spot in which the horses stood grazing. "I should not like to have ended my life here. Not now, especially."

He smiled wearily at his would-be assassin. "By the way, I'm taking your horse. I'll make better time with three."

Chapter Twenty-six

Gulliver was the first to hear it. He stood up from his place in front of the fireplace, ears pricked forward. An instant later, the big dog began to wag his tail.

Diana saw and rose from her chair. "Gulliver hears something," she told the witch. "It's David. I know it is!"

"Surely not," the witch said with a smile that admitted she lied, "it is far too soon for him to have returned." Then she added softly, "Unless he's a lovesick fool."

Diana didn't hear her. She was running with the dog for the door before the sound of hoofbeats came to them. Tearing it open, she rushed to the garden gate.

In the fading twilight, she saw them—a single mounted man and two led horses. Waving with all her might, she opened the gate and sent Gulliver running to greet him. She wished with all her heart that she could go, too. That she could fly down the lane to him as swiftly as the big dog. She waited, though, savaged by impatience, until he had halted his tired horse at the gate.

David looked utterly spent. There were deep lines of weariness carved beside his mouth, and his shoulders drooped the moment the horse stumbled to a halt.

With a little cry of concern, Diana held her arms up to him, and an exhausted David tumbled off his mount into them. As he did, he swept her into his own arms and hugged her fiercely.

"Are you all right? Did all go well here in my absence?"

"Yes, yes, of course. You carried the danger away with you, remember?"

He laughed as Gulliver bumped against him, demanding attention, and his legs threatened to betray him. "Egad. Two hard days in the saddle have finished me, it seems."

"Gulliver, leave him alone," Diana ordered. Then she scolded David, "You shouldn't have turned around and come right back. You should have rested a day or two."

He looked into her eyes, his own gaze tender. "I was afraid you'd worry if I stopped to rest. I couldn't have that."

Diana's eyes spoke volumes, as tender as his. "All went well?"

"Yes, the Archbishop knew exactly what to do with that wretched book, and God knows I was glad to be rid of it." He grinned at her, a tired, lopsided grin. "If your father gets the idea of buying another such book, tell him he is responsible for disposing of it himself, please."

He staggered as he took his first step. His legs were still reluctant to obey him.

Diana bit her lip and commanded briskly, "Here, lean on me until you have your legs back."

He laughed as he stumbled a step and accepted her invitation. "Very well. The horses are too tired to go anywhere. I'll get to them in a few minutes." Throwing his good arm around her shoulders, he let her guide him. For the first time since he'd hidden in the coachman's box at the beginning of their adventure, he thanked the Lord that he was very little bigger than his beloved.

Diana wavered once under his weight, took a deep breath, and walked determinedly up the garden path toward the cottage, her arm firmly around his slender waist, half-supporting him. The pressure of his body against her own gave her a heady feeling of intimacy. If she'd dared, she would have held him even closer.

Suddenly, the path through the little garden seemed all too short.

At the door, David turned his head and thanked her, his lips inches from Diana's. Another benefit of being almost the same height as his love discovered. He had only to lean forward just a little and . . .

Diana felt David's breath on her cheek and saw his mouth almost touching her own. She took a trembling breath and felt her eyelids begin to fall in anticipation of his kiss.

David's lips were . . .

"Ah, there you are!" The ex-witch yanked the door open. "Come in and let me tend your wound." Her words broke the spell.

"Wound!" Diana was stunned.

"It's nothing. A scratch." David sought to reassure her. "Only a graze."

"A graze!" Diana let go of him so quickly he almost fell. "A graze. Grazes come from rifle balls!"

"A pistol actually."

"A pistol." Diana's fear for him converted itself to anger. "'A pistol actually,'" she mimicked. "*Only* a pistol?" Her eyes blazed at him through tears that made them diamond bright. "How very nice that whoever shot you didn't use a cannon!"

David chuckled at her joke, saw that she didn't think it the least bit funny, and sought to calm her. "It's only a scratch, dearest. See?" He turned his wounded arm toward her to show her.

Unfortunately, he was unaware that his arduous ride had caused the wound to open and bleed again. In spite of the neat white bandage the Archbishop's physician had applied to his upper arm there was a soggy mass of rich, red blood soaking his entire sleeve.

"David!" Diana cried, turning pale.

"Oh, damn!"

"Sit down so that I can wash and dress that, Michael David." The witch pushed him toward a chair at the table. There was already a bowl of water and some clean linen rags on it. As seemed to be her habit, she'd known they would be needed.

David sat.

Diana hovered.

"Take off your coat," his would-be nurse instructed.

Diana stepped closer. "Here, let me help."

Together she and David eased the dark garment off, taking care not to hurt his wounded arm. David grinned at her. "You are a remarkably good valet, Diana."

"Be quiet and let us get you out of your shirt," the old witch said.

"No!" David's objection was almost a shout.

Their hostess looked into his face and read there his reluctance to have Diana see the whip scars on his back. "We can just cut off your sleeve."

David relaxed visibly. "Yes, that will do splendidly. The shirt is ruined anyway."

Diana backed away several steps. She knew exactly what had just transpired. He didn't want her to see the dreadful scars that crisscrossed his back. He'd no idea that she'd already seen them. She'd seen them at the river on the second morning of their trek.

Her stomach still tightened when she thought of that time. Hidden in the mists of morning, she had watched him bathe, admiring his chest and shoulders, thinking how beautifully muscled he was, how perfectly proportioned for a small man.

Then he'd turned to throw a stick for Gulliver to retrieve. Hurling it, he'd turned his back to where she stood in her swirl of vapor, and suddenly all she'd been able to think of was the pain he must have suffered as the whip scored his back again and again.

Recalling it now, she pressed one hand to her stomach and one to her mouth.

David looked up and started to rise to go to her. The witch pushed him back down on the chair, and said, "Stay still. That isn't what you think it is."

"She's faint," he protested. "*She* should sit."

"That isn't necessary."

David started to get up again. The witch shoved him back harder. "You'd better reassure him that you are all right, Baroness, or I shall have no opportunity to see properly to this ugly wound."

Diana was startled back to the present. "Of course I'm all right, David. Sit still and let us take care of you."

"You look faint, Diana." David was all concern for her.

"What nonsense. You're the one dripping blood all over the place. I am fine."

David shot her a scowling glance and muttered, "Well, you didn't look like it." Then he flinched as the witch poured something into the wound on his arm. Unprepared for her action, he burst out, "Gad, that stings!"

"Please blow on it for our hero, Baroness."

Diana pursed her lips, and bending down, blew on the wound until she saw David relax.

David forgot the sting. He was completely fascinated by the little pout Diana had to form to direct her breath on the abused flesh of his open wound. She was so sweet, so kind to do it, and so damned desirable with her hair escaping in ringlets around her flushed face and her lips ready for a kiss.

It was merely the sweet pucker with which she might kiss the cheek of her Godmother, but it set David afire. In no way were her lips formed for the hard, ravenous, open-mouthed kisses he wished he could bestow on them.

He began to breathe a little heavier. His lips parted and desire coursed through him as he thought of Diana's luscious mouth and what he wanted to do to it and to the rest of her.

The witch chuckled as she prepared the bandage she was about to apply, and David knew she had guessed what was in his mind. He heard her softly murmur, "All in good time, young David, all in good time." As a kindness, she dropped the rest of the clean linen cloths in his lap.

His heart thundered at the mere thought that someday he might hold and ravish the delightful woman who held his heart. Right now, he'd give anything and everything he owned to clasp her tight to his burning body and explore all her own with hot, fervent kisses.

The witch laughed again and brought him back from his daydream by tightening the bandage until he swore.

"David!" Diana was shocked.

"Sorry! Curse it, I'm sorry, Diana." He glared at the witch, though he supposed he should thank her for the lap full of linen.

Diana was instantly contrite. "There's no need to apologize. I imagine one has to let off an invective or two when the pain is really bad."

David's face flamed. He'd been cursing more out of the frustration of wanting her—cursing the acute discomfort that that wanting was causing him—than from the minor pain of bandaging his arm, but he could hardly tell her so.

Blast! If he hadn't used up his every reserve to get back to her, he could have controlled all of this! Weary as he was, control was simply beyond him.

The witch laughed again and picked up the bowl to go dispose of its bloody contents.

Both young people looked after her. Diana was puzzled that the old woman had found anything to laugh about in David's obvious discomfort.

As wave after wave of sharp desire for her shook him, Diana slipped an arm around his shoulders and breathed in his ear, "It's all right, David dear, I'm right here."

David thought he'd faint from her nearness.

Their witch-hostess threw back her head and howled with laughter.

David glared, knowing that she'd seen right through him to the heart of the terrible desire he was experiencing for Diana—a desire compounded into pain by her solicitous nearness.

Somehow, he didn't think that either kind of his pain should amuse her.

Of the two, however, David found the one in his arm by far the easiest to bear.

Chapter Twenty-seven

The witch brought a cup of tea to them at the table where Diana stood holding the seated David against her side. "Here. There's a little laudanum in it to help him sleep."

Diana held the cup to David's lips and instructed, "Drink this, dear. It will help you rest."

David gulped it down. He was thirsty from his long ride, it was true, but more than that, he was eager to get up and put enough distance between him and his beloved to enable him to stop his head from spinning with the desire her proximity continued to increase in him. His self-control was at the breaking point, and Diana was completely unaware that, with her arm around his shoulder, her breast was on a level with his chin. To kiss, to nuzzle, or only to lay his head against that softness? How he wished the choice were his to make!

He hadn't missed the fact that she had called him "dear," either. But was that just the tender word she would have called any injured object of her care, from Gulliver up? Or was it a word that expressed real affection for *him?* He'd cheerfully give a year of his life to know.

In his present debilitated state it was all too much for him. He groaned.

Diana gasped. "He's in pain! We must get him to bed."

The witch laughed again.

Diana glared at her as if she were ready to tear the woman's hair from her head for her laughter, and the witch laughed all the harder.

David thought he'd better take a hand in the confusion before the two came to blows. He lurched to his feet, and headed for the pallet of quilts that had been made for him in front of the fireplace. Kicking them away from the warmth the small fire offered, he tumbled down onto them.

"David," Diana scolded, "you shouldn't have moved your blankets. What if you cool down in the night?"

Oh, God, he thought, *what if I don't?* The last thing he needed was fire to warm him. He was already ablaze. How long was he going to be able to keep the need he felt for Diana from becoming evident even to her? The witch was hardly going to follow them around with handfuls of linen bandages!

The witch's laughter subsided to a deeply amused chuckle. A moment passed, then she sighed. Perhaps the young Duke's predicament wasn't something to be laughed at, for all that she found the tangle amusing. He *was* suffering, after all. Perhaps it was time she did her best to help them on their way. She looked at him carefully.

David was beginning to feel the effects of the laudanum. It, coupled with the vast weariness he felt from his strenuous two days in the saddle, was taking its toll. When Diana pulled the blanket up to cover him, he couldn't even hold his eyes open long enough to bid her good night.

Once certain he slept, the witch took Diana by the hand

and led her to the table. "Now," she told her, "we are going to remember where it is that your Godmother's new son-in-law has his estate. Do you agree?"

Diana, though still miffed at her hostess, nevertheless knew that if anyone could help her remember where the Grange that was Lord Anthony's address was located, it was she. She followed to the table, sat docilely, and closed her eyes to try to think. Recalling those happy days in her Godmother's house in London was pleasurable, but far from ordered. Memory collided with memory of the happy times and gay banter she had enjoyed there. Parties and balls, soirees and dinner parties all swirled through her mind like the kaleidoscopic whirl of a waltz.

Diana opened her eyes and regarded the smiling witch. "I'm sorry," she was distressed to have to say, "I simply can't remember."

"Ah, but you did, my dear. What a lovely time you had! And your Godmother's son-in-law lives just two miles outside of Appledore. That much was clearly in your memories."

"You read my mind!" It was as much accusation as question.

The witch sighed. "Yes. And for good cause, I think. But once you have gone, I shall have to settle down to ridding myself of all the abilities I gained while serving the dark master. My soul may have a chance if I can do so, because the Lord is merciful, and knows the heart. I hope I have but to prove my sincerity."

Diana reached out and clasped her hands. "Surely you will find your way. The Lord never departs from us, you know; it is we who turn away from Him."

The witch smiled. "Spoken like the true daughter of a vicar."

Diana smiled back. "I've forgotten many things since I

left my father to marry Baron Huntley, but I haven't forgotten the parable of the prodigal son."

Tears sprang to the witch's eyes once again. Her voice was choked with them as she told Diana, "Bless you, child."

The beginning of the night passed quietly. Outside the cottage, now that the danger was removed, the breezes were gentle and a lone nightingale filled the air with song.

Diana dreamed of a hero who was a composite of the Duke she adored and the simple seaman who seemed to have taken over her life. She awoke, unable to finish a dream, no matter how pleasant, that put her in such a quandary.

Clasping her arms around her drawn-up knees, she sat, wondering what her dreaming mind might have been striving to tell her.

Suddenly the peace of the cozy cottage was broken by an agonized cry. "Ahhhh, no!"

Diana leapt up to run to the pallet in front of the fireplace. "David!" She dropped to her knees beside him. "David, it's all right. It's just a dream." She shook his shoulder, but he didn't wake. His face showed her that his dream was one of something that had caused him great pain. "It's all right," she told him again. "I'm here."

David grasped her to him in desperation. "No. Run."

Diana couldn't have followed his orders if her life had depended upon it. He was holding her so tightly she could hardly breathe. She could feel every muscle in his body taut as a bowstring.

Stroking his hair back from his forehead, Diana pressed her lips there as a mother might to soothe a restless child. "There, there," she murmured, hoping to calm her friend. "It's all right, you're only having a bad dream."

When she saw that her words seemed to calm him a little, she relaxed in his arms, relieved that he no longer fought whatever unseen enemy he'd been struggling against. "You're safe, David. It's . . ."

Her words were cut off as the man who held her tightened his embrace. Once married, Diana had no difficulty interpreting the change in him. From warrior to lover, the change was instant. Her eyes flew to his. Was he awake? Did he know his body was fully aroused? No. His eyes were still closed, he was dreaming. Even without seeing the expression in his eyes, she could read naked desire in the lines of his face.

He nuzzled her neck, and the groan he released had nothing to do with the fear and pain his first cry had contained. Diana gasped as his hand slid to the middle of her back to press her more closely to him.

Panic touched her. Shouldn't she break free? He'd be embarrassed if he wakened to find himself . . . His hand found her breast, and the decision was taken from her. David clasped her more tightly still and took her mouth in a fierce kiss.

Her head went spinning as her body exploded with an answering passion she'd never known she possessed. Diana returned kiss for kiss, pressing herself as close as she could to the man holding her.

All thoughts of loyalty to her Duke went flying and there was only now, this moment . . . and David.

Then Gulliver barked from his position beside the door, and the sound hit Diana like a bucket of cold water. She shoved against David and rolled away from him, her breath coming quickly, her heart pounding.

Embarrassment, swift and hot, took the place of the former heat, and she began to rise from the floor.

David awakened, looked toward the dog, and shook his head to clear the fog of laudanum from it.

Diana used this respite to rise from her knees. As she did, she tripped on the hem of her nightgown, and stumbled toward David's pallet. She pretended she was rushing to his side as if she were coming from the bedroom. When David finally turned his head her way, she knelt next to him, saying, "David, did you injure your wounded arm in your sleep? I thought I heard you cry out."

She could feel the heat of a blush staining her face. Lying was uncomfortable for her still, but not as uncomfortable as it would have been to admit she had just been wrapped in his arms, plastered to his chest and kissing him as if the sun were never going to rise again.

He looked at her through the haze of the drug they'd given him to help him sleep, and she felt certain she had succeeded in deceiving him. The place his hand had rested on her breast blazed at her in accusation, and she hated the puzzled look that passed over his face as he looked at her and shifted the quilt he lay under to hide the condition of his body from her.

"No," he assured her, "I'm fine. Perhaps it was a nightmare."

Diana could have hurled herself back into his arms at seeing the bewildered look he wore, but that would only make matters worse, she knew. Wisely letting his explanation stand, she asked, "Is there anything you'd like?" At the wry grin that spread across his face at that, she amended hastily, "Anything I could get you?"

"No." He lay propped up on his good arm's elbow and looked up at her through the tangle of dark hair that lay across his forehead. "No." His voice was husky. "No, thank you. There is nothing that you could give me that would help."

Except myself, she thought, and longed to do so. *Except myself.*

Her hands clasped so tightly that they hurt, she told him, "Good night, then. Sleep well." Then, using all the willpower she possessed, she turned and went back into the bedroom.

David's breath exploded in a long sigh. Not for an instant, laudanum or no laudanum, would he give up the knowledge that she had been here in his makeshift bed. His passion-heightened sense of smell detected the light scent of her on his own body.

He lay back down again, his head spinning with the certainty that she had lain in his aching arms. He curled up into a tight ball to ease the pain as the iron claws of his need for her tore at him. Diana. His Diana.

Neither she nor David got any more sleep that night.

The morning dawned bright and clear. Light from the rising sun tinted the sky above the little thatched cottage with ribbons of gold and pale pink as its source rose to gild the world around them. Diana and David stood holding the horses they would ride, while the third waited, laden with their meager luggage.

"Take good care of Esmerelda," Diana admonished.

David added, "She should make it easier for you to gather firewood and to go to market." He smiled. "Even if she is no more than good company."

"I suppose I shall become known as the witch with a donkey as her familiar."

"You will become known as no witch at all, if you will only do as you've vowed to do." Diana hugged her hard and whispered, "I shall be praying."

David stepped forward and tenderly embraced her, too. "Thank you for all you've done. I have no doubt that we would not have fared well without your assistance. And remember, should you ever have need of anything, you have only to send to me for it."

"Oh?"

He laughed heartily. "Do not pretend that you do not know where to get in touch with me, for I know better than that now."

"Very well. But I shall not make any calls on your generosity if I can help it."

"In that case, you'll force me to send someone periodically to spy on you to see if there is anything you need."

The witch fought a smile and cut her eyes in Diana's direction.

David belatedly remembered that sailors don't have staffs of servants to send to check on friends.

The witch chuckled.

Diana frowned at him, clearly puzzled.

David sought to save the situation. "One of my companions will happen by every now and again, and I shall have a report of you, never fear."

He turned to Diana and lifted her into the saddle, wound or no.

Diana scowled. Even wounded, David was awfully strong to be no larger than he was.

Chapter Twenty-eight

Dusk had fallen and Diana was ready to fall off her horse by the time David finally called a halt. They'd arrived at the Grange. They were covered with dust and totally exhausted.

Driven by the memory of Diana in his arms last night, David had not dared to trust himself to spend a night on the road in her presence, and thus had forced the march. The control he had to exercise not to sweep her off her horse, cover her face with kisses, and declare his love for her was overwhelming. He kept from doing so only by summoning every shred of self control he could call on. He knew that if they stopped to spend the night anywhere, he'd need to hire an armed guard to keep him from her!

"We're here," he croaked in a voice choked with fatigue.

Diana barely heard his remark. She watched in a daze as the front door of the manse opened, light spilled out of it, and she saw her Godmother rushing toward her.

"Diana! Oh, my dear Diana! Tell me you are all right!"
Diana nodded.

David slipped from his mount and came to her. Raising
his arms without comment, he lifted Diana from her horse
and placed her where she could be enfolded in her Godmother's arms.

"Diana. Who is this person? Where have you been? I've
been frantic since I received word that you had arrived at
my house in Town without an escort and been turned away
by that idiot of a footman I left in charge."

That galvanized Diana. "He was very rude." She knew
she sounded like a simpleton, and had failed to identify the
subject of her disdain, but was too tired to care. "I wanted
a bath, and he wouldn't let me in."

"Yes, yes. I should have known better than to have left
him in charge. He was always more supercilious than sensible. At least he included the tale of your arrival in his
weekly report. He didn't know it was you he'd turned
away, of course."

David, leaning wearily against the shoulder of Diana's
horse, interrupted quietly. "Lady Diana still needs that
bath, Lady Bradford. And I shall require one myself as
soon as I've seen to the horses." He looked around.
"Where are the grooms?"

The butler who had accompanied his mistress out of the
house was her own faithful Jeffers whom she'd brought
from her London establishment. The fact that he was not
butler at the Grange didn't stop him from giving orders to
the servants who belonged there, however. Turning to the
footman behind him, he ordered, "Grooms. Immediately.
Can't you see these horses need attention?"

The footman hurried away.

Gulliver jumped down from his perch atop the horse
carrying the luggage. David had placed him there hours

ago. Footsore and as weary as his humans, he'd been glad to ride there. Now, though, there were strangers about. He must see to it that his humans were safe from them.

David called him to heel.

Casting a frown at David, Lady Bradford told her Goddaughter, "When I got the report from Town, I immediately sent a message to your father—"

"Oh, you didn't!" Diana was dismayed.

"I'm not a peahen, Goddaughter. I asked him how long I was to be permitted to keep you. After all, I didn't know what you were up to yet. I still don't."

"Oh." It was no more than a sigh of relief.

David interrupted them again. "Lady Bradford."

She turned to him, frowning slightly.

"May I suggest that you go inside and see to a bath and supper for your Goddaughter? She is exhausted, and she is filthy. She will be in a better frame to talk when your son-in-law's servants have seen to her needs."

"Yes. Yes, of course." The older woman led the younger to the house. At the door she looked back after she had given Diana into the competent hands of her daughter's housekeeper. "Who in the world *is* that man?" she murmured, staring hard at the slender figure ordering Tony's grooms about as if he were the lord of the manor. "Ah, well," she told herself softly, "no doubt all will come to light as the evening progresses."

She saw that Jeffers, with obvious deference and with no objection to the presence of the large dog at his side, was now escorting the young man with the regal bearing up the stairs. If she didn't wish to confront him just now, she had better go find out where the housekeeper had put Diana.

She hesitated only an instant. She very definitely didn't want to confront this worn-out but still confident gentle-

man just now, she decided. In fact, until she'd had a serious talk with her Goddaughter, she didn't want to confront
him at all!

She found herself fervently wishing that her precious
daughter Jessica and her dear son-in-law Anthony hadn't
gone to the neighbors for an evening of card playing. Or,
she admitted more honestly, she wished that she had gone
with them.

Just over an hour later, with their baths behind them, the
two road-weary travelers descended to the dining room,
where Lady Bradford had bespoken a lovely supper for
them. Both looked as if their baths had revived them a bit.

Diana was beautiful in one of Jessica's evening gowns,
but the man she had arrived with, clad in Tony's evening
attire, was nothing short of glorious.

His dark hair, free of the dust of his journey, had been
cut in the latest style by Tony's valet, and it rioted around
his head in that wind-swept perfection that only a well-
practiced hand can achieve with the Brutus cut. His slender form was shorter than Tony's so the evening jacket was
too long, if one were inclined to be picky. But Lady Bradford was too impressed to be by the fact that he filled it out
in the shoulders to perfection. The trousers had, no doubt,
been shortened a little, as Tony was taller, but his overall
appearance was indeed impressive.

Lady Bradford made a mental note. She *must* compli-
ment Tony on his valet.

Beyond anything even the best of valets could accomplish, however, the stranger wore Tony's clothes with such
an air of assurance that Lady Bradford wondered if her
Goddaughter were blind, dotty, or had been just plain lying
to her in the conversation they'd had while Diana was
being bathed. This man was certainly no ordinary seaman!

His table manners were impeccable, and his attitude to the servants as they served him was that of a man well used to such service. He was, in other words, a perfect dinner guest.

Which, she had to admit, was more than she could say for her Goddaughter, who was beginning to wilt. She frowned at Diana, who was leaning her elbows on the damask tablecloth, resting her chin in her hands.

Diana straightened, with a small apologetic smile, and ruined it all with a yawn she barely got her hand up to cover in time. "I'm sorry, Godmamma. We rode hard all day, and it has taken the starch out of me."

"Indeed." Lady Bradford reached out to pat Diana's hand. "I hope that you have enough 'starch' "—she made a little moue of distaste—"left in you to explain what is going on."

"I think that would be better left to me, your ladyship." Her male guest's tone of voice left no room for refusal. "Diana, you are exhausted. Why don't you go to bed and leave your Godmother and me to talk."

Diana shot him a glance that told him she'd refuse out of hand if she'd had the energy, then rose, stifling another yawn. "You are right, I am beyond weary. We shall all talk in the morning when I am rested." Having given her orders, she dragged out of the room and off to bed.

The "seaman" sat and watched her go until he could no longer see her and her footsteps had faded away. His posture was ramrod straight, and his face wore an expression that clearly told Lady Bradford that he would brook no interference in his plans from her. When he turned his intense brown eyes on her, she knew they were going to have the conversation her Goddaughter had sought to postpone till morning right now.

"We will get more quickly to the point if this is between

just the two of us," her guest told her. "Diana would interrupt to explain her reasons and attempt to persuade you to her point of view. The truth is she hasn't one. The girl has ruined herself by running away from home and spending almost a week alone with me day and night. Unchaperoned."

Lady Bradford looked as if she might faint. "A week alone with you . . ."

"Brandy!" the "seaman" snapped, and Jeffers was instantly there with it. Lady Bradford wondered if the two of them had foreseen the need.

"Permit me to tell you the story."

She nodded. "Please do."

When David had completed his concise description of Diana's flight from the vicarage to the present time, Lady Bradford downed her brandy in a single gulp, coughed, was patted on the back by Jeffers, and finally wheezed, "Together the whole time. Day and . . . *night?*"

He leveled that serious brown gaze at her. *"And night."* The words had the ring of a tolling funeral bell.

"And night," she gasped faintly.

"More brandy, milady?" Jeffers, at least, was unmoved.

She nodded. This time she sipped and considered. Looking at the man across the table from her, she could think of many more disagreeable ways to spend a night than in his arms. He was a compelling devil, with his commanding air of competence, those mesmerizing eyes, and that beautifully sculpted mouth. *Oh, dear,* she thought, *my poor Diana was doomed from the start.*

The brandy gave her courage. Her responsibility for her Goddaughter gave her the words. Lifting her chin at him, she demanded, "Have you seduced my Diana?"

Jeffers nearly dropped the brandy.

The "seaman" waited a moment for them all to regain

their composure then told her blandly, "No, I have not." He leveled a gaze at her that left no doubt about the sincerity of his next words. "But I can assure you that I fully intend to do so should she refuse to marry me simply in order to save her damaged reputation."

Lady Bradford just stared.

"Come now, Lady Bradford. You must admit that marriage is the only solution. Diana has been absent from home for almost a week. Various people have seen her with me. She has no choice but to marry me. And I assure you I do intend to have her."

Lady Bradford looked speculative. Regarding him carefully, she mused, "You seem a gentleman."

David nodded.

"And obviously, you are accustomed to the finer things in life."

His smile was twisted. "Do you refer to my proper use of your silverware?"

Lady Bradford recalled the way he'd ordered her son-in-law's servants around. Indeed, in the case of Diana's bath he had even ordered *her* around.

Her instincts told her to trust him, but her good sense bade her go carefully. They were deciding Diana's life, after all. He could be a gentleman who had lost his fortune and was down on his luck, or he could be a charlatan, out to trick her into helping him marry Diana. In either case he was probably a fortune hunter. She sighed. Diana had gotten herself into a pretty mess.

Closing her eyes, she leaned back in her chair and tried to think.

His voice came to her softly. "If it helps, I am in love with her. I have been for a very long time."

Her eyes flew wide. How could he have loved Diana for a long time when he had just met her less than a week ago?

The look in his eyes stopped her from remarking on that. That he loved her should be enough. Was enough. "Very well. I give you my permission to . . ."

"I don't need your permission, Lady Bradford."

She began to bristle. If he didn't want her permission, what had been his intention all this time?

Before she could speak, David informed her, "I need your insistence. You must command your Goddaughter to marry me. It is the only way we can save her from a lifetime of public scorn." He smiled then, and Lady Bradford's heart eased. "Though she may resist the thought, once wed, I promise she will be happy."

Lady Bradford sat another moment. Well she knew the way of the world. As matters stood, Diana had doomed herself to a lonely, childless life. Society would not accept her. No man would marry her. She would be shunned by all but a brave very few.

She couldn't bear the thought of such a life for her beloved Godchild. "Very well." She took a deep breath. "I shall permit you to marry Diana. What date shall we set?"

"Tomorrow."

"Tomorrow!" She nearly fell off her chair. "You can't even get a special license so quickly, much less do anything else."

"I had occasion to visit the Archbishop of Canterbury at his residence in Doctors Common the other day. I took that opportunity to procure a special license. We shall be married tomorrow. Please make the arrangements." He rose and bowed. "I'm afraid I must ask you to excuse me, Lady Bradford. I would like to be awake for my nuptials, and if I don't retire soon, I fear that won't be possible."

Lady Bradford waved a hand in dismissal. Her mind felt battered. She was beyond any further courtesies.

She watched the "seaman" leave the room with a pleasing natural grace, his dog at his heels, and turned to her butler. "Jeffers, you have been with me for over thirty years."

"Yes, milady."

"Will it be all right, Jeffers?"

"Yes, milady, I rather think it will."

"We don't even know who he is."

"We shall no doubt find that out in due time."

She flung herself back in her chair. "Oh, dear Jeffers. He is very much in the mold of one of the lords of creation, isn't he?"

"I must agree, your ladyship."

"At least she is safe."

Jeffers looked at the doorway through which Diana's future husband had just passed. "Yes, milady. And I think she will remain that way for the rest of her days."

Chapter Twenty-nine

Preparations for the wedding were going forward with the speed of a whirlwind. Footmen from various estates ran to and fro, delivering great vats of freshly cut blossoms. The chapel was being decorated with flowers begged and borrowed from every greenhouse in the vicinity. Their own greenhouse at the Grange was being stripped of every bloom as well.

It was there in the greenhouse that David finally found Diana. She was talking with Jessica, the pleasant young wife to whom, with her equally pleasant young husband, David had been introduced this morning at breakfast. They were trying to decide something about a tall fernlike plant, when David came up to them.

"Oh, David," Diana cried. "Can we talk?"

"Yes, I came to do just that." He bowed politely to Lady Jessica. He'd hoped to catch Diana alone. Alone was a relative term, though, he realized, with the whole house seemingly in motion. Postponing his own concern, he asked, "What was it you wanted to say?"

Diana glanced at Jessica. She wanted to talk to David without being heard by anyone else, too, but she didn't especially want to be alone with him just now. Friends before, she was nervous about the change in their relationship.

Since the other night on his pallet, she knew how she felt about him, but she was still unsure that her feelings were reciprocated. He hadn't really been awake, after all, and she didn't want to enter another loveless marriage, no matter how much more pleasant one to David would be than the disaster she had experienced with Huntley.

Furthermore, she was baffled by the sudden change in his demeanor. Her casual, smiling—and rather deferential—companion of the road had suddenly taken on a stern and lordly air. She hated to admit it, but he was making her nervous.

"Yes?" David prompted, the lordly manner still in evidence.

Taking a big breath, Diana plunged in. "David, I think it is only fair to tell you . . ." She hesitated before his intent regard. Another deep breath and she all but blurted, "You should know that I am in love with someone else."

Jessica gasped.

David looked as if she had knifed him. White-faced, he demanded, "Who is he?"

Faced with this new David, Diana felt a moment's fear for her other love. Nevertheless, she raised her chin and told him. "The Duke of Smythington."

For an instant David was totally still. Then he threw back his head and burst into full-throated laughter.

Jessica couldn't bear it. "David! How insensitive! You mustn't."

"Oh, I mustn't, mustn't I?" To Diana he said only, "I wish we could have been a bit more private for this, my love. However . . ." It was all he said before he reached out and grabbed his betrothed, snatching her to him so hard that he knocked the breath out of her as she slammed into his hard body.

Kissing her with all the pent-up passion he'd ever felt for her, he held her tight against him until she began to respond. Then his kiss softened and he stood holding her gently as he led her to return kiss for kiss.

When he released her, he let her stagger back a step before he caught and steadied her.

With a smile that, for David, could only be called wicked, he told her solemnly, "I'm very glad you told me of your love for the Duke, my dear. It was gallant of you to do so, and I shall always cherish the knowledge. However"—he gave her a little shake—"you are going to marry *me!*"

"Yes," she pledged, more than willing after his kisses, but hating the fact that she sounded so meek about it. She saw him start to leave her, and grasped his arm to demand more strongly, "What is this change that has come over you, David? You stalk around the Grange as if you imagine yourself a lord of the realm!"

David stopped. Mischief lit his eyes. "Do I, my love? Now fancy that."

Diana stomped her foot. "David!" Her tone was anything but meek and loving now.

Deciding he had best give her an explanation that would serve to satisfy her, he offered, "Do you think your Godmother would so willingly have given me your hand if I comported myself like a common seaman?"

Diana was stunned by the question.

David had no more time to spend talking. He pecked

her on the cheek, saluted Jessica, and told them both, "Pray hold me excused. I must go make the plans for our wedding trip, and I have precious little time left in which to accomplish it."

"Oh, David." Jessica's eyes were still round from the passionate scene she had just witnessed. "Oh, my!"

David smiled kindly at her confusion and turned again to his fiancée. "We are going to be wed at three, Diana. Resign yourself to it."

After he had gone, Diana turned to her long-time friend. "Oh, Jessica. What if I *am* marrying a common seaman?"

Jessica watched through the glass of the conservatory as David met the groom bringing his horse and vaulted lightly into its saddle. Always a dreamer, a misty look filled her eyes. A silly smile came over her lips. She was living in . . . or rather beside . . . a lovers' tale.

After David had galloped off, she could finally speak. "Oh, yes, Diana . . ." She sighed. "What if you are?"

Diana looked at her companion and gritted her teeth. Jessica was clearly enchanted. "Jessica!" she started to scold her dear friend. Then she remembered the way David's arms had felt around her and how masterfully he had held and kissed her and . . . "Oh, well," she said at last, "if he is only a seaman, he's a very special one, and I have enough money for us both."

"And," Jessica added in an attempt to offer something as practical as her friend's last statement, "he *is* saving you from absolute disgrace, and that must count for something." She sighed. "And he is so handsome. And he rides so well. And when he was kissing you . . ." She wrapped her arms around herself and shivered. "It was as if the very angels were singing. I felt sheer bliss clear down to my toes."

Diana looked at her as if she had just fallen out of a fairy tale.

The old stone chapel was as beautiful as loving hands and every flower in a ten-mile radius could make it. The guests were eager to be present for the auspicious event, for all that they were so hastily assembled.

Everyone thought the bridal couple exceptionally attractive. The bride was beautiful, and the groom, for all that he was only a hint taller than his bride, was commanding as well as handsome.

Everyone thought it a beautiful setting and a lovely ceremony. All except Diana and David, for they saw nothing the whole time but each other.

Earlier, David had asked Diana if she wanted to be married by her father. And while it might have made for a touchy situation if the Vicar recognized his patron, David would have risked it for her, but Diana had answered, "My father wants me married, and I shall be married; that should suffice."

As she stood looking into the dear face of the man she was marrying, she thought about that offer and how typically considerate of him it was.

She couldn't help wondering, however, if her father would have been as kind as David. He might easily have objected to her marrying a commoner. After all, his family and her mother's were both noble, and though her father was quite democratic when it came to his treatment of the common people in his parish, it might well be another thing entirely when it came to accepting one into his family. She refused to chance him hurting David, for she loved him and would marry him even if her father objected.

Perhaps she should feel odd about marrying a lowly seaman. Heaven knew she could hear her ancestors spinning in their graves, but it didn't matter to her. All she knew was that she'd been happy with David, walking the countryside, and miserable while he'd been away facing danger without her.

The night David had cried out from his pallet, and she had ended up in his arms, had been the turning point of her life. His holding her had given rise to the proof that she cared for him as a man with whom to spend a lifetime.

As the curate pronounced them man and wife, she turned into David's embrace and accepted the kiss that sealed their future together.

When they parted, the guests all crowded around to wish them the best. Lady Bradford and Jessica cried for joy, while Jessica's Tony laughed at his romantic wife and her sentimental mother.

Then Diana and her new husband were in the landau that was to take them to the yacht David had procured for their wedding trip. The guests gathered round and tossed flowers into the carriage as David threw handfuls of gold coins out to them.

The yacht David had summoned for their wedding trip was lovely, long and sleek and white with a great deal of well-polished shining brass. As they arrived at the top of the gangplank with Gulliver at their heels, the captain saluted David and said, "Welcome aboard—" His eyes widened as he remembered his orders not to use the Duke's honorific and realized he didn't know what to say next. "Er, sir and madam," he managed, looking as if he wished the deck would open and swallow him.

David laughed and clapped him on the shoulder. "How was your voyage, Hendricks?"

"Hasty, sir." The captain relaxed at last.

"My message from Canterbury didn't give you many

hours to get ready to sail, I know. I congratulate you on making it in time."

"We had fair winds, er, sir." He led the way to the spacious cabin on the stern, opened the door, and bowed them in. "Just ring if there is anything you require, Your G . . . s-*servant,*" he saved just in time, bowing again and adding "sir and madam." Blushing brightly, he stepped out and closed the door, taking a reluctant Gulliver with him.

As he did, a laughing David called out, "Well done, Captain!"

And they were alone.

Chapter Thirty

Silence filled the cabin except for the soft sounds of waves lapping against the hull of the yacht and the mew of the gulls flying overhead. Beyond the many-paned windows in the stern, sunset filled the sky with glorious bands of russet and gold.

After a moment, the captain called orders to his crew. Quiet movement could be heard on the deck outside. The graceful ship moved smoothly away from the pier.

Diana stood in the middle of the cabin, listening to her own heartbeat. She was breathless with a mixture of apprehension and anticipation. She was married again, but this time it was to someone she loved, and she could hardly believe her flight had ended in such radiant happiness.

David stood by the door they had entered through and she thought he had never been handsomer. When he moved toward her, his eyes were full of love, and when he touched her, her knees threatened to betray her.

David turned her to face the windows and the glorious

sunset. Standing behind her with his arms around her, he kissed her shoulder. Then her neck just above that spot. Then her ear. "I love you, Diana," he breathed into it.

"Oh, David. I love you, too."

His voice infinitely gentle, he said, "But you love your Duke as well?"

She turned in his arms then, wanting to face him, wanting to make him understand. "He was my hero, David. I was a young girl. Only sixteen, and I was married to a horrible brute. A man who . . ." She stopped herself. Not for the world was she going to let Huntley and his brutality intrude on this golden moment.

David placed a kiss just beside her mouth, his hands lightly resting on her waist.

"The Duke rescued me from Lord Calverson and his bullies when I was trying to save a little dog from them."

David kissed the other side of her mouth, and Diana found it was becoming difficult to order her thoughts.

"They were tossing the puppy back and forth between them, you see, and . . . and . . . David! I can't think when you do that."

"Then don't."

She shrugged a shoulder at him to try to keep him from kissing her again. "I can't explain to you how I feel when I can't think."

"Then don't."

"David. I am trying very hard to tell you about the other man I love!"

"That you *love.*"

"Yes."

"But not that you are *in love with.*"

"Stop confusing me with nonsensical statements," she ordered. Her voice lacked conviction, though.

"There is a world of difference between *loving* and

being in love with, my angel. I have no objection to your loving your Duke."

Diana was scandalized. She tried to twist around to look into his face, but he held her fast. "You don't?"

"None in the least." He kissed her on the nape of her neck, swung her up into his arms, and walked easily and purposefully toward the huge bed built into one corner of the cabin. "Just so long as you never permit him to do this."

Diana didn't say a word. She couldn't, the look in her new husband's eyes had taken her breath away. She hid her face in his neck, almost frightened by the look of fierce possession she saw in his.

When he reached the side of the bed, David let her slide down the length of his body till she was standing, clasped tightly against him, facing him. Tilting her chin up, he regarded her seriously. "Any regrets?"

Diana knew that the degree of happiness they would experience for the rest of their lives depended on her answer. Her heart almost quailed at the thought.

She knew he was asking if she were ready to give up society to live whatever sort of life a seaman's wife enjoyed—or, she thought with a hint of sadness, endured, if her husband was gone at sea. She would do so gladly, if that was the price she had to pay for the joy of spending the rest of her life with him, her David. And she'd let go of the memory of her rescuer from long ago, as well.

For five long years she'd clung to that dear memory of the Duke of Smythington. Now she was ready to let it go. It had been her strength and her reassurance. Yes, and her protection, too. But she was married to David now. Her friend, her boon companion, and her soul's true mate.

Suddenly she knew she could answer his question

freely and with all her heart. "No. No, my dearest David, I have no regrets."

Such relief dawned in his dear face that she could hardly bear it. Sliding her arms around his neck, she kissed him sweetly, pulled back again, and repeated, "No regrets."

He kissed her again, and heat began to build between them. When David slipped the shoulders of her gown down to her waist, and kissed her breasts, Diana could only hold on to him, fearful she would melt to the floor without support.

David removed the rest of her clothing, interspersing each move he made with more kisses until Diana was mindless with desire. By the time he picked her up and placed her on the bed, she wanted him more than she wanted her next breath.

He was beside her an instant later, his beautiful body showing clearly his need for her. She met him in a fierce embrace that left no doubt in his mind that she loved him. Loved him as a man—common seaman, intruder, cherished friend. All of it was David, her husband. If he were more, she didn't care, for she knew he could never be less. She loved him, David, she realized at last, not the exalted Duke of Smythington. In soft murmurs interspersed with the little moans of pleasure his caresses drew from her, she managed to tell him so.

That knowledge was burning brightly in David's mind when he made her his own. Both his dearest wishes were granted. Diana was his at last, *and she loved him for himself!*

The next morning they stood in the bow, David's arms around his cherished wife, their faces turned homeward.

"Are you happy?" He couldn't stop himself from asking.

"Hmmm. Deliriously." She caught the hand he had raised to touch her hair and rubbed her cheek against it.

Just then the captain joined them to say, "We'll be in port in another half hour."

"Thank you," David told him. "And thank you for a peaceful voyage."

"Ay, ay, Your . . . you're welcome," he finished lamely. David laughed again.

"Why did you laugh at him," Diana wanted to know, scolding a little.

"You'll see soon enough, my love. Only be patient." He changed the subject. He wanted to be just her David for as long as he could. "Did you like sailing? I thought after all those days in the saddle you just might like to ride the wind home."

"Ride the wind home." She turned her face to smile at him. "What a lovely thought."

He nuzzled her neck. "Hmmm."

"Are you a poet as well as a seaman, David?"

He chuckled. "Among other things."

She turned in his arms and touched his cheek. "Are you being mysterious, my love?"

"Would you be angry to find that I was something other than your 'common seaman'?"

She looked deep into his eyes for a long moment. "I'm certain that whatever else you are, it is noble and good, my dearest, whatever it may be."

Relief coursed through him. He kissed her softly. "And you will love me still?"

"Of course."

"Promise?"

"How very strange you are being, dearest." Her eyes showed that she was puzzled, curious.

"Promise?"

She regarded him solemnly for several heartbeats, and David could feel his own accelerating. Finally she answered, "I promise."

Not a moment too soon, either. Looking ahead, he saw his harbor coming into view. When they landed, keeping his true identity secret was quite likely going to be an impossible task, and David didn't know how he was going to handle it.

David could see the curricle he had ordered standing on the shore, the perfectly matched pair harnessed to it, tied and waiting patiently. As he'd requested, there was no one in evidence. He would have the unheard-of privilege of driving his bride peacefully to his home, alone and unattended.

Nothing could mar the happiness that filled his heart to overflowing.

Chapter Thirty-one

As soon as the noble couple had disembarked and the gangplank had been taken back aboard, the yacht pulled away from the handsome stone pier. Silently it ghosted out to its anchorage in the spacious harbor. Soon it was enveloped in the evening mist that was rising from the water.

David lifted Diana toward her place in the curricle, changed his mind, and brought her back to earth for one more kiss that left her quivering. "I can't seem to get enough of you, Diana."

She looked into his eyes, her own full of the love they shared. Her voice was husky as she told him, "We have the rest of our lives, dearest."

"Which won't be long if you don't get the hell out of here!" a voice shouted at them from the top of the low hill beside them.

"Calverson!" David cried, stepping quickly in front of Diana. "What the devil!"

"The devil's right behind me, Smythe," Calverson replied, using the name he'd called the Duke when they'd served together under Wellington, "and he's after your hide!"

"David, what is this?" Diana demanded.

"Ah"—Calverson sketched a hasty bow—"so the fat boy has won the fair Diana."

"Have you run mad, Lord Calverson?" Diana demanded. "What in the world are you talking about?"

Calverson threw a glance behind him. "No time now! He's here!"

"*Who's* here?" Diana demanded. Then she gasped as David tossed her unceremoniously into the curricle.

David leapt in beside her. Grabbing the whip, he sent the horses flying up the only lane that led away from the cove. He had to get Diana to safety!

They'd only gotten a hundred yards, however, when they were met by a horseman brandishing a pistol in each hand.

Calverson galloped up beside them and rode down on Ewing in an effort to turn him from his murderous purpose. Sir Joseph shot him off his horse.

David let go a string of curses that amazed Diana and began to pull the team up. "Calverson!" he shouted, ready to go to the fallen man's aid, more concerned with the man who had attempted to save him than for his own safety. Shoving the reins into Diana's hands, and ordering her, "Drive! Go!" he prepared to jump.

Diana, however, had no intention of being widowed when she had just barely been made a wife! "No, David," she shouted, "don't!"

The man aimed his second pistol at David almost point-blank. Before he could get the shot off, Diana snatched the whip, struck the assailant's arm up, and slashed him across the face with the long lash. His shot went wild.

The man fell from his horse, howling, his hand pressed against the livid welt she'd raised on his cheek. Diana leapt from the still moving curricle, and David was left to fight the frantic horses to a standstill.

Diana brought the butt of the whipstock smashing down on the head of the would-be murderer of her beloved. "There! You villian! You'll not harm *my* husband!"

David leapt from the curricle to Diana's side. "Blast it, Diana! You could have been killed!"

The terrified horses tore off. The curricle swung from one side of the lane to the other as the team galloped for the comfort and safety of the stables at Smythington Park.

"I," Diana informed David at the top of her lungs, "was not the one he was trying to shoot!"

Calverson was sitting up, holding his shoulder. "My God, Diana. You are well named." He looked at his hand as if he had hoped he wouldn't find blood, then nodded in disgusted resignation as if he'd known he would. "Wasn't Diana the huntress?"

Diana turned to look at her long-ago nemesis. "Yes, she was. And, thanks partly to you, I have been training for the past year to be able to emulate her should the need arise." She tossed back her disheveled hair and glared triumphantly at their downed foe. "And the need finally did arise!"

"Dear lord," Calverson remarked faintly.

David could only stare. Then he remembered all that Jonathan had told him about his "dreadful cousin Diana." Suddenly all the training and all the trying and all the seeming abuse of her younger cousin made sense. She'd been preparing to defend herself and her own, and by George, she'd done so, remarkably.

His mind still had to work to grasp the fact that his beloved Diana had thrown herself into action and saved the day. He was stunned with admiration. Or just stunned. He couldn't seem to decide which.

Diana took charge. Pulling the sash from her dress, she thrust it at David. "Hadn't you better tie him up?"

Still thunderstruck at his wife's brave and capable actions, David did as she commanded.

Diana went to Calverson, knelt, and looked at his wound. Having the ability to do so without feeling queasy gave her a wonderful sense of power. She was able to because she'd helped take care of the wound on her beloved's arm. "It's only a graze. We can dress it properly when we get to David's house."

Calverson shot an astonished look at David. "'To David's *house'?*" He was vastly amused at something.

David just stood there, striving to find words for a prickly situation.

Diana turned on David. "You *do* have a house, don't you?" She frowned. "I may have a lot of money, David, but we will need shelter of some kind, you know. Especially since we must take care of Lord Calverson. He risked his life to warn you, after all. And he very nearly lost it, too. Surely you at least have a bed he can rest on until he is recovered."

David's face was flaming. Words eluded him.

Calverson was convulsed with laughter and gasping with the pain it was causing him.

Diana stamped her foot. "What is it?" She glared from one to the other of them, angry at being left out of whatever knowledge they obviously shared. "What are you laughing at, Calverson?" she demanded.

"She doesn't know?" he asked David, his expression incredulous.

There was a thunder of hoofbeats in the distance.

"She doesn't know!" Calverson answered his own question and went into gales of laughter.

Before Diana could react to this, a band of men in the livery of the Duke of Smythington arrived and flung themselves from their horses. "Your Grace! Are you all right?"

David sighed and addressed the leader who'd just inquired for his health — and let the proverbial cat out of the bag. "Thanks to my Duchess, we are fine, thank you. We are grateful for your prompt arrival and your retrieval of our curricle, however."

David smiled shyly at his astounded bride. The cat was very definitely out of the bag, and his wife looked as if she were going to help it claw.

David's fond fantasy lay in figurative broken shards around them. Gone was his dream of driving his beautiful bride quietly through the calm serenity of twilight up the long carriage drive to his palatial home. His dream of watching the wonder in her face give way to the dawning realization that she, just like him, had achieved her dearest wish and married her Duke had just been shattered.

He'd longed to watch her dear face as she discovered that she'd not only married the man she loved now, but had married the Duke she'd held in her heart for so long, as well. Now, thanks to his cousin, Calverson, and a pair of pistol shots, it was not to be.

Diana looked from the liveried servants to David and back again. She put a hand to her forehead as if it ached. Then the truth was borne in on her, and she realized whom she had married. If she hadn't understood from the brief exchange between David and his men, she would have deduced it from the deep bows now being directed at her.

Her senses rioted. She couldn't seem to put it all together. For Diana, who prided herself on her good sense and powers of observation, it was too much. How could she have been so blind? How could she have misinterpreted his commanding air and believed him a lowly seaman? He would have had to captain a ship-of-the-line, at least, to have become so . . . so high-handed!

He'd deceived her. David had *tricked* her into accepting his escort by pretending to be of the servant class. Never would she have accepted him had she known him to be her equal, and well he'd known it! She understood it all now.

In spite of understanding, she couldn't forgive David for having chosen to deceive her as he had! Could she? She stood stock-still, fighting to regain her equilibrium.

Anger came to her rescue. Turning on her newly acquired husband, she fixed him with a glare that would have felled a lesser man. Then she turned her back on him and said to the men awaiting orders from their master, "Put Lord Calverson into the curricle, please. I shall drive him to Smythington Park. The Duke can ride his lordship's horse."

Without so much as another glance at David, Diana strode to the waiting curricle, jumped lightly into it, and took up the reins. Managing the fractious horses with the consummate skill she had learned from her grandfather, she held them steady as Calverson was helped in. Then, she turned the curricle and sent it on up the lane at a spanking pace.

Calverson, a devilish grin on his handsome face, hung on with his good hand so that he could turn around and laugh at David without falling out of the light vehicle.

David stood in the middle of the narrow road, surrounded by solicitous servants, stunned by the turn of events. He closed his eyes briefly against the excruciating pain. He put his hand against the center of his chest and pressed hard. His heart actually ached.

The very worst had happened. The shining dream he'd treasured throughout his trek with Diana had been utterly destroyed.

Chapter Thirty-two

A man, whom David had obviously ordered to ride ahead and announce her arrival to those at his palace, galloped past. For an instant, Diana clutched the whip tighter.

Calverson saw and grinned. "It's beneath your new dignity to race a servant, Duchess."

Diana clenched her teeth against the scathing reply that rose to her lips and drove on, pulling the horses down to a more sedate pace.

"Good girl."

"That was hardly a remark commensurate with my 'new dignity,' Lord Calverson." She managed to glare at him even as she settled the team into a rhythmic trot.

"You're angry."

Diana snorted. Calverson was evidently attempting to master understatement.

"Hmmm. Yes, you are angry." He furrowed his brow. "Let me try to understand this." He flashed her a rather charming smile, and Diana was instantly suspicious.

Calverson was not a man given to charm. "You ran away from home. Is that correct?"

"Yes. I had no intention of marrying a second one of you scoundrels, and Father had invited Runsford to visit with just that in mind."

"Ah. Never liked Runsford, myself." He waited for her to continue.

His interest drove her to do so. "I ran away to my Godmother, Lady Bradford, in London."

"Then why . . . ?" Calverson was puzzled.

"She wasn't in residence," Diana snapped at him, recalling her rude reception in London.

"Oh, I see." Calverson used his oiliest voice. "And David ran across you there and decided to take advantage of you, a young, beautiful woman all alone."

"Don't be absurd! That was left to your kind as they ganged up on me at the coaching inn." Diana's chin came up. "David—His Grace, I should say—had followed me from home. He'd been taking refuge in the vicarage barn."

"I say!"

"Well, he was dressed as a sailor for some reason and he saw me go past the barn and followed to be certain I was safe."

It was Calverson's turn to snort. The sound seemed more natural coming from him than it had from Diana.

"He rescued me from *your* sort."

"How dastardly!"

"Stop playing the fool, Calverson."

He was silent a long moment. "You've changed a great deal since I last saw you, Diana." His hard gray eyes held a pensive expression.

"Yes, I have." She eased the horses to a walk, seeing the palace that was to be her home in the distance. "Anyway, to make a long story short, His Grace pretended to be, and acted like, a servant to me for the rest of my misadventure."

"And now you find yourself in this awful predicament. Married to a man you obviously love as a lowly seaman, only to discover that he is an exalted peer of the realm. You poor darling."

"You are being facetious," Diana accused.

The horses walked on, cooling out before being returned to their stalls, unaware of the drama being played out in the curricle behind them.

Calverson regarded Diana's profile steadily for a moment.

In a voice unfamiliar to her because of its sincerity, she heard him say quietly, "Be careful you don't ruin everything, Diana."

Somehow Diana made it through the army of servants hastily assembled to greet their new Duchess. She graciously accepted the heartfelt congratulations of the kind, elderly gentleman who told her he was her husband's secretary Carrington, and was finally escorted to her rooms.

There, soaking in her bath, she thought about Calverson's warning. It had angered her when he made it. Who, after all, had more right than she to be angry with David? Even if . . . but her thoughts seemed to grind to a halt there.

What nonsense was she about to tell herself? That he had protected her from her own folly to the best of his ability? That he'd been wise enough to know that she would have balked like Esmerelda if he'd tried to return her to her father? That, had he disclosed his true identity, she would have . . . But she wasn't certain what she would have done. Declared undying love of five years' duration? Hardly!

Then what? She worked to be objective, Calverson's warning bright in her mind.

Last night beside their marriage bed, she had used her good sense to answer David when she had told him she had no regrets. And she'd had none, for she'd known that she loved him with all her heart.

If she had known his identity as the Duke, she would never have gotten to know him as the man.

Her heart quailed at that thought. She would never have known her dear David because of the image of the Duke she had kept enshrined in her heart.

She dropped her head back to rest on the high edge of the tub and let her thoughts flow.

And there in the yacht's cabin in the moonlight, hadn't David led her to realize there was a difference between what she felt for the Duke and what she felt for him? And hadn't that been the most important discovery of her life?

And later—she blushed as she recalled the passion they had shared and her own unbounded response to his love-making—hadn't he asked her for promises? Promises she had freely and lovingly given him?

She sat up so suddenly, the maid bathing her asked, "Are you all right, Your Grace?"

"Yes," Diana managed to reply around her anger at having been such a complete fool. "Thank you, I am fine." She stood to be rinsed, and the second maid came bearing the large pitcher of water she'd been keeping warm by the fire and poured it over Diana.

When she was wrapped in a huge drying sheet, one of her attendants went to the nearest wardrobe and threw open the doors.

Diana gasped. Dear glory! It was full of her own gowns! All the lovely clothes she'd had made for her in London were here! She turned puzzled eyes to the maids. "How . . . ?"

"There was a message from the Archbishop of Canterbury a few days ago, Your Grace. It ordered the yacht that brought you home and also told Carrington to get your clothes so that . . ." She trailed off at seeing the expression dawning on her mistress's face.

Diana found that she couldn't immediately speak because of the lump in her throat. David! David had even thought to see to her having her things about her. She saw, now that she was looking, the little items she had always cherished. On a small table by the bed stood the silver-framed miniature of her mother, and her favorite worn book of poetry. On the mantel were several china figurines she'd loved from her childhood. And he had even caused someone to bring her her own clothes to wear.

When she could finally speak, she asked slowly, "Was there a muslin dress among those things you've unpacked? An old yellow muslin dress with grass stains on the skirt?"

"Yes, Your Grace, there was," both maids answered as one.

"It was in your things they brought from the ship," the younger one added.

"His Grace was most specific that nothing happen to that dress, Your Grace," the older maid told her. Then, a little anxiously, "Though it is ruined, you know."

"Yes." Diana smiled radiantly. "I know."

Downstairs in the blue drawing room, David was resplendent in his proper garments. Calverson was a little pale from loss of blood, but bathed and comfortable in dinner dress borrowed from the Duke's secretary. He was, of course, too large to borrow anything from David. Together with Carrington they awaited the appearance of the new Duchess in the luxuriously appointed drawing room.

David's heart was heavy. The knowledge that his beloved was angry over his presumed trickery weighed heavily on him. Try as he would, however, he could think of no other way he could have protected her. Only as a lowly servant could he have accompanied her on her journey. Only as her servant could he have stolen the time he'd had with her.

Of course, he could have revealed his true identity immediately and offered to take her to one of his friends' mother's for safekeeping until he could locate her Godmother. He could have. Perhaps he should have. He sighed.

Calverson and Carrington both turned to assess David's state of mind.

Of course, if he had done that, he would never have caused her to love him for himself. He sighed again.

"For the Lord's sake, Smythington, don't blow all the candles out!" Calverson gestured toward the unthreatened candleabras with the wineglass held in the hand of his uninjured arm.

David was forced to laugh. Then he took a deep breath and smiled. He could trust his Duchess, however incensed she might be for having become one.

"What is it that troubles you, Your Grace?" Carrington used the proper form of address because there was a guest present, but he wanted to say, "My boy."

David's smile widened. "Nothing, now, Carry. I've thought it through, and I think, if I have rightly read my Duchess, that all is well."

He turned to his guest. "I haven't thanked you properly for the good turn you did in warning us of my cousin's presence, Calverson."

"I couldn't very well let the bastard kill you after he'd been so abusive to me for having failed to do so."

Carry choked on his wine.

David patted him on the back. "It's all right, Carry." His eyes glinted with mischief. "He missed."

It was Calverson's turn to choke on his wine.

David went on before his rescuer could proclaim that he never missed. The whole army knew that was so, but there was no need to worry Carrington.

"How the blazes did Cousin Joseph know I was sailing home? How did he know to lie in wait for me here?"

"Simple," Calverson told him. "He deduced, from what Runsford hinted you carried and the direction I helpfully told him you were riding in, that you were headed to Canterbury to get rid of that cursed book of spells. From there, it was a simple matter to go find someone to bribe who had the information that you'd ordered your yacht to come and fetch you home."

"You make me sound like a dog's bone."

"You'd have been cold bones indeed if you hadn't had Diana with you," Calverson told him. "She was magnificent."

Suddenly, Gulliver rose from in front of the fireplace and stared at the door.

"Why, thank you, Lord Calverson." Diana spoke from the doorway.

David's face lit up like the sun as his gaze traveled her.

She glided into the drawing room and stood like a queen in the full light of the many-candled chandelier. David's heart soared when he saw she had accepted the gift he'd sent in to her.

The famous Smythington diamonds sparkled at her throat, glittered at her wrists, and rivaled the highlights in her golden hair.

They looked rather strange with the grass-stained yellow muslin gown.

PENGUIN PUTNAM INC.
Online

Your Internet gateway to a virtual environment with
hundreds of entertaining and enlightening books
from Penguin Putnam Inc.

*While you're there, get the latest buzz on
the best authors and books around—*

Tom Clancy, Patricia Cornwell, W.E.B. Griffin,
Nora Roberts, William Gibson, Robin Cook,
Brian Jacques, Catherine Coulter, Stephen King,
Ken Follett, Terry McMillan, and many more!

**Penguin Putnam Online is located at
http://www.penguinputnam.com**

PENGUIN PUTNAM NEWS

Every month you'll get an inside look at our upcom-
ing books and new features on our site. This is an
ongoing effort to provide you with the most
up-to-date information about
our books and authors.

**Subscribe to Penguin Putnam News at
http://www.penguinputnam.com/newsletters**